Sacrifice 2086
Book Three
Daughter of Time Travel

WAL OZELLO

THE
DAUGHTER OF TIME TRAVEL
SERIES

Book One:
Assignment 1989

Book Two:
Revolution 1990

Book Three:
Sacrifice 2086

"I have noticed even people who claim everything is predestined, and that we can do nothing to change it, look before they cross the road."
Stephen Hawking

PROLOGUE

President Tobias Mack had lived a wondrous life. Even though he grew up in 1970s in Urban Washington D.C., and saw firsthand the cruelty of the Nazi occupation of U.S. after the Germans won World War II, he eventually helped drive the Nazis out of North America and restored his nation to greatness. Leading the rebellion helped solidify his stature with the American people who elected him the first U.S. President, post-World War II. He oversaw the reconstruction of the nation and convinced war torn Canada to join the Union.

There was a time, though, where he almost didn't become President. His storied past is a well-known fact. He was a drug runner. Worse yet, some considered him a mobster – an organized crime boss, coordinating drug operations across the country during the Nazi Regime. "It is true," he would often say. "I am not proud of how we kept ourselves alive during that time, but I am grateful that we are alive."

Americans easily remembered the dark decades when the Nazis conquered the U.S. and made it theirs. The relief from the oppressive rule was enough to balance out whatever anyone needed to do to stay alive. Since President Mack had led the rebellion and overthrew the Nazi overlords to regain America's freedom, he was declared a hero, and his dark history was forgiven.

But President Mack still had secrets. Secrets that he never told to anyone. All Americans will always remember how he led the attack on the Capital, Smithsonian, and White House and assassinated three of the top Nazis rulers in America. It's the details that have been forgotten. The rebels that traveled with President Mack disappeared and their where-a-bouts afterwards were never explained. Legend that he was helped by a red haired woman called the "Falls Jumper" who led the attack on the Niagara Outpost faded away. Tales of a scraggly old Russian and a broad shouldered Canadian that helped him plan and conduct the attacks were dismissed as rumors. Eventually they all slipped out of the history books.

President Mack couldn't explain their where-a-bouts. He couldn't confess where they came from, or where they disappeared to because his cohorts were not from here. They were foreigners. Not just people from a different country… but from a different time. They were from the future – time travelers who were stuck in the past. They explained to President Mack that he was living through an altered past and that in reality the Americans had won World War II back in 1945. Instead, the Nazis had gone back in time to change the past so the outcome of the war would tilt in their favor. His friends were there to correct things and make it the way it was supposed to be.

At first, President Mack found it hard to believe them, until he traveled through time as well.

On the historic night when President Mack and his rebel army entered the Smithsonian Castle to kill the Nazi leaders, they found something odd – over two dozen children and teenagers imprisoned in the basement. These were great minds – Da Vinci, Imhotep, Aristotle, Newton, Benjamin Franklin - all brilliant thinkers of their own time. The Nazis had gathered them all in one location there at the Smithsonian. For what reasons, President Mack and the rebels never discovered.

But each of the children had to go home. Home to the time from which they came from. Most of the rebels were dead or already returned to the future. It was up to President Mack and his Russian rebel friend, Mojmir, to help escort each of them back in time. In addition, they found other scientists deeper in the castle. They were old in age and from the recent past, some even from that year. They returned them as well. Mojmir explained it was important that they get back to work to help correct the temporal shift.

When they were done, President Mack and his friend looked at each other for a moment, exhausted but overwhelmed with joy. When they first met, President Mack didn't like Mojmir. He looked like a unkempt starving bear with long gray matted hair. When he opened his mouth, the President hated him even more. He had a deep hatred of

Russians since they had deserted the Americans during their quest for freedom.

Mojmir had his reservations as well. President Mack looked like a thug. One you'd avoid even in the light of day.

But Mojmir and President Mack had both been prisoners of war, held captive in a concentration camp and tortured on an almost daily basis. They were block-mates and it's amazing how quickly friendships are forged when you have a common enemy. He and Mojmir had been through so much together: escaping the concentration camp, leading the rebellion, overthrowing the American Nazi government, and traveling through time. When they had to say good-bye, it's as if he was losing a brother.

President Mack remembered their final words to each other as if it was yesterday.

"It's been a great ride," President Mack said to Mojmir after returning all the children and scientists. "I'm glad we got to do the things we did. You know, save the world and stuff." The President stuck out his hand for a hearty handshake.

Mojmir grabbed it and pulled him in for a bear hug. For a skinny guy, his handshake was firm and his hug was strong. It must be how Russians say good-bye.

"It's not over," Mojmir told him. "Your job has just begun. You must track down every Nazi in this country, chase them down every rat hole they'll hide in, pull off every veil they try to disguise themselves with, and imprison them. Kill them. Mercilessly. Promise me you'll track them down."

"I promise you, my friend, that I'll destroy every ounce of Nazi blood in this country and beyond. I'll rid the world of these scumbags. You got my word."

With that, Mojmir released his hug. He took a step back and pulled out a stick. In a few seconds it extended steel tentacles which unfolded and circled around Mojmir in a big shiny orb.

"Good-bye," Mojmir could be heard through the orb. "Watch your back and keep your promise."

These were the last thoughts President Mack had on his

deathbed. Not the drug running, not the glory of reconstruction, not his wife, family, or grandchildren. He remembered the pledge he made to his Russian friend Mojmir.

President Mack had led the rebels to defeat all the Nazis and drive them from America and Canada. As he laid there in his final moments of life, his hospice nurse could hear him mumbling, "I kept my promise."

President Tobias Mack died knowing he fulfilled his commitment to his friend and completely cleaned America of its Nazi scum.

ONE

I think I'm being followed by Nazis. Which is worse than it sounds, because I'm the one that should be doing the following. In my past, I'd be hunting down Nazis and disposing of them by any means necessary. Today is different. My assignment is to observe. I'm not to engage by any means. But while avoiding making contact, I think I've put myself at risk. Plus, I'm out of my element and in unfamiliar territory.

On the other hand, my assignment in 1989 was to observe as well, and we all know where that led to. I helped ignite the rebellion, demolished a Nazi outpost, swam over the Niagara Falls, and then led the attack on the American Nazi Government. On the scale between a participant and an audience, I definitely tipped the scale towards a participant.

At the end of it all my father dragged me back home. Did I return here as a hero? Not in his eyes. He immediately put me back to work as a temporal researcher, sending Frank and me back in time to help him figure out how exactly the Nazis manipulated the past.

This time, my orders aren't from the government; they are from my father. If I don't follow them, there will be a multitude of punishments, but nothing will be worse than his disappointment and disdain during the weeks ahead. On top of that, they'll be no more missions.

So I'm standing in the shadows in between a few columns of the Brandenburg Gate back in 1933, waiting for the Nazis to pass me. I'm alone and at the edge of a huge city park. Frank's on the other side of the park, about a one hundred and fifty yards away. If I'm discovered I can scream loud enough and I'm sure he'll come running. So, if I need his help, I know it's there. But my goal is to stay undetected. I don't move.

From behind me, I can hear a small group of men shuffling. They're not talking and trying to keep quiet themselves so no one discovers their mission – to burn down the Reichstag Building. It's the German equivalent of the White House and in actual history communists started a fire there, but it only caused minor damage. The small fire made the Germans hate the communists, which is how the Nazi political party came into power. But as part of their plan to alter the past, extend World War II, and create long-time German world domination, the Nazis somehow got the Communists to torch the whole Reichstag Building to ashes.

In 2086, all the communicators are two-way ear buds that fit in like miniature hearing aids. It emits an audio signal so I can hear the sender and absorbs the sound waves when I speak for the receiver. Back in 1989, we used the Walkman to communicate with the future but now I'm using a two-way ear bud to my dad back at the lab. A click signals he's about to speak.

"You must not make contact, Alex," my father's voice commands. "This is not the Nazi party you know and understand. Your mission here is to determine how many people are involved, not to stop them."

"I still don't understand why I can't just take them out," I whisper. "I can stop the Nazi party right here and now if I prevent them from starting the fire."

"Do not engage," my dad directs. "We need them to start the fire. If they don't start the fire and blame it on the communists, then the Nazi party won't come to power there in 1933."

"I still don't get why that's not a good thing," I say.

"We've discussed this," my dad explains impatiently. "The Nazi party will come to power. It's their destiny. If we put it off for a year, or even months, we don't know what the ripple effect will be. It will change American History drastically and could put its fate back into the hands of the Nazis. What we need to know is how they've manipulated their past. If there are more than a handful of Nazis conspiring to light the Reichstag on fire, than that means they didn't trust their initial historical plan. Understand, Alex?... Alex?"

I don't respond. The group of Nazis are a few feet from me and if I speak, they'll hear me. They don't look like your average Nazi, dolled up in crisp black uniforms with swastika armbands and silver eagle crusted hats. Instead, they look like common 1933 street thugs.

See, this is pre-World War II Nazis, just as the party was coming to fruition. In fact, the fire at the Reichstag Building is what catapults them into power. The building was the home of the German parliament and on this day it caught on fire. Investigators declared it was arson and started by Marinus van der Lubbe. He was a communist. At the time, the Germans hated communists more than Nazis so the Nazis were able to arrest all communists and in essence, take over rule of Germany. It was the catalyst for everything. A big huge "node" on the temporal river of history. If you want to make big swings in the course of history, like prolong World War II, this is the node to manipulate.

"Alex! Will you answer me?" my father shouts into my ear bud. I ignore him. I peer through the darkness at the group of Nazis. There are six men. I scan through their faces, looking for the Dutch boy with the big quiff of hair, but Marinus is not there. I watch them pass in the night while my father yells for me in my ear bud.

"Dad," I whisper when it's safe, "He's not in this group. He must be with Frank." Neither of us have heard from Frank since we landed here an hour ago. Frank and I split off so he can reach the Reichstag Building from the East side and I from the West.

"I'm bringing you both back," says Dad, "This is too risky."

"No, not yet," I argue. "We have to know how big this really is."

My dad wants to know how they went about changing the course of time. We know that in our manipulated history the fire was larger than the real historical one. It's one of the moments of history that helped them split off the temporal gravitational pull and forced all the aberrations in time – extending World War II and allowing the U.S. to be conquered by the Nazis.

My theory here is the Nazis infiltrated the Communist Party, convinced several members to burn the Reichstag Building to the ground, blamed it on Marinus, and then claim that communists were out to overthrow Germany. That's how the Nazis gained immense, long lasting power.

"Follow them," Dad directs in my ear bud. "Stay close but not too close."

"Dad," I whisper, "I know what I'm doing. I've been through several missions before."

"You're not back in 1989," Dad reminds me. "This is different. You're a woman in 1933 Berlin. You're not supposed to be out this late alone. I can't even imagine what they'll do to you if you get caught."

"Well, then," I say, "I won't get caught."

The group of Nazi street thugs are far enough away to follow so I step out of my shadow and head up Ebertstraße to track them, with the Reichstag Building just a block away. As we reach the building, they walk around it to the front. Suddenly, out of the city park another group of about ten men step out to meet them and start speaking in German.

My ear bud translates any language into my ear. It's new cool 2086 technology. But I'm not close enough to hear what's being said. I dip into the trees to observe. The total group is about fifteen guys and I scan the crowd to find Marinus. He looks nervous, but the other guys keep on patting him on the back. Most of the other men look like typical German men in their 30s. One has his back to me, and seems a little odd compared to the rest. His clothes don't fit as well and doesn't quite match the others. He anxiously looks around, turning his head towards me, and I discover why he looks out of place. It's because he is. It's Frank.

"Dad," I whisper. "We've got a problem. That order you gave Frank and me to just observe? He may have not been listening that well."

"WHAT!" Dad screams into my ear bud. Dad was crystal clear that we weren't to get involved. He told us we are research scientists that are just supposed to observe.

"Come on, Dad," I argue. "When in the past two years have Frank and I not been participatory?"

"I'm pulling you two back, right now," my dad insists.

"You can't, Dad," I say, "Frank is in full view of the others. They'll figure out he's a time traveler and it may cause more problems that we want. I'm moving in closer."

I sneak through the forest in the shadows to get a better look at the crowd. I'm close enough to hear their conversation.

"You will be a hero, Marinus," one of the guys tell him. "You'll be the biggest hero of the Communist Party. Stalin will celebrate you. They'll make a statue of you right here in the park."

"Yes," says another. "Burning down the Reichstag is the correct thing to do. It's a great statement to the Nazi Party. They will be devastated."

"But why won't you guys stay with me once the firemen come?" asks Marinus. "Don't you want to be a hero, too?" Marinus talks rather slowly, as if he has brain damage or something.

The tallest man among them, with wide droopy shoulders, steps up to Marinus and just from his presence you can tell he's the leader. He's got an elongated jaw and protruding forehead that adds to his dominate posture. His eyes are sunken into his face and his brow juts out farther than most people. He looks like one of those people who never smile, with baggy jowls and thin lips. I'm not going to like this guy.

"You deserve this," the tallest man clearly states. I recognize his voice instantly. It's General Stefan Kaiser – head of the Gestapo in the future, and orchestrator of the Temporal Shift.

I can't get too close. He'll recognize me. He knows who I am, especially since I threatened to hunt him down and kill him after the attack on the Niagara Outpost.

General Kaiser looks up from his watch. "It's 9 p.m. It's time to start." The group of men head towards the front entrance. Frank is still part of the gang, glancing around to see if he can catch a glimpse of me. He knows I'm here, but he wants to know where.

As the group gets closer, a few peel off towards a window that's to the right of the main stairs. They kick at it several times and bust it open. They return to the whole group and walk through the main door.

"They must be leaving evidence for false entryway," I say.

"The history report says the police claim Marinus entered through a window by the main door," states my dad.

When the coast is clear, I head up the stairs and through the door, following the group. I don't know what I'm going to do, but it's got to be something. They have Frank. If we return now, he'll vanish in thin air and we'll break a bunch of temporal laws. I move down the hallway and towards the Parliament Library where the fire was supposed to start.

That's where I find the gang.

They're pouring oil over furniture, book cases, and books. Frank is tied to a chair and General Kaiser is beating him.

"Who are you?" the general yells at Frank. "Where have you come from?"

Frank says nothing and looks forward stoically.

The general hits him again.

"You will tell me who you are or you will burn with all these books," he explains. "You think you can just show up, blend in with this crowd in the park? You don't think I knew you were an outsider? Do you think you can outsmart us? I know you don't look German. Are you French? Dutch? Canadian?"

"Stefan," shouts Marinus. "We are almost done."

"Yes, Marinus, your hero moment is upon you," confirms the general. "But let me finish interrogating the prisoner."

The general hits Frank full force in his gut. Frank cries out and doubles over as far as he can, pulling on the ropes tied behind the chair.

"What is your name?" he asks.

Then it hits me. The general should know exactly who Frank is. When we were back in 1989 and 1990, General Stefan Kaiser was the man behind the scenes trying to hunt us down. I spoke to him after the Battle of Niagara. He has to remember us.

Unless, this is still the past! It must be before 2086! The

general probably time traveled from an earlier year, back to 1933, to change the past and create the temporal shift in 1989 that Frank and I lived through. So at this point in his personal timeline, he hasn't met Frank and me yet, which is why he doesn't know Frank. But he is suspicious.

So now I need to save Frank, which means I have to stop the fire. Even if it means going against my dad's instructions. Maybe even take the opportunity to kill the general and stop it all.

"Very well, then," says the general to Frank. "Keep your secret. It will be the last thing you do." He hits Frank one more time. His face is now a bloody pulp.

"Alright, men," says the general. "Let's gather our things and get out of here before the fire brigade shows up. Marinus will light the fire and take it from here. Leave no trace."

"But what about the prisoner?" asks Marinus. "Won't he leave a trace?"

The general picks up a can of oil and doses him with it. "No. Light him first."

One by one the general's men gather their stuff and begin to leave the room. I stand in the shadows, in the archway, up against the wall. If I start a fight now, I'll be easily subdued by the gang. I have to be patient and wait for my chance. Which of course, is a very hard thing for me to do.

They begin to pass by me and seem not to notice I'm there. I see the general finally walk by me, smiling. He turns around back to Marinus. "Remember: wait several moments for us to leave, then begin the fire. Thank you for your service, Marinus. You will be marked a hero for this day. A true hero of Germany."

The general turns around and starts walking away. Poor Marinus. The general convinced him that he was being a hero for his Communist Party. Instead, the Nazis will use this moment to stop the Communist uprising and turn Germany into Nazi rule. This is how the general made a stronger change and increased the hatred of communists. Marinus didn't do this solo, he had the general's help.

But there's no time to explain this all to Marinus. He's already getting his flint and steel together. He has a mission, and it starts with killing Frank.

"You are communist scum," says Marinus. "You look like a Russian. I know it in my bones. It will be my pleasure to kill you." He bends over a wooden stick wrapped in an oil rag and begins striking the flint and steel over it, trying to spark up the torch.

This is my moment to attack. I rush across the room and try to tackle him. He's caught off balance and starts to fall, but not before a final spark flies off the flint and catches the torch on fire.

Marinus rolls over to see me staring at him. It registers that I am a woman and the look of shock increases. Then as the torch flickers to his left, he is reminded that there's a mission he must complete.

I raise my fist in the air and bring it down to pummel him, but he moves to his left and grabs the torch. My fist makes contact with the wooden floor, and the pain rockets up my arm and down my spine.

I don't have time to console myself because Marinus has moved out from under me, pushed me down on my belly and is now swinging the torch in my direction. I can smell burnt hair in the air and realize that some of my curly red hair is getting singed.

I roll over and he swings the torch straight at me. I move to my right, jump to my feet and grab his torch arm from the side. I dig my thumb into the pit of his elbow and hold it there. This instantly collapses his arm and forces his hand holding the torch to his head. He screams in pain as the fire burns his face. He struggles to release himself but I hold my thumb in place firmly.

After a few moments he passes out from the pain of the flames and heat. As he drops to the ground, I grab the torch from his hand and run over to Frank.

"Are you okay?" I say to him, he head still slumped to his chest.

"Alex?" he mumbles out. "Is that you?"

"Yep," I confirm, pulling out a knife from inside my jacket and begin to cut off his ropes. Relieving the pressure of his binds seems to help him come to.

"Just once," he says. "Just once, I'd like to save you."

I smile. Even with him being a bloody mess, he's trying to make me smile.

"Come on, let's get you out of here," he pulls his arms free. Suddenly, I see his eyes widen and he pushes me to the side to avoid an attack from Marinus. Instead of a fireplace poker hitting me square in the back of the head, it hits Frank on his thighs. He stands up out of the chair and towers over Marinus. He's got at least a foot on him.

"You messed with my girlfriend," he explains. "Now you're going to pay."

In the shuffle, I have fallen backwards onto my butt. The torch I was holding in my left hand went flying across the room and has ignited an oil covered bookshelf.

"Frank," I yell. "There's no time for chivalry. We gotta get out of here. The place is going up in flames."

Marinus positions himself between us and the one exit. He's blocking the only way out. "You'll have to go through me," he declares.

"I don't think we're just observers anymore," says Frank, "We got to stop this. I'll get Marinus, you go get the general." Frank grabs Marinus by the shoulders and bends him forwards towards his knee, making contact with his gut.

I'm going against my father's instructions, but Frank's right. We have to try and stop the general. If I can keep him from returning to the future, and capture or kill him, then maybe I can stop this whole Nazi Temporal War from ever happening.

I run down the hallway and head to the front door, hoping I can catch him and it's not too late. As I turn the corner, I run smack into someone and lose my balance. The person I ran into reacted much quicker, holding his footing. In fact, he holds me up, as well. Now I'm stuck in his hands.

It's the general.

"Well," he chuckles. "What do I have here? A rogue Irish Red?"

"If you're smart," I claim. "You'll let me go."

"Hmm… and an English speaker. Not much of an Irish accent. My guess is you're American," he says. "I'm smarter than you think I am. There are things I know and understand that you can never fathom. My gut says you're a companion of the man I left for dead with Marinus. But why a red-haired Ami is paired with him, I haven't quite figured out."

He tightens his grip on my left shoulder. It's solid, there's no way I can wriggle out. I could call out to my father to pull us back, but I've cut off my communicator. The general slowly clamps his right hand over my throat and starts to squeeze.

"Maybe I can convince you to tell me. I've been told that I'm quite persuasive." His grip on my throat tightens and I start gasping for air. I see some flashing white dots and the world around me starts to get a little hazy.

"ALEX!" I hear from behind me. It's Frank. He's coming to save me. Suddenly, the general loosens his grip.

"Red hair. Irish-American. Time traveler," he smiles. "Do I have the famous Alex Eviston right here in my grip?"

I struggle, but he tightens his grip on my throat again.

"I came back in here because I thought Marinus would fail me, that I'd find him in the library still trying to make a spark with steel and flint. Instead I have a prize now."

"I swear to God if you hurt her general, you're a dead man," says Frank.

"Don't take another step forward," he commands. "Or I will kill her."

He looks at Frank, then deep into my eyes.

"You both know me," he realizes. "You've seen me before. In the future. Let me see, last I heard of Alex Eviston, you were banished to 1989 – the year of misfits. You must have seen my temporal shift plan come to fruition. Tell me, what's it like to live in Nazi America? How does one come to terms with the fact that Nazi Germans are superior?"

"Tah…" I can barely breathe, let alone say anything.

"Let me guess," says the general. "You defeat us in the future and now you've come back in time to stop me. To stop each change I'm making to cause the temporal shift. Sad. You can't change destiny. Germany is destined to rule the world and there's nothing you can do about it. See, you're the one that's being defeated here. Because instead of stopping me, I'm going to stop you, now"

The general's grip tightens and in my last breath I'm able to bellow out, "Two vs. One!"

Frank realizes we're outnumbering the general and at least one of us can come out of this alive. He charges the general and tackles him to the ground. He loses his grip on my throat and I fall to the ground, trying to gulp in air – renewing oxygen to my lungs. Frank and the general roll around on the ground exchanging punches. It all seems like a blur to me, the world is spinning. I shake my head and try to snap out of it. I fight the urge to pass out. I stand up and pull out the knife from my jacket. Still a little dazed, I watch the wrestling battle before me. The general rolls over and has Frank on the ground, pummeling him. I stumble forward, quickly grab the general by his hair, pull his head back and place my knife against his jugular vein.

"It's over," I say to him.

Suddenly, osmium tentacles push my hands and force me away. The general is enveloped by an osmium cocoon.

"Have fun trying to track me," yells the general through the metal casing. "I'll be watching for you. Now I know your plans and there's no way you can thwart me. I'll be expecting you."

Heat is pulled from my body and the light around him begins to bend as if I was looking at him through a prism. A rush of energy is sucked from my body as the return sequence begins.

The general is gone.

I crawl over to Frank. I'm sore from being thrown back from temporal gravity, and the fight with Marinus, plus I'm still woozy from almost being choked to death. Frank is rubbing his head and checking for blood.

"We gotta get out of here," he explains.

"Okay, call my dad," I don't want to talk to him and have to explain what happened. I'm still trying to avoid my dad.

"I've lost my communicator," responds Frank. "You're going to have to call him this time."

I hate disappointing my dad.

There are voices outside. Smoke is filling the hallways. The building is on fire. If we try to hide inside, we'll get caught in the fire. If we run outside, we'll get caught by the police. Our mission is done here anyways.

I turn on my communicator.

"Dad." I say solemnly. "Bring us home."

TWO

"What in God's name were you thinking?" my father yells at us. "I expect something like this from you, Alex. But Frank? You're supposed to be the level headed one. You're supposed to keep her in check."

"I'm sorry," is all I can manage to get out.

Dad is a scientist. I've learned over the years that when God's name comes into play then he's really pissed off. I don't want to fuel his anger any more so I decide to focus on cleaning up Frank's face. Most of the dried blood is washed off but he's got gauze stuffed up his nose and his jaw is bruised from his left ear to his chin. He's gonna have a left black eye as well. I was really worried about him while we were in the fire. I don't want to lose him again now that we have finally taken our relationship to the next level. That kiss we had back on the airstrip in 1990 was our first kiss with many more that came after it. I've found someone that wants to be a part of my life and looks after me. I really haven't had that type of connection since my mom and I don't want to let that feeling go.

I'm bending over Frank, treating his wounds while he's sitting on a stool in my dad's private bathroom. He looks up and smiles at me for a moment. I know he's glad I'm here for him, even if he's got to deal with my domineering father as well.

"Do you understand the implications this has? The ripple effect?" Dad admonishes from the doorway of the bathroom. "Stefan knows his plan works. In fact, you did nothing to change it! But worse yet, he knows you're out to stop him. He will track you forever. You were supposed to just observe, not interact! Now we have no idea how this changes everything!"

"Sorry, Dr. Eviston, but I had to call an audible the moment Alex and I split up," Frank explains. "In the park I ran right into those guys. And when I say right into them, I mean it. I knocked over that Marinus guy and he twisted his ankle. I had to pretend I was one of their gang. Turns out they figured me out. It's all my fault. Don't take it out on your daughter."

"I'm blaming the both of you," my dad shouts. "You both should have known better. Do you know the paperwork I have to file? We have to alert your superiors that General Kaiser knows you were there, and then I have to explain to the head of the base why you were there in the first place!"

I sigh. My father is all about the rules. Rules must be followed. Always. Even if they aren't his. Once my mom and dad bought a new car. The dealer miscalculated the tax and we shorted him $2000. Dad insisted we go back to the Dealer and pay the difference. Mom said she'd take care of it. Dad never worried about it again. A week later I asked her about it. Mom replied with, "If the Dealer made a mistake, then that's his fault. And what Dad doesn't know, doesn't hurt him." Mom never took care of it, and never told Dad.

"Dad," I softly said. "Why don't you let me file the paperwork? Since Frank and I were the ones that messed up, we'll take care of it. Think of it as our way of making things better."

"I want to see the paperwork before you file it," my dad acquiesces. "Don't think I don't realize what you're doing. You're not as smooth as your mom. I'm going back to my lab to finish some research. You should be leaving soon to get to your lecture. One more thing, I'm extremely disappointed in you. You specifically went against my clear orders. You're better than that."

Dad walks out of his office and back towards the particle accelerator.

"I don't think I'm ever going to please him," I sigh to Frank.

"Forget about it, Sunshine," says Frank.

Frank's taken to calling me "Sunshine" as his pet name for me. Says my hair makes him think of the sun rise. I think it's because I make him feel warm and fuzzy. Never the less, I kind of like it.

I smile to myself. I like the nickname – Sunshine. It makes me feel good that Frank recognizes how happy I make him. I hope he calls me 'Sunshine' for the rest of our lives.

I glance over at the digital display on the mirror. "Time," I say.

The numbers 12:18 appear on the edge of the mirror. "It's eighteen minutes past Noon," explains a voice that sounds very much like a drunk Irishman. It's an interactive computer with sound recognition. My dad programmed it to sound like a bartender from Kilkenny in Ireland. "Your lecture starts in about three hours. It's gonna take yah about sixty minutes to get there. If I were you, I'd finish it up and make yah way to Columbus."

As annoying as the computer's voice is, it's right. It's a good hour from my dad's lab at Wright-Patterson Air Force Base to The Ohio State University where I'm a guest lecturer. I have to get moving.

"Frank," I say. "Can you do me a favor?"

"You want me to do that paperwork, don't you?" he smiles.

"No. We're not doing any paperwork," I explain. "I need the keys to your car. I drove here with Dad and I need to get back for the lecture."

"No, no, no," he argues. "You're not leaving me here with your dad. I'll drive you." Frank gets up and slowly starts hobbling over to the bathroom door.

"Give me the keys," I tell him. "I'll drive you. Then after the lecture, I'm taking you to the doctor."

Frank gingerly reaches into his pocket and hands me the keys. "I'll be fine," he argues. "You can drive to Columbus, but they'll be no doctor's visit."

We slowly start walking down the hall to the elevator. We press the button and the doors open, as if it was waiting for us. This isn't that unusual since my dad's lab is on the bottom level and it's easier for the elevator to be waiting on the lowest floor rather than on an upper floor. But as I step through the doors and turn around, I look up and find a pencil camera that pans over to me, following my movement. Security cameras are everywhere at Wright-Patterson Air Force Base, but I don't remember that one being there. And it gives me the chills, thinking that it's following me.

Over the past few days, little things like that have been going on: a car that curiously follows me all the way from Dayton to Columbus, someone watching me in the grocery store, a couple at a restaurant several tables over who seemed more interested in watching me than paying attention to each other. Frank thinks I'm paranoid. I think that with all that's happened to me, I have the right to be paranoid.

As the doors close, I nod to Frank to point out the cameras. But a hand pops through the closing doors and holds them open. After a moment, the doors recede and a woman steps through. She's got on a lab coat and carrys a clip board but it's the only evidence that she's a scientist. She's dressed a little too racy for the lab, wearing a pencil skirt and black high heels as if she's going somewhere to impress a guy. Her sandy brown hair is pulled back in a tight ballet bun which accentuates her ocean blue eyes. She turns and smiles at us with that kind of look that says, "I'm smiling because I have to." Complete with long legs, she looks a lot like an attractive Alpine Skier Frank used to date back when he was in school. I've seen the pictures. I'm not going to like this woman, at all.

The doors to the elevator close.

"Ground floor," I say. The elevator begins moving up.

"Hello," she offers her hand to Frank first, "I'm Dr. Mackenzie Radkowski," she explains.

"Hello," Frank smiles warmly and shakes her hand.

"Yes. Hello," I butt in. "I'm sure you know who we are."

"Yes," she smiles and laughs, tilting her head a bit. "You're the infamous Frank Bouchard and Alex Eviston. You're legends here. Your frizzy red hair is like a beacon. No one could mistake you."

I hate this woman already. First, who wears black high heels in a temporal research lab and second, don't be commenting about my hair with your perfect ballet bun and ocean blue eyes.

"So, how's the research going?" She asks us.

"Good," smiles back Frank. "We had a little run in but it's going good."

"Well, it looks like you had a run in," she says concerningly.

She reaches her hand up to Frank's face and touches his cheek. "You're still a little puffy. What happened?"

"Well, we had a run in with-" starts Frank.

"Research." I cut Frank off. "We're doing top secret research." The hairs must be standing up on my neck. She's touched my guy and I'm not happy about it.

"Hmpf," she says and turns around to face the doors. We stand in silence as the elevator smoothly brings us to the ground floor. It takes a few moments since his lab is so far down into the basement. The silence is a bit awkward but that's okay. I typically use this time to rethink through some of the research I did in dad's lab, but all I can think about is why this woman thinks she can touch my boyfriend's face.

That's when it hits me. Dad's lab is the only lab on his floor. Where did this woman come from? What was she doing on his floor?

Before I can ask we reach the ground floor, the doors open, and she steps out, disappearing into the crowd shuffling about the Air Force base.

"Didn't you find that odd?" I say to Frank.

"Yeah," he admits. "She did look a lot like my ex-girlfriend, Diane. She even used to wear her hair like that when she wasn't skiing."

"No," I say and hit his shoulder. "Don't you find it odd that she got on at my dad's floor? There are only a few people that ever get on there. My dad, me, now you, and his lab assistants.

"Maybe he's got a new lab assistant?" he offers.

"He would have mentioned a new lab assistant to me," I counter.

"Maybe she was assigned to him and he didn't know it, yet," Frank says as we make our way to his car.

This argument could go on forever.

"I wish you'd trust me more. Believe me more," I say.

"You have a lot of stuff swirling around in your head," he says. "I just want to help you think about the right things and not let some of your dark past make you live in fear. I want to start thinking about happy times."

Frank reaches out and takes my hand as we walk to his car. Maybe he's right. Maybe it is time to let go of my demons.

"How long do you think it will be until Homeland Security gives us a new assignment?" asks Frank, trying to pass the time on the stretch of road between Dayton and Columbus. "I'm itching to get back out to the field."

I'm not as anxious as Frank. My dad needs me here to help him with his research and I have the lecturing job at The Ohio State University. Frank must be a little bored. He's been working with my dad as well, but he's not doing much else. Frank needs something else to do when I'm not around during the day.

"Maybe you can be a coach for a kids' hockey team while we're waiting?" I suggest.

"Hmm… seems like a long term commitment. What if we have to go back out to the field? I don't want to leave those kids stranded without a coach," he counters.

Obviously, Frank wants to get back into action. We'll both have to get back to work eventually, but Frank wants to go sooner than later. I have to stay with Dad and OSU for a while. Maybe I can let him go ahead of me?

I'm not sure about separating from Frank, again. We split up after the attack on Cleveland back in 1990 and I almost never saw him again. I ended up in a concentration camp and if I didn't find Mojmir and Toby, then I might still be there today.

Frank and I are definitely a couple now and kind of on a fast track to permanent status. Once things settle down a bit more, we'll probably start discussing our future together but for now there's a lot of gray area about what we'll be doing. I don't really care what my new assignment is, as long as it's with Frank.

I know he feels the same way. He had his moment of glory shooting down the Nazi's B-52 over the ocean and saving Washington D.C. from being destroyed with an atomic bomb.

He's a hero now and brought back respect to his family name. He's ready to create a life together with me. But like all men, he's got to do something. He can't relax. Together, I'm sure we'll figure something out. The world around us is settling down, so we'll be able to finally do the same. The good news is with all the work he's done with my dad, I think Frank already has his approval.

Mrs. Alexandria Bouchard? I'm pretty sure that name is in my future.

Suddenly, there's a multitude of brake lights ahead of me and my thoughts refocus on driving. I quickly slow down and come to rest at a full stop a few inches from the car in front of us.

"Looks like a traffic jam of some sort," states Frank. "I'll turn on the information channel so we can see what's going on."

Frank presses the touch screen on the dashboard and navigates to the information channel which broadcasts all the important news and things people are talking about online within a hundred foot radius.

"There's an overturned tractor trailer," says one voice, "Hauling corn grain, spilled all over the freeway and blocking the road."

"I see a police car several feet blocking all the traffic," says another voice, "A patrolman's leaning over the hood of his car, pointing his gun at a minivan parked between himself and the tractor trailer."

"This is more than a car accident," says Frank.

"Call the Columbus office," I say, "See if they think we should help?"

The Information Channel chimes back in, "I'm parked behind the police car and can see everything," the voice says, "The driver of the truck is slumped over the steering wheel. He's out cold. There's a family in the minivan and some guy in the back seat with the kids, flashing his gun at the police man."

Frank opens the car door. "Pop the trunk. We don't have time to call the office."

"Open trunk," I command and get out of the car. I meet Frank around back and he hands me a 9mm and a rifle. He grabs his own and we double time it to the front of the accident. We can see the tractor trailer up ahead and reach the police car in a few moments, crouching down low against the side fender of the car. There's a highway patrolman leaning over the car, taking aim at the van. He looks at us in surprise.

"I'm Colonel Alex Eviston," I explain, "This is Colonel Frank Bouchard. What's the situation?"

He drops down and leans against the tire between us. "Thank God you're here," he anxiously blurts out. Beads of sweat are dripping from his forehead and his hands are shaking. "It all happened so quickly, I didn't know what to do. I was looking for speeders and out of nowhere this guy popped out of the grass and ran onto the freeway. Shot the guy driving the truck. When the minivan spun out of control to avoid hitting it, the guy pulled open the hatch and climbed in. He's in the back with a couple of kids, with the Mom and Dad in the front. I called for some additional units but with the traffic backed up they ain't gonna get here very soon. I don't know what to do. All I ever do is give out traffic tickets."

Poor guy. Was probably never trained for moments like these. With all the medical and technological advancements over the past few decades, you'd think doctors would have solve for crazy people by now but they haven't. Frank and I have to play heroes again and save this family from the insane guy who hopped in their van.

Frank slowly gets to his feet and peers through the police car's window at the van, then at the tractor trailer. After a few seconds, he returns to his spot next to us.

"I got a plan," he explains. "What's your name, Deputy?"

"Dwight," he nervously explains.

"Okay, Dwight, we're going to get through this," Frank calmly explains. "I want you to return to your stance on the hood of the car. Keep your aim on the intruder. Don't take your aim off. Don't shoot. Just make it look like you have him completely in your sights. Can you do that for me?"

"Yes," says Dwight.

"Alex," Frank changes his focus to me, "I need you to distract the crazy guy, keep him talking to you, looking at you, whatever. Okay?"

"What are you going to do?" I ask. But it's too late, Frank has already gone running towards the shoulder of the road and into the tall grass.

"He takes down one B-52 and saves the world. Now he thinks he's invincible," I scoff at Dwight. He looks back at me in confusion. "Take your position," I instruct, "I'm going to distract him."

Dwight gets back onto the hood of the car and into his stance. I peer around the front bumper and see my options are limited. There's nothing between us and the minivan. The guy in the back seat is shouting and moving his gun to the Dad, to the Mom, and then back to the kids. Frightened expressions and tears are on everyone's faces.

"Hey," I yell at him, standing up behind the police car, "You want to point that thing somewhere else?"

He turns and sees me. His eyes widen and eyebrows raise. He must realize there's more out here than one Highway Patrolman. A sinister look moves over his face and he slowly and deliberately takes aim on me. I quickly fall to the ground and roll over behind a tire. I hear screams from the minivan.

"Are you okay?" asks Dwight. "Should I shoot back?"

"No," I instruct. "What happened?"

"He took a shot at you," he explains. "It busted through the window and through the exact spot you were standing. The guy has accurate aim."

"You missed me!" I yell and crouch-walk over to the rear part of the car. I peer around the trunk to see a broken window in the back seat, a freaked out family, and the intruder frantically trying to find out where I am. His aim keeps switching to all points of the car.

Why hasn't he taken out the patrolman? Dwight is completely exposed on the hood of the car. Instead, the shooter keeps on aiming at me.

"Looking for me?" I shout as I pop my head up over the trunk then fall back down.

A shot rings out and again I feel a bullet whiz over my head. I wish I knew what Frank was up to so I knew how long I had to keep this up.

"You missed me again," I yell. "That's two shots and I'm guessing you expended only one shot on the driver. So I'm wondering if you have a six round gun or nine round gun. You want to let me in on the details so I know how many more times we have to do this?"

Except for the pleading mother in the front seat of the car, I don't hear anything. Frank better do something soon, I don't know how many more times I can make this guy shoot and miss.

I shuffle over to the patrol car's driver door and open it up. After climbing over the front seat, I peer out over the window frame. As soon as my red hair clears the frame, a shot rings out. I'm not quick enough to duck my head back down but it doesn't matter. The bullet hits the glass and the window splinters but doesn't break. It must be bulletproof glass.

I hear more screams from the van, but I can't see through the glass.

"He's in there," I hear Dwight yell. "Your partner climbed in through the back hatch. They're struggling."

I open the car door, climb out, and run as fast as I can to the van. I pull open the back passenger door and look over the toddler inside to find the crazy guy on the floor unconscious. Frank is staring at him in shock.

"Is everyone okay?" I ask.

The toddler burst into tears and her older brother in the other seat, who looks like he's seen a ghost, nods in confirmation.

"Is it over?" the Dad asks.

"Yes," I explain, "It's safe. Why don't you take your kids over to the patrol car?"

The parents get out of the car. I help unbuckle the toddler and pass her off to the Dad. Mom on the other side, grabs her son's hand and they run over to the patrol car, wanting to get away as soon as possible.

I turn back to the minivan and see Frank still staring at the dead crazy guy.

"You okay, fly boy?" I chuckle at him. "You want to explain the whole plan next time before you go running off to save the world?"

Frank doesn't answer. He stares at the intruder who's laying on the floor of the minivan, dead. Bruises are around his neck, Frank had choked him to death.

"I've seen him before," Frank finally mutters out, "In Columbus."

"That doesn't surprise me," I say, "We're about 20 miles from Columbus. This guy could have easily traveled here from our neighborhood."

"I saw him at the train station," Frank explains further.

"Are you sure? I don't remember you going to the train station since we've been back," I'm confused. "When were you there?"

"In 1990, on the train ride to the kill the Nazis in Washington D.C." he replies. "Toby and I got off the train together when we stopped to refuel in Columbus. Ran into this guy who was asking a bunch of questions. I thought he was a common Nazi guard at the time. I didn't know he was a time traveler."

I look down at the dead guy. Plain black pants. Plain black shirt. Blond hair. Blue eyes. No swastika anywhere. You'd never know he was a Nazi.

"He was aiming for me," I say. "Didn't shoot at the Deputy at all. He wanted me dead."

THREE

I try to make sense of all this during the rest of the drive to Columbus. Frank and I had to stay back and give some quick explanation of the events and promise that we'd file a full report later. I'm still going to be able to drop off Frank and make it to my lecture, but I'm going to cut it close. I can't stop wondering why the guy from the train station tried to kill me. It's as if he knew we were going to be there, so he caused the traffic jam as a cover for trying to kill us.

"I thought Toby took care of all the Nazis," I tell Frank. "What the heck was that guy doing there? He was waiting for us to show up. He wanted the authorities to think he was looney, but he wanted me dead."

"Maybe this guy went rogue," Frank says. "Maybe we just changed something in the past that made this guy come after us."

"Now that I think about it," I say, "I'm not sure if this was an isolated incident."

"What do you mean?" he asks.

"I've been seeing things, out of the corner of my eye I've caught people staring at us," I explain. "I chalked it up to us being celebrities, and a little bit of paranoia. Maybe it's something more? Maybe there are Nazis still throughout the United States and they are tracking us down for revenge sake?"

"You know I love you, Honey," starts Frank, "But with all you've been through sometimes you over think things. I don't think this was part of some grand plan. I trust that Mack Truck took care of the Nazis. He promised Mojmir. This has to be an isolated incident and your first gut reaction to people watching you is correct. We're heroes and everyone notices us."

"All right," I concede. "But don't be shocked if I'm still always looking over my shoulder."

I drop off Frank at my dad's house. We haven't rented our own place since we've only been back a few weeks and we don't know where we're going. It's kind of weird for us to be living with my dad, but most of his time is spent in the Lab and we rarely see him at home except for mornings.

I head to The Ohio State University to start my class, parking my car in the Stadium parking lot with fifteen minutes to spare. I grab the bag out of the trunk and look around. There are students milling about but nothing strange. No one is watching me. At least I don't think anyone is.

I head up the hill to Hitchcock Hall, enter the building, and go directly to Room 131. It's one of the largest lecture halls on campus and it's going to be packed today. The class is Introduction to Temporal History and it's typically taught by my father, which you could imagine draws a large crowd.

But today's crowd will be even more than typical because I'm giving today's lecture. Since I'm a famous scientist and a war hero – they let anyone come in here and listen.

I step up on stage and the podium senses I'm there. It lifts from its resting position and levitates towards me.

"Greetings Professor Eviston," says the computer in the style of Keanu Reeves. "Today's lecture will be most excellent." Someone in the A/V Department must have thought it would be fun to program the voice as Ted "Theodore" Logan from *Bill and Ted's Excellent Adventure*, a time travel film released in 1989.

"I'm not a Professor," I explain to the computer. "I'm a guest lecturer. You can call me Doctor or Colonel Eviston. Actually, Alex will be just fine."

"Whoa," the computer trails off. "Okay, Professor Eviston, I mean, Alex."

I roll my eyes. Couldn't they have programmed the voice as John Cusack from *Say Anything*? He was dreamy. Or at least Harrison Ford from *The Last Crusade*? No… I get the doofus who almost flunked out of San Dimas High School. I wave my hand over the display on the podium. The ring I'm wearing is very fashionable but also functional. It shares my lecture notes with the podium and they appear on the screen. The ring also acts as my music player, phone, and a dozen other apps.

"Dude," the computer responds. "These notes are awesome. Have a most triumphant lecture. It's 2:01. Shall we start?"

"Yes," I say hesitantly because I know the computer is programmed to call everyone to attention.

"Ladies and gentleman," the computer bellows through the room's PA. "Honored guests and distinguished dignitaries. Put your hands together, than apart, then back together again. It is my pleasure to introduce you to the most excellent Professor Alex Eviston!"

Synthesized hard rock music from the 1980s fills the air and lights above the stage move around and then settle on me. The crowd erupts in applause.

"Thanks computer," I respond. "That's enough folks, that's enough. Applause isn't needed. I apologize for the computer's exuberance."

"Dude," responds the computer. "Don't be such a dickweed."

The lecture hall fills with chuckles. They are used to the computers being so comedic.

"Okay, computer," I say. "That's enough. Time for me to lecture."

The crowd settles in and en masse they all reach for their preferred device, a ring, a necklace, an earring, a watch, or whatever. They engage their audio recorder and sit back to listen.

Today's lecture is all about prehistoric temporal shifts and how they shaped the Dawn of Humans. I begin my lecture and as I speak, images automatically appear on the screen behind me. The slideshow I've selected is programmed to sync to my voice so I don't have to advance my own slides. The computer just hears me say, "Cambrian Period," and a huge slide of a trilobite appears on the screen.

I pretty much have my notes memorized so I spend my time looking out in the audience. All the chairs are full and people are sitting in the aisles. The doors are open and there are people out in the hallway, listening. The balcony is packed as well. It's as if everyone on campus wants to hear me speak. Or everyone is watching. All this attention I've received since our return is kind of unnerving, but Frank says I have to get used to it. It's who we are now.

Towards the end of the lecture I recognize someone down front. It's Sonia Montilla. She's a good friend of mine, my Venezuelan counterpart back in 1989. An inspector. I haven't seen her in over four years. We ran into each other at a resort in Aruba when I was taking a vacation there and she was inspecting the island. At first, we didn't know the other person was from the future, but one night I found her drunk and talking to her door lock to get into her room. Since she was trying to use modern day voice recognition to unlock her hotel room door, I instantly knew she was from the future. It was her first tour of duty and my second. We hung out the rest of the week, became close friends and stayed in contact. After her third tour of duty, she was assigned another year to monitor and I never heard from her again.

I haven't reached out to her since I returned, mainly because the U.S. isn't that friendly with Venezuela right now. We're in a Cold War with Russia, and Venezuela is aligned with them.

That's also why I can't talk to our Russian friend, Mojmir, which really pisses me off. He was always there for Frank and I. Mojmir was the one that first saw the aberrations in the Madonna video which helped warn us of the Temporal Shift. He protected us from being captured below Saint Patrick's Cathedral and helped me break out of the concentration camp in Leavenworth. He was part of the raid on Washington D.C. and worked with Mack Truck to get all the scientists back home. But while he helped us save America from the Nazis, he's now considered a spy and the enemy. I don't get it, but I can't argue it.

So, it strikes me as extremely odd that Sonia is sitting in my lecture right now. She's risking her life to be here. If she's caught, she'll go to a prison for enemies and war criminals, which is not much different from the concentration camp I was in back during the Revolution.

I try not to look at her or call attention to her, but now that she knows I've noticed her, she's staring very intently at me. As if she's trying to tell me something. Give me a visual warning.

When I make eye contact, she shifts her gaze to the man in front of her. He's got slicked back black hair, a full black beard and mustache, and circular rimmed glasses. His beard hangs off his jaw line an inch or two. Enough to claim full beard status, but not long enough to be unkempt.

He's sitting with his elbows up on the arm rest. He's tapping his fingertips onto the ones on his opposite hand, finger by finger, as if his left hand is a piano and he's playing the keys with his right hand. I try to ignore him but it's hard to avert my gaze now that I've noticed him. He's dressed in a black jacket and white shirt, too fancy to be a college student.

Once Sonia realizes I've noticed him, she gets up and walks out of my lecture. The people in the aisle move aside to let her go by. She heads straight to the doors and walks out, never turning around to wave good-bye.

Someone who was sitting on the floor in the aisle has already taken her seat.

The finger tapper never noticed her leave.

Every time I look his way, he's staring right at me with dagger eyes. He doesn't look away and his fingers keep rolling onto each other, rhythmically. Never missing a beat.

It's 2:45 and my lecture is supposed to go another five minutes. I'm so unnerved by the finger tapper that I decide to end the lecture early, which is so unlike me.

"Well since we have a full house," I begin to explain, "I'm going to end a bit early today to give you more time to get to your next class."

"Whoa," chimes in the computer. "That's most excellent indeed. Thanks. Party on, dudes."

The lights come on and the crowd begins to shuffle towards the doors. I grab my bag and walk off the stage. A group of students have gathered by the steps to talk to me, ask for autographs. But I wave them off.

"Sorry, folks," I explain. "I need to get back to some important research. It's going to have to be next week."

There's a collective sigh, but I don't wait to take it in. I follow the crowd out the doors and into the Atrium. I look around for the finger tapper and his black-slicked back hair.

I scan the crowd: about seven hundred people, all trying to get out eight doors. Talk about a fire hazard.

I keep on shifting my head east and west. There's two sets of doors out of the building and the finger tapper can walk out of either of them. For all I know he's already gone.

Sonia wanted me to follow him. I'm sure of it.

As I scan the East doors again, I see flash of greasy flat black hair and spot him. Except he's not going outside, he's heading to another hallway that leads to the stairwell. He reaches the landing and starts to go downstairs. I push my way through the crowd.

"Excuse me," I say. Those who notice me give me some room to get through. Those that don't just make me wait with everyone else. After several moments I make it to the stairwell and head down to the basement. I get to the bottom of the stairs and peek around the corner. The halls are deserted. No one's around.

I creep down the hallway. I have no reason to be down here since my office is on the top floor, spaced reserved for the honored professors and distinguished guest lecturers like myself. This floor is for graduate students. Lab area for projects that are less than worthy to be listed on the university's website. The emeritus professors get offices down here when they stop coming in. Even though my first lab was on the other side of this floor, that was years ago and people would be shocked to see me down here.

Still, I got to find the finger tapper. I look through every door window I can. When I don't see him, I stop and listen. Faintly, I hear voices from around the corner. I slowly step down the hallway, heel to toe, trying not to make a sound. I get to the corner and peer around. The hallway is empty but a few doors down there's a lab door that's cracked open and a light shining through. The voices are coming from inside. I gingerly step across the hall and lean up against the wall. I work my way over to the lab and crane my head to see through the crack. The finger tapper is in there and he's talking to Dr. Mackenzie Radkowski, the tall girl with her hair in a ballet bun from the elevator at my dad's lab. I knew there was something fishy about her.

"Her lecture was soooo boorish," claims the finger tapper. "I could barely stay focused. There is nothing she's doing to incite the students here. No coded messages in her lecture. Trust me, she is up to nothing."

"She is definitely up to something," argues Dr. Radkowski. "Frank was beaten to a pulp this morning. They came from her dad's lab. When he checked through security at 7am he was fine, but when I met him in the elevator later he looked more purple than a plum. They time traveled this morning. To where I don't know, but they got into a fight and my guess is it was with us."

"The father is not stupid," argues the finger tapper. "There is no way he would go after Nazis. He wouldn't put his daughter at risk like that."

"He is a scientist," she replies. "His goal is to uncover the mysteries of the world and be famous. He is all about his research. I'm not sure he cares about his daughter or anything else other than making the next big discovery."

"So you think he stumbled his way into something this morning?" asks the man, "By complete accident?"

"I believe so," she responds. "James Eviston is not a Nazi hunter. He's simply a researcher."

"I'm concerned about him doing more stumbling," says the bearded man. "I don't want him to find out our plans by accident. He may appear to be an absent-minded professor, but he's smart enough to start to put pieces of the puzzle together. He'll figure out what we're all really up to."

"Do you think Dr. Eviston knows about Wright-Patterson?" she asks.

"That his lab and air force base is run by Nazis pretending they are Americans?" chuckles the finger tapper. "Dr. Eviston is book smart, not street smart. I'm sure he thinks Wright-

Patterson is as American as apple pie."

She laughs back at him. "Still, we shouldn't trust any of them. Let's continue making sure all three are being followed twenty four by seven. I'll keep an eye on him while he's at the base. You need to be vigilant while he's not in his lab."

"The father is constantly being followed by one of our agents," he explains. "Frank is being watched also. We have a car outside the Eviston home right now making sure he doesn't leave."

"And what about the girl?" asks Dr. Radkowski.

"We have orders to take her out," he responds. "Almost did it this morning with a Freeway diversion, but her boyfriend, Frank, ruined our efforts."

"What?" says a shocked Dr. Radkowski, "Killing her is a terrible idea. It will cause too much attention. I'm overruling those orders. You are to follow and monitor."

"That won't be an issue. I've hacked into her ring," he proudly announces. "I know where she is at all times, I can activate the recorder and hear what she's saying, and turn the camera on to see what she's looking at. I know all her activities in the last fifteen days. I can call it up right now if you wish."

Tracked? I think to myself. They've known my every movement, every conversation. This is worse than 1989. They know exactly where I am at all times and what I've done. That's how they knew I was on the freeway. That must be how they were able to send the Train Station Guy after me. It wasn't coincidence, it was planned. I have to figure out a way to escape. I have to talk to Frank and my dad.

I take off running from the basement and fly up the stairs. I hit the atrium and quickly move through all the people milling about. I race through the doors, down the hill, and to my car. I pull out of the stadium parking lot and head west down Woody Hayes Drive. As I pass over the Olentangy River I roll down my window and toss the ring out. It bounces off the stone rail of the bridge and flies through the air, plummeting down into the river.

I look down at the dashboard of my car and see the touch

screen monitors. There are computers everywhere. I'll need to get rid of much more than my ring.

FOUR

"They are following us," I whisper into Frank's ear. "They are watching our every move."

Frank and I are hugging in my kitchen. My head is buried in his neck with my mouth inches from his ear. I'm whispering so softly that you could barely hear me even if you're standing next to me. If you were watching me from afar, you couldn't see me talking to him either.

He smells my hair.

"Are you sure?" he questions.

"Yes." I confirm.

"Follow me," Frank goes upstairs. He takes off his watch, necklace and his belt. All three carry his electronic devices. I remove my bracelets and place them on the dresser.

I head back downstairs and he follows in silence. We climb into his car and pull out of the driveway. It's after dinner and the sun has set. It's dark outside. If someone's following us, which I assume they are, it's going to be difficult for them to track us tonight since there's no moon. We drive to the closest neighborhood park, get out of the car and start walking. As we move into the trees, I take off my earrings and cast them away. Frank slips out of his shoes and I follow his lead. I take off my belt, slip my hands into my shirt and remove my bra, just in case they placed a bug into the underwire. We're walking barefoot in the woods in just our pants and t-shirts. If I wasn't so damn scared right now, I'd be turned on.

After a few moments, Frank stops and pulls me close. He kisses me full on the lips.

"Frank," I say. "This is no time for hanky panky."

"Shh," he says. "This is our cover. I saw a car following us. He parked on the side street and may follow us into the woods. You still need to whisper out here."

"Okay," I say, keeping him in my arms. I feel all warm up against him.

"Now, tell me everything," he insists.

I tell him about the lecture, about Sonia, the finger tapper, and Dr. Radkowski.

"She's a spy?" he says disappointedly.

"Yes," I explain. "They are following us. All of them. Worse, yet. Nazis are running the lab."

"The lab in Hitchcock? Where you do all your lectures?"

"No. My father's lab. In fact, they are running the whole base."

"This is impossible," argues Frank. "Toby hunted down every last Nazi sympathizer. Tried them. Jailed them. Executed some of them. He wiped the slate clean and set up the Cold War against the Russians. We agreed in the car, the Train Station Guy was an isolated incident. Toby cleansed this nation of Nazis."

"Maybe we're facing a different reality since we altered the past back during the Reichstag Fire," I say. "There are now Nazis still here in America and they are controlling things we can't even imagine."

"If they are running the base, then they have access to your dad's computers. They know exactly what we did this morning," realizes Frank. "They know your dad is trying to find out how the Nazis changed history."

"He's safe. We're safe. Dad keeps his research on a separate private computer. In fact, most of it he stores in his head," I explain. "And now I'm never going to file the paperwork I said I would."

"We have to tell someone," says Frank. "Someone who can do something about this. This can't be just us this time. We don't have the resources to battle the enemy from within."

I think about this for a moment. My first instinct is to attack the issue head on… reignite the war against the Nazis, take down the Wright-Patterson Air Force base. But Frank makes some good points. We don't have the means to do this. There's no rebel army for us to inspire. It's just the two of us. This can't be just our battle.

"I don't have any solutions, yet," I confess. "But I do know one thing. We can't talk about it anymore. We're being tracked, watched, and listened to. There are probably cameras and audio equipment everywhere. Don't talk at the lab, the office, school, in the car, at the house, anywhere. Get rid of all your computer devices. They know our every move and every thought this time."

"We're going to get through this, Sunshine," responds Frank. "I don't care if you, your dad and I need to escape out of the country, hide in some remote village, and forget that time travel even exists. We'll survive this."

I grab Frank and squeeze him. He always knows what to say.

"This is fixable," he reassures. "We've been through much worse. This is a cake walk compared to jumping over Niagara Falls. We just can't do this one alone."

"We need to talk to my father," I admit. "He needs to know they are watching. He'll know what to do next."

FIVE

Frank and I head back to the house. We make small talk, giggle like a couple in love should. We flirt, turn on the TV and snuggle up on the couch together. All the things you'd expect out of two love birds, but things Frank and I find difficult to do. Maybe one day when all this is behind us we can have a normal relationship, but right now as we sit watching television I'm wondering who's watching me. I know there's a camera somewhere in my living room and am trying to figure out where it is. I can't enjoy being nestled up in Frank's arms because I'm glancing out of the corner of my eye wondering if there's a pencil camera hidden in an intricate frame of a picture of my mom and dad in front of the Cathedral of Saint John the Baptist.

I've always found it odd that of all the pictures my dad keeps of him and my mom, the one in front of a church in Italy hangs over the fireplace. Dad and the Catholic church aren't on great terms so why he's got a picture of the most famous Cathedral in Torino on his wall is beyond me. I guess there's a memory behind it that he's never explained to me.

Frank and I have been passing the time, waiting for my dad to get home so we can explain what's going on. I need to tell him about Dr. Radkowski, but it's getting late for our typical bedtime routine and we don't want to alert anyone that may be monitoring us. So, we brush our teeth, put on our PJs and crawl into bed. I cringe thinking there's a camera in our bedroom as well, wondering what other things they've heard and seen since Frank and I have been back, including all the intimate things we've said and done. I barely get any sleep that night, worrying about our future and listening for my dad to come through the door.

I know it seems like I've been through worse. I know I'm the Falls Jumper. But I'm in a much different situation right now. Before, I was part of a rebel army in a war-torn world. Now I'm living in a normal world that's really not normal, and this time I have my dad to worry about as well.

Morning comes too soon and I barely got any sleep. I crawl out of bed and step into the hallway. My dad's bedroom door is still open so I check if he's there and find it empty. He must have never came home last night, which isn't that odd. He frequently gets lost in his work at Wright-Patterson and sleeps there in a bedroom they set up for him. I'll catch up with him later today. Frank and I can always drive down to his lab at some point since I don't have any lectures this afternoon.

In the shower, I wash off yesterday's grime and think through the day. First, Frank and I need to go into work to file a report on the Train Station Guy that Frank strangled and killed on the freeway yesterday morning. We shouldn't report we saw him back in 1990 so instead, we'll keep that a secret.

Plus, we need to touch base with our boss. While we have the freedom to come and go as we please right now, and don't have any real assignments, we are still part of the Homeland Security Temporal Force. At any moment they can reassign us to anything. We're heroes and all that, but we're not immune to the workings of the military and government. So we have to check in every now and then to make sure we keep our jobs.

If the Nazis have infiltrated the Department of Homeland Security just like Wright-Patterson, my guess is they are not going to reassign us anywhere just yet. They want to keep an eye on us and see what we'll do. Maybe that's why they are keeping us here and giving us the freedom to do what we want? Damn it. I should have argued for an assignment and to be part of the action instead of just spending time recuperating.

After stopping in at work, we'll go out to my father's lab. We'll talk to him one on one. There's a special test module there that's set up to analyze sonic waves. It creates a vacuum and sucks up all the sound. If you crank it up all the way, you can't hear anything unless you're directly talking into someone's ear.

After the shower, I get dressed and make breakfast while Frank is finishing his morning routine. I have several friends who developed a relationship with someone during a moment of crisis and when the crisis is over the relationship goes sour.

Frank and I enjoyed each other's company before the war, we just never consummated it. Now that the war is over, and the crisis has settle, we can go back to being friends, except friends with benefits. Maybe this new revelation with Nazis in the U.S. is someone else's problem. Maybe Frank and I can worry about "us" now instead of the "U.S."

Frank comes down to the kitchen, grabs a plate of eggs and a Greek yogurt.

"Morning, Sunshine," he says, "I was thinking we should stop by the office this morning and finally file the report from the traffic accident and hostage situation," he says. We already decided this last night. He knows what our plan is today. He's just saying it aloud in case we're being monitored.

"Yes," I play along. "I don't have any lectures scheduled today. We should check in and see if there are any assignments they need us to get started on."

The Homeland Security office is located in downtown Columbus. The city has become somewhat of a hub with the University here and Wright-Patterson only an hour away. Our offices are on the 60th floor of the Neil Armstrong Tower. Built in 2069 and named after the first man to step on the moon, it's tall and thin, made of spiraling white mirrored glass of diamond shaped panels. A bluish metal structure winds around the outside of the glass, adding to the feeling of upward movement and mobility. The top of the tower curves to simulate the projection of a rocket after take-off and leans a whole two blocks over the river. They had to create gravitational plates on the top floors to keep people from falling out of their chairs. It's a modern day marvel of architecture and a tribute to a man who was a modern day marvel in his time and one of Ohio's most famous sons. Dad's never mentioned it, but deep down inside I think he's proud of me for working for the Department of Homeland Security and having offices in the most prestigious building in Ohio. Frank and I ride the elevator up alone and continue the small chat.

"I think we're out of milk," Frank says.

"We should pick some up on the way home," I respond.

"And coffee. We need coffee," he adds.

"Did you like the Italian Roast, Columbian-Costa Rican Blend?" I offer.

"Is that what your dad has been buying?" he asks.

"Yep."

"Yeah, we should pick up some more," he says.

We get off the elevator and onto our floor. We step up to double glass doors.

"Alex Eviston," I speak loudly.

"Frank Bouchard," says Frank in the same tone.

As the doors slide open a voice much like Vincent Price from the old black and white horror films says, "Enter at your own risk."

"Floyd in IT must be programing the voice security now," I chuckle.

Frank and I walk across the floor. People look up and stare, heads snap in our direction. We don't come to the office that much, but when we do we still get our celebrity reception since we saved the world from the Nazi scum. Each and every one of these agents aspire to be us. I'm convinced they would have done the same if they were in our shoes.

But there might be some among their ranks that have evil behind their eyes, those that are reminiscent of the ruling party from less than 100 years ago. That's our mission this morning. Frank and I want to discover if our boss, Associate Director Jeremy Barben, is on our side or their side. We're not really here to file a report and don't plan to.

The Associate Director sits in the large office overlooking the Scioto River. We stop at his assistant's desk to see if we can interrupt him.

"Good morning, Tammie," Frank grins.

Tammie sits back in her chair. "Let me guess, you want some time with the big guy," she smiles.

"Well... yeah," Frank reveals. "It's kind of why we came in this morning."

"His 10 am was canceled," she responds.

"Great," I reply. "Can we just go in?"

"Not so fast," she says picking up the phone. "He said he didn't want to be bothered by anyone."

"Crap," blurts out Frank.

"But you're not just anyone," she smiles. Tammie leans towards the phone and whispers into the receiver, "Han and Leia are here today. Do you want to speak with them?"

I mouth to Frank, "Han? Leia?"

Frank shrugs his shoulders.

Tammie turns back to us. "That's your code names," she explains. "Associate Director Barben has code names for everyone. Originally, he wanted to call you guys Harry and Sally from the movie *When Harry Met Sally* but I didn't really think Frank was as pessimistic as Harry, and Alex isn't as high-strung as Sally. I made him pick Han and Leia from *Star Wars* instead. You guys can go in."

Associate Director Barben is a balding, silver gray-haired man in his late 50s with the energy of a college student. Everything is fascinating to him. He's a constant observer of the world around him and his personal processing speed is record fast. He scores so high on the IQ test that they don't even calculate it. When they say he's in the 130 and above range, he's in the "above" category. We enter into his office and find him staring out his window.

"Come here," he instructs, "But slowly. I want you to see something amazing."

We inch over to him.

"You don't want to disturb them or let them think you're a threat," he begins, not knowing we're not yet by his side. "This one time I jumped up from my desk to check them out and the mother tried to attack me. Of course, she didn't get far because there's a plate glass window between us, but she tried."

When we finally reach the window, we see a bird's nest in the metal trusses outside with several small blackish baby birds in it. A larger bird is looking over them while a smaller bird is doing the feeding.

"They are Peregrine Falcons," explains Associate Director

Barben. "They nest here every year and give birth to new family. Fortunately, this brood is rather large. The birds themselves are rare now, due to all the nuclear destruction up North in Canada. They are the fastest animal on earth. When they dive for their prey they can reach upwards of 240 miles per hour. By comparison the fastest land animal is the Cheetah at 100 miles per hour and the speed of sound is 727 miles per hour. Think about that. The speed of sound is only three times as fast as this animal in front of us. It's a majestic and magnificent creature of God and the damn Nazis almost drove it to extinction."

"The mother does a great job feeding her young," Frank says.

"Oh no, she doesn't," argues the Associate Director Barben. "The mother is the larger bird watching over the nest. She's the protector. The father does the hunting and the feeding."

We stand there for a few more moments in silence watching the birds on the building ledge.

"Associate Director Barben," I say. Everyone is required to refer to him as his full title. He won't speak to you otherwise. He reciprocates.

"Yes, Colonel Eviston," he replies.

"Colonel Bouchard and I have come here to see if there are any assignments for us," I explain.

He pauses for several moments still staring at the falcons nest on the ledge. He steps away, sits behind his desk and motions for us to sit down, rubbing his forehead.

"Tell me about the White House again," he states.

"Associate Director Barben," sighs Frank. "We've been through this a million times. We've told you every detail."

"Then let's talk about the Capitol Building," he says.

"We've spent hours and hours talking to you about every detail and everything we did in 1989 and 1990," I counter.

"You told me about places, things you did," he says. "I want to know more about the people. Tell me about Mojmir."

"You can read his file," says Frank coldly. "You have him

listed under known terrorists."

Associate Director Barben stands up and walks around to us and leans against his desk. "Tell me about Tut. The drug runner from St. Louis. Did he survive?"

"Yes," I blurt out, letting my annoyance slip out. "He and his sister became close friends of President Mack. He appointed him Ambassador to Egypt. We told you about Mojmir, President Mack, Roach, Ella, Tut, Rat-tailed Jimmy, everyone we ever met that we could remember. What else do you need to know?"

"I want to know more about yesterday's traffic altercation," he says. "I analyzed the initial report and the Highway Patrolman on the hood of the car explained the assailant kept aiming at Alex. Why do you think that?"

"Don't know," replies Frank. "Maybe he knew she was a threat? Maybe her red hair was an easy target?"

Associate Director Barben drops his head into his hand and rubs his forehead again. "There are details I need to put together still, things I need to know," he says, "yet they are all still a bit blurry in my head and it looks like I'm going to lose you."

"What?" asks Frank.

"I think you're being reassigned," he confesses. "I'm not sure to where. Or to what year for that matter."

"When?" I say.

"You're getting your orders tonight," he looks up at us, staring us in the eye, reading our reaction.

I'm in shock. Frank and I can't leave my father in his lab by himself, stalked by Nazis.

"We can't go," I immediately react. "I... I have my guest lectureship at the University. We have a lot to do around the house. We have work to do here."

"We have a wedding to plan," Frank exclaims.

My head quickly snaps his way. Sure, I want to plan a wedding all right, but this is not how I wanted to be proposed to. But I have to admit, it's a damn good cover.

"Yes," I join in. "A wedding. Well, there's no ring, yet.

We're kind of planning to plan a wedding."

Associate Director Barben looks at us thoughtfully, as if the answer he's been looking for has been revealed. His body relaxes and he places his hands on his desk. It's his way of saying I'm going to be honest with you now.

"I have nothing to do with this," he admits. "This is coming from far above me. So far that they wouldn't explain who. They told me it was top secret. The orders are coming tonight, to your house."

Frank and I exchange glances.

"And as for the report about yesterday's accident, I've been told you don't have to file anything," he adds. "The Highway Patrol took care of it."

At that moment there's a rap at the door and Tammie peaks her head in. "Your 11 am is here," she says and stands in the doorway.

"I need to take this meeting," explains Associate Director Barben. "Call me tonight after the orders come in, if you need to touch base."

I want to tell him more. Tell him about our suspicions, about Dr. Radkowski's conversation, about yesterday's assailant being from the past. But Tammie hasn't left. She's standing there as a sign we must leave. We get up to walk out and Associate Director Barben starts shuffling some papers on his desk, rather loudly.

"Be careful out there," he whispers. "There are strange things afoot that I haven't quite yet figured out."

"You be careful, as well," I whisper, "And keep your eyes open."

He nods his head and walk out of his office. I now know that we can trust him. He's knows there's something going on but he just can't quite figure out the details. I want to come back and talk to him about what I know, but I got a bad feeling this is the last time I'll ever see Associate Director Barben.

SIX

We leave the Neil Armstrong Building and make our way towards my dad's lab. I've been trying to get a hold of him all morning long but he hasn't been answering my calls. This isn't anything unusual, he's typically so immersed in his work that he doesn't realize there's a world around him that's trying to engage with him. But given the current circumstances, I'm a little worried about him.

Frank and I make small talk in the car. We talk about the weather, about the Columbus Blue Jacket's upcoming season, how he wants to get season tickets, and I prefer to stay with Ohio State Hockey because the tickets are cheaper. You never realize how difficult it is to say something meaningless until you try. We go a whole sixty minutes talking about nothing important and trying not to reveal any secrets or feelings.

When we arrive at the base, we stop at security. The sensors at the gate recognize my car but the soldiers in the gatehouse look up for a visual confirmation. They notice it's Frank and me, then smile and open the window.

"Sorry about the wait," the soldier adds, "The base is on heightened security this morning and the computer didn't have you guys on the personnel list today."

"My dad must have forgotten to put us on," I reply.

"It's okay. Sorry for your wait. We're just following protocol. We'll let you in," he retorts, "You did save the world from the Nazis. Have a great day!"

The soldier opens the gate and waves us through.

The whole thing seems a little odd to me. The soldier was overly apologetic and gave the impression he was covering something up. Maybe I'm being paranoid and over cautious. These security soldiers can't be in on it as well? Maybe no one is out to get us. Maybe what Dr. Radkowski and the finger tapper were lying about Wright-Patterson Air Force base being controlled by the Nazis.

We park and enter the main research building. There's no one else on the elevator and we travel all the way down the basement to dad's lab. The doors open and we begin walking down the hallway. We get to the double glass doors to find a hand written sign by my dad. It's posted from the inside and says: "Busy with research. Do not enter. Do not bother."

I try to open the doors and they are locked.

"Alex Eviston," I say. "Doors open."

"I'm sorry, Alex Eviston," the computer says, programmed as my mom's voice. "You do not have permission to enter. Go away." Dad would always program the lab's computer to sound like my mom's voice when he wanted me to do something. In fact, Mom was the disciplinary in the family. Unless it was academics, Dad always left Mom to do the parenting.

"I need to speak with Dr. Eviston," I instruct the computer, knowing it's not my mom.

"Dr. Eviston is not available right now," explains the computer. "I've been instructed to tell Alex Eviston to go away."

"Frank Bouchard," states Frank. "Open Doors."

"Frank Bouchard does not have access," explains the computer. "I've been instructed to tell Frank Bouchard to take Alex Eviston and go home immediately."

This is a bit strange. The computer is doing more than just denying access, it's giving us some specific directions. I'm not sure I trust this computer. The Nazis could have programmed it to say what it's saying. They could be torturing my dad right now and there's nothing I can do about it. I peer through the glass doors trying to see if I can find any evidence that my dad is still in there.

"Step away from the doors," instructs my mom's computer voice.

"I must speak with my father," I demand, "Immediately."

The computer pauses and we wait.

"Dr. James Eviston cannot be bothered right now," the computer finally chimes back in. "He is deep in research. Return to your house and he will meet you for dinner. A steak is in the fridge."

Steak? I pause. Dad is giving me clues.

"Oh, well," I say to Frank. "Looks like we're not going to get in. Let's head back home. I'll be making steak for dinner."

Frank looks at me oddly. He's not used to me being told what to do. He hesitates for a moment, wanting to stay here and argue some more with the computer.

Instead, I grab his hand and lead him back towards the elevator, to the car, and head home.

So there's two clues Dad gave me to send me away. First, he programmed the computer to be my mom's voice. He's never done that before. After mom passed away, it was tough for him to be reminded of her daily so he tried to remove any reference to her. Her favorite books were donated to libraries. He threw out the bed and bought a smaller one. He removed the pictures from the walls and repainted them to cover up the faded spots left behind. The only one he kept was the picture of him and Mom in front of the Cathedral in Italy that he hangs over the fireplace.

Dad couldn't handle constant reminders of Mom. He always thought it was his fault she died because he didn't find a cure. But he knew that I longed for time with Mom and must figure that I still listen to her sage advice, even if it was a memory. He knew that if he programmed the computer as her voice, that I might listen to her since she was the disciplinarian in the family.

The second clue was about dinner. In college my dad and I became even more distant and rarely spoke to each other. But when he had something important for us to discuss, he always invited me to dinner and bribed me with my favorite meal – filet mignon. Dad was telling me there was a steak in the fridge and that there was something super important he had to say to me at dinner.

I couldn't tell any of this to Frank. It would take too long to explain and we're guessing the car is bugged, the Nazis will hear everything. Frank has learned to finally trust me and not to doubt my actions. I've finally found someone that believes in me more than I believe in myself.

My dad is a complicated person. On the surface he appears

as the "absent minded professor," oblivious to all the actions of the world around him. He's a brilliant scientist who gets hyper focused on his work, forgetting that there's a world around him. But sometimes I think it's just an act. There are things he notices that no one else does. When he steps back and realizes that there's something going on other than his research then he begins to analyze everything. Dad has thought through the reality that General Kaiser knows we're trying to go back in time and to observe his actions that caused the temporal shift. He's analyzed every nuance of that and probably figured out that the Nazis have control over his lab before I realized it. That's why he's keeping Frank and me away from his lab; he must not want us all to get trapped together.

Or at the very least, he doesn't want Frank and me looking like we're doing research with him. The Nazis might get even more nervous than they already are.

I've made my favorite meal for us: grilled filet mignon with a garlic sauce, sea salt steamed broccoli, and baked sweet potato. Dad is sure to be happy. Dinner was ready at 6:30 pm, our traditional "time to talk" dinner appointment time. I also set out dad's plate at Mom's regular spot at the dinner table so he can realize I had picked up on his clues.

I'm flipping the steak for the final turn on the grill when I look up to see Dad pull in the driveway. It's 6:15 and he's right on time. He opens the car door and nods in approval, knowing that I've figured it out.

"How was work today?" I asked him. It's something Mom said to him each time he came home.

Dad smiled and cringed at little at the same time. I imagine after all these years memories of mom still hit him hard.

"Good day," he says, "Just trying to make a little progress." That was dad's typical response to Mom.

"Dinner will be ready at 6:30 p.m.," I explain. "Frank's already inside finishing the broccoli and sweet baked potatoes."

Dad nods again as he walks in through the back door.

Frank and I have the evening completely figured out. After we left dad's lab, we drove back to the woods we went to the night before and analyzed all our options. We have a plan to share with Dad after dinner. Frank will piece by piece tell him this evening while they are watching the hockey game on TV. There'll be enough noise and shouting from the game to cover any dialogue they have. We don't know where the bugs are in the house, but we're sure there are plenty that can pick up our conversation so we must be careful.

When the orders come in tonight for a new assignment, Frank and I are going to ask Homeland Security for a transfer to the main office in Washington D.C instead. From there, we can secretly assess how deep the Nazis have infiltrated the government and then craft a plan to expose or fight it. While there's a Nazi wolf in the hen house, there are still many patriotic Americans who believe in freedom. If it's a fight they want, it's a fight they'll get. I won the last battle. I'll win this one, too.

What to do with my dad was a tougher call. His work has always been at Wright-Patterson Air Force Base. For him to leave would be a huge red flag, the Nazis would definitely realize we're onto them. We're going to advise Dad to start researching something else… something that will throw the Nazis off completely. Instead of researching the temporal nodes to understand where exactly the Nazis altered time, we'd like him to research Ancient Egypt for evidence that someone traveled back in time to teach them architecture, ship making, irrigation, and pharmacy.

This is obviously a false theory and predicated on the racist view that the African culture could not innovate on their own. But the invention of time travel fueled that fire. We're going to ask Dad to dispel it. He'll throw the Nazis off our track analyzing something that has nothing to do with them.

In the meantime, during dinner, we're going to make small talk and bide our time until the hockey game.

The steaks are now a perfect medium rare. I take them off the grill, place them on a serving tray and take them inside.

Dad has cracked open one of Frank's beers and the two of them are at the dining room table laughing. It's already completely set with the steamed broccoli, sweet baked potatoes, silverware, cloth napkins and plates. Frank's poured me a glass of red wine because he knows I don't drink beer. He's shocked that an Irish woman shuns beer and is convinced there's a bit of Italian running through me. The fact is, Mom and Dad were always into Italian wines so I just followed into place.

We sit down and say a quick Grace, catholic style, out of habit, and begin to eat.

"So work went well today?" I say, making small talk.

"Frank, Alex," my father says, "There's something I've been meaning to address for some time."

Frank and I shoot each other a glance. What's Dad getting to? This isn't part of the script we've determined. This is supposed to be small talk. It sounds like dad's getting right to the deep stuff and throwing caution to the wind. There are bugs in here.

"Dad," I say softly, "I'm not sure this is the right time to talk about this."

"It's the exact time to talk about it," my dad counters. "It's been on my mind since the two of you have come back and it has to stop."

"Dr. Eviston, can we table this until later?" adds Frank.

"No," he says. "Now I appreciate that you've made this wonderful meal, and I understand that the two of you are adults. Whatever choices you have made about your living arrangements in the past is your business. But while you're living in my house, you'll sleep in separate beds. I'll have no cohabitation going on under my roof. You were raised respectably. Your mother would have none of it, and frankly I'm surprised I tolerated it this long."

Smart move, Dad. Separate Frank and I within the house. If there's cameras and bugs in here, we don't want to give them access to any conversations... or intimate things, either.

"Yes, Dr. Eviston," responds Frank. "I'm sorry for being

disrespectful. I'll start sleeping on the couch tonight and rearrange the office tomorrow so I can sleep there."

"That's the other thing we need to discuss," adds my father. "If you're going to show me you can be a formidable partner to Alex, then I'd like to see you being more career minded. Get a job at the University, get your next assignment at Homeland Security, or get a job in the Private Sector. I don't care but it's time you go back to work."

"Yes, sir," he responds. "In fact, we stopped by Homeland Security's offices today. They are coming by tonight with orders for a new assignment."

"Tonight?" my dad jumped a little in his seat. "I... I... That's terrible timing."

"Dad, why is tonight a bad thing?" I look at him thoughtfully, seeing if I can discover any emotional reaction behind his eyes. His eyes are darting back and forth, not looking at anything particular. It's what he does when's he's trying to think quickly. He knows the Nazis are tracking us. He must know that Nazis are controlling his lab and now they want us. He probably thinks they are coming for us tonight. And dad's a good judge of Nazis, so if he thinks they are coming tonight than maybe they are.

"I need to head back into work to finish some research," Dad rambles out. "In fact, I need the two of you to go with me. I need your help."

"Sure," replies Frank. "We'll be glad to help."

"Good," says my dad and starts to gobble down his food. "We'll leave in a few minutes."

For some reason, I don't think we're going to the lab to do research. My guess is Dad wants to make a run for it. With the particle accelerator, we can go anywhere in any time.

Suddenly, there's a knock on the door. We're too late.

I place my napkin on the table and walk out to the front room. Looking out the living room window, I discover a black sedan with two American Flags ordaining its hood.

"It's government all right," I say. "Not sure which division or branch."

They knock again, louder and longer. I look through the peep hole to find two men at the door, one military and the other civilian.

The civilian raises his hand to knock again but I open it before he does. It leaves him in an awkward position as we stand face-to-face, his hand raised between us forming half a fist. I recognize him and plastic smile from all the commercials and advertisements, it's Senator Stiener. He's running for re-election. He's always so happy to be wherever he is at the time, and right now it's on my front porch.

"Colonel Eviston," he coos, extending his hand. "What an absolute pleasure it is to meet someone so distinguished and patriotic as you. Thank you for your service and courage. I'm sure you recognize me as Senator Stiener. This is Lieutenant Shank from the 53rd Armory Unit here in Columbus. The exact unit your Great-Great-Great-Great Grandfather belonged to that raided the Nazi warehouse back in the Great Ohio Valley Rebellion."

The Lieutenant salutes and I return the gesture.

"Colonel," says the Lieutenant. "Thank you for meeting us this evening. Is your father home as well? Colonel Bouchard?"

I take pause and figure out my options here. Fight or flee? If I fight, that may give Frank and Dad time to escape. If I flee as well, then we may all be caught. The place could be surrounded and even if it isn't, I'm not about to take out this innocent soldier. I need more information before I can make a decision about how to react.

"Colonel Eviston, may we come in?" requests the Senator.

"Yes, Senator, Lieutenant, please come in," I respond. "Dad? Frank?" I yell. "Can you join me in the living room? Senator Stiener is here, along with a Lieutenant Shank. Please gentlemen, sit." I motion to the couches in the front room. They are rather out of style. My dad bought them after Mom passed away and he never replaced them. They are in great condition since they are rarely used but they look a bit odd because they are more than ten years old.

"My goodness this is a beautiful home," states Senator

Stiener with extremely forced sincerity. "I love how you've kept it a bit retro. It gives me a nostalgic feeling."

"My dad's never gotten around to updating furniture. It was my mom who used to keep up with that," I confess as Frank and my father walk in to join us.

"Ah," his face turns overly compassionate. "Your mother. She was a brilliant woman. Much like you in so many ways. So sad we lost her when we did."

"Senator," my father states with disdain. The kind you have for people that speak about your loved ones as if they knew them when they really didn't. "Why are you here tonight?"

"Yes," the Senator stands and extends his hand towards my dad. "The infamous Dr. James Eviston. It is truly an honor to meet you. What a treasure this evening is and what an astonishing family you have. A brilliant psychologist, a scientific phenomenon, and a patriotic savior. Not to mention, Frank Bouchard, Canada's most prized and esteemed citizen. It is so special to be here with you all this evening."

"Senator," my father continues with the disdain, never shaking hands. "We are well aware of my family's stature. We are in the middle of dinner. What can we help you with this evening?"

"A man of science gets straight to the point," the Senator smiles. "Well, it is my pleasure and privilege to invite you to our nation's Capital for a special celebration."

"Celebration?" I interrupt him. This doesn't sound like an assignment or a trap.

"Yes!" the Senator says with exuberance. "A celebration in your honor! You, your dad, Frank... all are special honorees of President Austin. I'm here to personally invite you."

Frank looks at me, stunned. Moments ago we all thought we would have to be fugitives from our own government. Instead, we are being honored by it.

"When? How?" asks my dad, equally bewildered.

"This is all so exciting," explains the Senator. "You will be recognized in front of a large crowd on the National Mall in Washington D.C.! Typically, these types of events are held at the Kennedy Center, but you are the biggest heroes of our generation and maybe even since George Washington himself! I'll be by your side the whole time of course, my office will make all the arrangements and put out a local press release as well. You, all three of you, will have a special place of honor in American History. Truly this is the most amazing thing that's ever happened to the Great State of Ohio and I hope you'll allow me to thank you on behalf of all our citizens."

"Thank you," I manage to stumble out.

"The Lieutenant here has your formal invite with the itinerary and details. Don't hesitate to call my office with any questions," he states heading for the door. The Lieutenant stands to hand my dad an envelope.

The Senator stops in mid-stride. "Oops," he says. "I almost forgot something. How foolish of me." He reaches in his jacket, pulls out his phone, and hands it to the Lieutenant.

"Can you take a picture for us?" he asks the Lieutenant as he steps in between us and gathers us around. "Hold on," he instructs and turns us a little to get the picture on the wall of my mom and dad. "Perfect," he says and grins with his plastic smile again.

The Lieutenant begrudgingly snaps the photo.

"Take one more," instruct the Senator. "In case I blinked. This is for my webpage. It's a historical moment."

The Lieutenant takes another. "Okay, Senator, let's leave the family so they can celebrate," he insists.

"Again," says the Senator, "If you need anything please contact my office. The number is in the invitation package. Thank you, thank you, and thank you," he says shaking all our hands.

The Lieutenant practically has to pull him out onto the front porch and to the driveway.

My dad closes the door and opens up the envelope.

"Pack your bags," he says as he's reading in the invitation. "The ceremony is in three days. We're leaving tomorrow morning."

SEVEN

The last time I was in Washington, D.C., I was being shot at by Nazis. This time I am chauffeured in with a military escort. We're staying at the Plaza Hotel for the first two nights and the ceremony will be on the National Mall. Afterwards, there will be a private reception where we get to meet the President and the First Lady.

Yesterday, my dad, Frank, and I all got together in his lab at Wright-Patterson and talked in the Sound Test Module. The vacuum absorbs 99.9% of all sound waves so we're fairly confident that no one knows what we said, but we still had to make it brief since we didn't want to be suspicious. Our plan is now rather fool proof.

We figure the President is the only one we can trust, so during the private reception we're going to explain to him that the Nazis have infiltrated the military and possibly Homeland Security. But we're going to need a little more evidence than dad's hunches and conversation I overhead in the halls of OSU.

So once we get to D.C. we're going to split up and do some reconnaissance. Dad has a few friends at the Smithsonian that he's going to touch base with, mainly in the Air and Space Building. He'll discover if there's been any odd research done, or rumblings in the scientific community there. Whenever a government takes action against something, the military is always first to find out with the scientific community being second.

Frank is going to Toby Mack's old neighborhood to find out what's the word on the streets. He doesn't know anyone there, but we figure that they know him and can trust him. President Mack is like a king to his old neighborhood and we figure they'll trust an old friend of President Mack's like Frank.

Oddly enough, I'm going to go sightseeing. Originally, my plan was to go to the Department of Homeland Security and do some snooping around the office. Frank nixed the idea thinking that they'd be onto me. He said if there's one person they're watching out for, it's Alex Eviston.

Which gave me an idea, if they're watching out for me, why don't I lead them astray? Make them think I'm looking for something when I'm really not. It also gives me the opportunity to discover who exactly is following me and maybe even what they're up to.

I have a few historical stops on my schedule but mostly government buildings. Through Senator Stiener's office and his gracious offer to help with anything I needed, I have a tour of the White House planned, the Capitol Building, the Supreme Court Building, NASA Headquarters, and the FBI Headquarters. While my intent on all these tours are harmless, if I'm being stalked it gives them the impression I'm up to something and at the same time gives me the opportunity to see if anything is wrong at the surface level.

In the late afternoon, Dad, Frank, and I will gather together at M.E. Swings for coffee, just like Frank and I did back in 1989, to report in anything odd we discovered.

On the day before the event, I'm touring the White House. It's a good three hours before I need to meet up with Dad and Frank at the coffee shop. I'm on a private tour along with celebrity broadcaster Stan Stepanowich, the President General of The Daughters of the Republic of Texas and her family, and one of the members of the General Authority of The Church of Jesus Christ of Latter-day Saints. I know this because he keeps on reminding me how it was the Mormons that helped me plan and execute my attack on Washington D.C.

The President General was thrilled to be on the tour with me and almost instantly asked for a picture. She gave me an open invitation to visit her at the Alamo anytime I was in San Antonio and she'd give me a behind the scenes, private tour. Stan Stepanowich was less than thrilled to be with me and ignored me for most of it. My guess is he's used to being the center of attention. His digital streaming video show gets over five million impressions a week.

I've been through the White House before, but I have to admit it was a complete blur. When you're running room to room under gunfire, chasing after the most wanted American

Nazi who ever lived, you don't really take the time to notice the beautiful mix of blue and red hues in Theodore Roosevelt's equestrian portrait by Tade Styka titled *Rough Rider*.

For each room we enter, the tour guide asks me, "Were you in this room?" and if I answer "Yes," she proceeds to pummel me with more questions about my activities in each and trying to point out where maybe they filled in holes from gunfire. The President General from Texas was in awe of my stories and Stan Stepanowich kept on trying to turn the conversation to him, usually about a segment he did on his digital video show. The Mormon on the other hand fell quiet over time.

To stop the annoying routine of questions from the tour guide, shock and awe reactions from the President General and non-stop nonsense banter from the Stan Stepanowich, I eventually began denying that I had ever been in any of the rooms. Stan Stepanowich still embellished every story and made it about him, but it kept the tour guide from harassing me and stopped the President General from swooning over me.

Thankfully, now I have the time to look around corners and inspect hallways to see if I can get a glimpse of some suspicious activity. If I could discover some strange happenings at the White House, I could get the President to believe that the situation is dire and must be dealt with.

We enter a reception room in the West Wing and the tour guide leads us to an old mahogany bookshelf. "This bookshelf dates all the way back to 1770 and is the oldest piece of furniture in the building. Miraculously, it survived the Nazi occupation and any damage from Alex's assault on the White House," the guide explains.

"What's really fascinating is how the books change based on the President," adds Stan Stepanowich. He begins to drone on about what Presidents like to read, a segment he recently featured in one of his blogs.

"Check out that wall," the Mormon whispers in my ear.

I look over my left shoulder and notice a blank wall with a framing hook and a square of paint that's slightly off-color, obviously a space where a tall painting used to hang.

"What's supposed to be there?" I ask, interrupting Stan's speech about how President Jefferson could read in several different languages.

"I'm sorry," says the Tour Guide, turning her attention to me, "I don't understand."

"That wall," I point, "What painting used to hang there?"

"The space in this lobby is always reserved for some of the most important Presidents in history," she announces. "President Washington crossing the Delaware River hangs over that couch, and *The Peacemakers* with President Lincoln and President Grant hangs over the other couch. The space on the wall in question is reserved for President Mack's portrait."

"Where is it now?" I ask.

"Well," she smiles, "I'm sure you're interested in seeing your friend's portrait but it's currently under restoration."

"It's only some eighty years old? Why does it need restoring?" I wonder aloud.

"I'm not sure," she responds. "Now if you follow me down this hallway, we'll pass by the Bullpen on the way to the Vice-President's office."

We all follow the tour guide onto the next room. The Mormon comes up close and whispers, "That's not the whole story. Rumor is that it's restoration is due to vandalism. Someone wrote 'ahnungslos' on it."

"Sounds German," I whisper back.

"Yes," he replies, "It means clueless."

I want to ask him more but I'm suddenly the center of attention. The walk towards the Vice-President's office goes through staff room. It's filled with people who are popping up over cubicle walls, peering down hallways, and stepping out of their offices, all to get a look at me.

"Is it her?" one says.

"It has to be," another replies.

"The red hair is a giveaway," someone adds.

"She's a hero," I hear.

Finally, someone starts clapping and the whole room

instantly stands and erupts in applause. They all smile at me with pride.

"She won the war," I see one of the assistants say to the other. "She's why we are free today."

While I hate the attention, I felt proud for a moment. I helped these people have freedom again.

"Don't be fooled by all of their patriotism," the Mormon whispers in my ear.

"What?" I turn to him. "Is this more about the painting?"

"It's bigger than the painting," he explains, "Keep following the tour guide, face forward, and listen while we walk. I don't have much more time."

"Okay," I say, waving to the people in the cube and following my guide.

"You are in danger," he explains. "Things are not as they seem."

"Tell me something I don't know," I whisper.

"Your friend, President Mack, didn't vanquish the Nazi sympathizers," he continues. "They quietly retreated but stayed within the fabric of society, holding important business positions in banks, telecomm, technology, and yes, even within the government. They are waiting to return. Waiting to make their move and strike at the opportune moment. We believe that moment is soon."

"What proof do you have?" I ask.

"I am Mormon. We have maintained our network of spies across the nation." he reminds me.

I should have remembered.

"How deep does it run?" I ask.

"Very deep," he explains. "The Nazi sympathizers are worried about you and think you're a detriment to their plans. They want you dead. You, Frank, your dad. You're best to leave the country," he adds, "Before it's too late."

I want to know more but I'm cut off.

"And you must be Colonel Alex Eviston." The Vice-President of the United States is standing right in front of me extending her hand. She's towering over me at least a foot and a half, having played volleyball for the University of Wisconsin. She's blonde, gorgeous, and oozes that slick oily saleswoman personality. She's your typical Vice-President politician, waiting in the wings until it's her turn, an eye on the President's chair. I've read about her and she's not very effective or smart. But when you can take a state like Wisconsin and win the mind of voters around the country with good looks, well, brains don't quite matter.

Which is sad. Not just because she's one heartbeat away from the Office of the President, but because she should be a role model for women everywhere. And she's not someone I want to represent us.

"Madam, Vice-President," I shake her hand politely.

"I went into politics because of you," she smiles. "You are my inspiration," she adds as she starts to fake an emotional reaction. Pathetic.

"You know," interrupts Stan Stepanowich, "I did a whole show on the Pioneers of Women in politics. A fascinating subject and phenomenal show, I must say. It featured you at the end. You were still the Senator of Wisconsin, but I talked about how you were the perfect candidate to become President."

"I still am," she chuckled to Stan and tilted her head with that flirty nod that says thanks for the attention. How annoying.

As they engaged in their celebrity camaraderie routine, I turned to continue my conversation with the Mormon.

He was gone.

EIGHT

"Mmm…," grins Dad as he takes a sip of coffee, "This is almost the best Italian Roast Costa Rican Tarrazú blend I've ever had. It reminds me of your mom. When we were doing research at the University of Torino, we'd wake up in the morning, brew some fresh coffee, and sit out on the balcony staring at the mountains. We used to dream about retiring there. Italy."

We sat at M.E. Swings drinking wonderful coffee, but I couldn't savor the chocolaty nutty notes. Instead, I'm still worried about Nazis. I told Frank and Dad about everything, the people on the tour, the guide, where we walked through, what the Mormon said – word for word, the interruption by the Vice President, and how my Latter-day friend vanished.

"How do you disappear from the White House?" asks Frank.

"Poof," I say. "He was gone. Like magic."

"We should listen to him," says Frank. "Leave the country."

"Head to Canada?" I say. "Remember what happened the last time we set out to go there? Ambushed by rebels and never made it across the border."

"No," retorts Frank. "Canada is part of the U.S. now. Instead, we go south. Mexico."

"I don't know any Spanish and neither do you," I argue. "Besides my red hair will stick out like a sore thumb."

"Listen, I don't want to lose you," confesses Frank, "I spent half a decade in 1989 pining over you and now that I got you, I'm not going to give you up. We're not getting jailed. We're not going to get killed. If not Mexico, then it's Europe we go to, somewhere else we can fight this battle from. We should align with another country that would enjoy taking down the Nazis. In fact, Russia might be our best option. We can contact Mojmir."

"Keep your voices down," my dad whispers, "You're not going to Russia, Mexico, or Canada. You're going to do exactly as I say. Tomorrow morning, you're going to wake up and go to the National Mall to receive your medals. You're going to accept it with honor, grace, and dignity. Then you're going to ask for an assignment here, infiltrate the Nazis from the inside, take them out, and save the world again."

"But Dr. Eviston," argues Frank. "They want her dead. I can't let that happen. If that means disappearing to another country, than that's what that means."

"You're going to do it my way," my dad says as he gets up. "There's no discussion here."

"But –," Frank tries to argue.

"I have to leave," my dad states. "I have an old colleague to catch up with. I'll see you for breakfast tomorrow." Dad turns to me and looks into my eyes, "You're going to accept that medal. Am I clear, Alexandria?"

"Yes, Father," I respond. Dad only calls me Alexandria when he's completely serious.

I watch him walk out of the coffee shop, across the street, and meld into the traffic of people walking about.

"You're going to have to stand up to him one day," Frank says to me.

"It's not that easy," I reply. "I can't disappoint him. He's all I got left."

"You've got me, Sunshine," responds Frank.

I turn, smile, and take his hand in mine. "It's different, honey," I explain softly. "For better or for worse, dad's part of my past. Memories that I enjoy. He's the gateway to the happy times with my mom. He can be difficult to please, like he is now, but I love him. I need him. He's *my dad*. I'm *his* daughter. We're all I've got."

"But you don't have to always listen to him," Frank argues.

"I know," I say. "But most of the time he's right. And this time, maybe he's right. We were able to find the rebels and defeat the Nazis on our homeland before, I think we can do it again."

Frank squeezes my hand. "I'll follow you wherever you want to go. But at some point we need to stop this. At some point we have to step back and let someone else save the world."

"I know," I reassure him. "One day, maybe we'll retire to the Italian Alps, just like my dad keeps talking about how he and Mom planned to be there. But not right now. There's still a chance to save this country. We have to tell the President tomorrow. Then we have to help and get into the D.C. bureau to begin to uncover whatever network of Nazis spies there are. Once we do that, I promise we'll stop and settle down."

Frank leans over and kisses me on the cheek. "I like the sounds of that," he smiles.

"What did you discover in Toby's old neighborhood?" I ask.

"I have to admit," he starts, "I felt like a fish out of water. It was obvious I wasn't part of the neighborhood and I was worried that no one would be comfortable talking to a clean-cut white guy like me. Eventually, I walked into a corner grocery looking for anything... clues... someone to talk to... anything."

"Did you have any luck?" I ask.

"Well, at first I thought I did. There were a few older men outside the grocery smoking cigars and playing chess," he says. "They nodded at me. As I walked up they welcomed me back to the neighborhood. They recognized me and knew I was a friend of President Mack's, so this made me more comfortable. I relaxed and felt a little more accepted. My confidence grew and I went inside and walked around hoping they'd follow me in but they never did. I was about go out to the sidewalk and strike up a conversation with them but I was stopped by two bodyguard types. They were bigger than me. Two wide shouldered men in a small corner grocery store. There was no room for me to go anywhere, and that's when I started getting concerned. They asked me what I was doing there. Why I was in their neighborhood. I told them the truth, said I was looking for information. They forced me to come with them. One in front of me, the other in back. Told me they'd show me the truth. My heart was racing a bit and I could feel beads of sweat forming on my forehead, and I was hoping these guys saw me as a friend. I mean, the old guys in front of the grocer recognized me, these guys had to as well. They took me to the back alley, between all the apartment buildings. Led me around a few corners. I was lost and had no idea where I was. I tried talking to them once or twice but they didn't respond. They were super secretive. It seemed we walked through a dozen or so buildings. At the back of one, they opened a door and let me into a dark hallway. Again, a few turns, a staircase down, a few more turns, and then a few flights back up. Finally we stopped at a door. They banged on it. An old decrepit voice answered back something inaudible. The leader opened the door. I was blinded by sunlight. He told me to go in."

"Holy crap," I chime in. "This story is way better than mine."

"It gets crazier," Frank acknowledges. "I step out into the sunlight and I'm on a brownstone roof. At first I think this is it, that they're going to throw me off the roof for being in their neighborhood. But the bodyguards close the door behind me and leave me on the roof by myself. As my eyes adjust to the sunlight, in the middle of the roof I see an old man on a rocking chair with his feet in a kiddie pool. I step up to him and I see scars all over his legs, like he's been badly burned. He looks up at me and this guy is old. I mean super old, at least 100. He had moles all over his face with dark patches and white patches everywhere. White bushy hair. His cheeks were sagging and his skin looked rough, like sandpaper. He slowly raised his hand and pointed at me."

"Come closer," he told me. "Ain't no old black man gonna hurt you. Come closer so I can see you."

"I stepped up to him," Frank says to me, "And his eyes opened wide. He smiled. It's almost as if he saw an old friend. I'm a little relieved but immensely confused. I don't have any idea who this guy is."

"I remember you," he pointed at me. "I was nine years old the last time I saw you. It was dark times back then, yep. Dark times. Them damn Nazis ruled our neighborhood. Every day those Krauts would come in here and harass someone. Make sure they put us in our place. Smacked around the women. Teased us kids, told us we were no good 'cause the color of our skin. Sometimes they'd come in with a few brutes and beat up the strongest guy they could find. That's how I lost my dad. Took him away. Took my momma, too. I had to live with my aunt and uncle."

The old man paused and looked out to the sun, then he leaned down and poured a cup of water over his legs.

"Those Nazis give you those burns?" I asked him.

"Nah," he chuckles, "I wear these scars with pride. Got 'em the night you came to town. I watched you and President Mack from the window of my Uncle's apartment on New Hampshire Avenue. My older cousin said some serious shit was going to go down. She remembered Mack Truck running this neighborhood. Saw him with a bunch of strange white people with guns, knew he still had lots of friends here. When the Nazis showed up my uncle told me to get out, said things were gonna get hairy. Then he pulled a couple empty beer bottles outta the trash and ran up to the roof."

"Did you follow him?" I asked.

"Heck no," the old man said. "I was curious but I wasn't stupid. Knew he'd whip my ass for tagging along. But I still wanted to see a couple of white people and one big black man stand up to those Nazis rats. So I hid in the basement and looked out the window to watch you and everyone. I remember your jawline. Never saw a white man built like you, shoulders as wide a doorway and such a squared jaw. Then the oil started raining down. Some spilled into the basement and onto my legs. That's how I got these scars."

"I told him I was sorry," says Frank.

"Small price to pay," he said smiling at me with half a mouth of teeth. "I got to see President Mack and his gang at their finest hour. I'd never forget you. Glad I got to see you again."

I stood there in silence for a while. He seemed to be lost in thought, as if he were remembering and savoring the moment. Then he poured more water over his scars.

"I used to run this neighborhood for thirty years," he finally says. "Used to be councilman when President Mack was in the White House. I still know everything that goes on here. The gangs, the reverends, and the local government all pay homage to me. They are my eyes and ears out on the street. My brain's still good. Always thinking. A couple weeks ago, cops come askin' for me."

"Cops?" I interrupted, "They come asking about Nazis?"

"Shit, boy," he snaps, "You don't know nothin' about a neighborhood like this, do you? See we don't trust cops. They're almost as bad as the Nazis used to be. Tellin' us what we can't do, tellin' us where we got to be, when we gotta go home. Ain't nobody tell me what I can or can't do."

"I was scared that I upset him and that he wouldn't continue," Frank tells me. "But after a few moments, he started explaining."

"See, when a cop comes to your neighborhood askin' you about stuff you seen," he explains, "You don't tell them nothin'. You just listen. You get the information on what they're looking for, then pass it onto your friends if you want to. The gangs saw you walking the neighborhood. They came to me asking if you were a friend. When they described you, and talked about your wide shoulders and jaw, I knew it had to be you. Told them to bring you here. I had a message for you."

"I finally felt relieved," Frank tells me, "This guy knew me as a friend."

"Those cops asked me about you," he finally explains, "Wanted to know if I seen you lately. Seen that red-haired girlfriend of yours, too."

"Damn it," I interrupt Frank. "The Nazis are a few steps ahead of us. How'd they figure we'd be here?"

"Don't know," Frank replies, "But the old man says they're asking the whole neighborhood about the past. Wanting to talk to whoever was alive back in 1990. The neighborhood tried to hide him, but the cops knew where he was."

The old man said, "They told me to tell them if I see ya, but I said my eye sight ain't too good at my age and I can't tell one white man from another these days. Told the cops that you white folk all look the same to me."

"He smiled and chuckled a bit after that," Frank added.

"Besides," said the old man, "I ain't never trust no white cop and I ain't gonna start now. You shouldn't either. Watch your back, my friend. Someone wants to put a knife in it."

"The old man then poured some water over his legs," explained Frank, "Leaned back in the sunlight and started snoring. I left the roof and the same young boy led me back to the street level, gave me directions back to the National Mall. From there, I came straight here."

"Frank..." I begin to say but he interrupts me.

"I know, I know what you're going to say - these people need us, we're their only hope. It's just like the rebels back in 1989 except worse, yet, they don't know they're being oppressed. Only we can save them and we have to try our hardest to bring freedom back to everyone." Frank sighs, "Tomorrow we have to tell the President everything and ask him to get us assigned to the D.C. office on special duty just like your dad said we need to. We have to convince the President that only we can solve this problem and clean the Nazis out from inside the ranks."

"Well," I say, "I was going to say that Mexican beaches look really beautiful this time of year but now that you mentioned all that save the world stuff, well, I'm in."

Frank shoves me hard, "You're lucky you're cute or I would have left you a long time ago."

NINE

I wake up after the third snooze alarm and sit up to stretch. Frank rolls over and mumbles something about letting me get in the shower first, which really means he wants to sleep longer. We stayed up late last night arguing about the best approach to explain the situation to the President. Eventually, we decided during the photo opportunity we'd whisper to him that we suspect Nazis are infiltrating the government, and we need five minutes with him to give him the details. Originally, I wanted to slip him a note but Frank thought that for security reasons the Secret Service would try to stop us. If they were in on it, we'd never get our moment. Frank lobbied for a quick conversation during the photo op. There's no way the President could refuse the concern of two heroes.

My body is craving some caffeine, so I crawl out of bed and fill the automatic coffee machine with some of the Costa Rican blend that we took home from M.E. Swings. I open up the curtain and look out the window. Towering above the rest of the city is the Washington Monument. The sun is rising behind it but even as its white marble stone is shadowed, I can still tell that there is no Nazi flag hanging from the tallest Obelisk in the world. I breathe a sigh of relief knowing that today the Americans are still in charge of the country.

Leaving my great view behind, I head to the shower, shed my pajamas, and hop in the shower. The warm water wakes me up and I wash up for the amazing day ahead. It will be a great moment to get honored by my country today, but now I have an even greater duty. I need to save it again. I step out to towel off and find Frank already in the bathroom shaving.

"Good morning, Sunshine," he says, making that weird guy stretchy face as he pulls the razor over his skin.

"I like waking up with you," I say and kiss him on his shoulder. "Don't take too long in the shower."

My business suit and skirt are pressed and hanging in the closet. I slip into my clothes and check myself in the mirror, I look good and feel good.

"We have to meet my dad in another fifteen minutes," I yell

to Frank, still hearing the shower going. "You should finish up. I don't want to be late."

"Okay, Sunshine," he yells back.

I pour two cups of coffee and look out the window again, observing the hub-bub that's started on the National Mall. I'm kind of surprised that people are already gathering by the reflection pool to get a spot closest to the stage. That's when I realize that the stage is on the steps of the Lincoln Memorial. I'm going to be honored in front of my favorite U.S. president. I take a moment to revel in what I've achieved.

Frank sits down next to me on the bed and we stare out the window while we sip coffee together.

"It's a different city than we're used to, isn't it?" he says.

"Yep," I say. "Big day ahead."

"What do we do if he doesn't want to do a photo op?" Frank asks.

"Remember Senator Stiener scrambling for a picture before he left our house? All politicians want a photo op with heroes," I smirk. "He'll want his moment in the sun. It will make for a great political ad one day. Most likely it will be in his Presidential Library."

Frank laughs.

"You better get dressed," I tell him. "My dad hates it when I'm late."

We were supposed to meet my dad at 7:30 a.m. It's now 8:00 a.m. and he's still not here. In fifteen minutes we leave for our protocol meeting and then need to be in our seats by 9:30 a.m. since the ceremony begins promptly at 10:00 a.m. I would have sent my dad a dozen messages by now but we've decided to go dark after we left Columbus – no electronic communication whatsoever.

Across the room Frank is chatting and laughing with Howard Perhach, the assistant deputy communications White House liaison or something like that. In between chuckles, Frank sips his coffee then glances my way and at the clock. He's just as worried about where my dad is as I am. We don't really know what Dad was planning to do here in D.C. nor where he was going. He told us he was catching up with old friends. I hope they all weren't a bunch of absent minded professors like Dad who got themselves into trouble while snooping around to find Nazis. Dad should really leave this Nazi hunting stuff to us. He never fully explained to us how he survived all those years under Nazi rule before we corrected the past.

"It's time to head over to the Lincoln Memorial for the protocol meeting, Sunshine," says Frank. He and the assistant communications something or other are now standing at my table.

"Did your dad oversleep? We can send a military escort to his hotel room to see if he's awake," offers Howard.

"No," I explain. "My dad is a scientist. He wakes up precisely at 6 a.m., whether he's gone to bed at midnight or five."

"Maybe he expects to meet you at the Protocol Meeting?" thinks Howard aloud. "It is on the itinerary that we gave him."

"I'm sure that's what it is," Frank says. "Dad's probably going to meet us at the Protocol Meeting."

We start gathering up our things.

"Do you want a cup of coffee to go?" asks Howard. "There's nothing at the Memorial, so if you need some more pick me up, now's the time for it."

A third cup of coffee would be a good thing for me right now. I got little sleep last night and I have to be awake when we talk to the President. It will be good getting back into the Bureau. The lecturing and research was fun but I want to go back to serving my country where they need me the most and that's in the field, battling the enemy. There will be lots of time for lecturing and researching when I retire.

I turn the lever and the coffee flows into my cup. I inhale the smell of deep roasted nutty coffee and it relaxes me. Frank stands next to me waiting to fill his cup.

"I have to admit," Frank whispers. "I'm starting to get concerned about your dad missing. He isn't like this. He wouldn't miss this. Sure he's a little absent minded, but I think he'd stick pretty close to his schedule on this one."

"Let's see if he joins us at the Protocol Meeting," I say. "We won't panic until the end."

"It's time to go," instructs Howard. "We must depart now in order to make it to the Memorial in time for the Protocol Meeting."

In the motorcade over, I look out the window and take in Washington D.C. 2086. For the past five years I had been living the same year over and over again and had not experienced any change except the seasons. But this version of Washington D.C. is much different than 1989 and my memory of it in present time. The past was altered, and while the war has been over for decades, this version of Washington D.C. hasn't completely corrected, yet. It's still an amalgamation of the altered past and what it should be.

Think about it this way. There's a river of time. You dam it up and all this water accumulates behind the dam and the river beyond it dries up. When you remove the dam all the water explodes onto the lower river, rushing miles away. Eventually the raging river settles down and begins flowing again normally.

We're still in the raging waters. My dad predicts it will be a decade or so before time calms down and returns to normal. That's what his research has really been about. He's trying to understand the impact the Nazis made on the past to predict how long it will take to revert the temporal flow back to normal.

But now that we've discovered there's still the enemy among us, we may have to help that course correction along. We're going to have to kick some Nazis ass and get things back to normal.

The motorcade proceeds down Henry Bacon Drive and stops along Lincoln Memorial Circle. We step out of the car and I stare up at the Washington Monument in all its glory and marvel at its reflection in the pool below. During my tour of duty in 1989, this is the path I jogged every morning which ended right here at the Lincoln Memorial.

I follow Howard and Frank across the front of the Memorial and into its base. We meet up with a security guard and Howard flashes our credentials.

"Have you seen Dr. Eviston?" Howard asks.

"No," says the guard. "I was told he would be arriving with you."

"We think he got confused and may come straight here," responds Howard. "Keep a look out for him and let us know if he arrives. Direct him to the Administration office behind the gift shop."

"Will do, Sir," the guard responds.

We follow Howard through security and to a gift shop at the base of the stairs. Inside, we go through a back hallway and into a back room with chairs, a table, and a projection panel. Seated at the table is the most impeccably dressed man I've ever met. His suit jacket and shirt are neatly pressed. He's wearing a traditional navy blue suit and baby blue shirt with a lilac tie. It's perfectly tied into one of those fancy Eldredge knots.

"Good morning, Colonel Eviston," he says to me, extending his hand, "I am Rex McClure, Chief White House Protocol Officer. This morning I'll be teaching you, along with Colonel Bouchard, on how to properly experience this celebration in your honor. As you can see, I've chosen a specific spot for each of you to sit. Please take your seats so we can begin."

I look at the table and there are piles of paper neatly stacked at each chair. At the top of each pile is an individual picture of us, indicating where we should sit.

"I've placed Alex next to me," explains Rex, "Since you are our most important guest of honor. I don't want you to miss any details and embarrass yourself."

"Thank you," I reply and sit down, hoping this is going to be super short. I sit opposite my dad's spot which is obviously empty.

"Do we want to wait a few moments for your dad to arrive?" asks Howard.

"We are on a tight timeline," argues Rex, "We cannot wait any longer."

"Dad's usually on time," I respond. I begin to shake a little and not from the caffeine. I'm not sure what Frank is thinking, but my dad is not like this and I'm concerned he may be in trouble. I want to leave right now and go look for him, but that would be awkward, and leave a trail of clues to any Nazi sympathizer that we know what's up.

"Colonel Eviston," Howard says slowly. He can sense my nervousness. "Would you like us to send out a search party for your father? We can contact the D.C. Police for help…"

"No," responds Frank. "We don't need to get the police involved. I'm sure he'll turn up."

"Well then, let's get started," says Rex, "Howard, can you get the lights, please? Thank you."

Rex then begins to talk and talk and talk and talk about the importance of political etiquette at these events and what is expected of each of us. I glance over to Frank who's absorbing every word he says. Being from Canada, Frank's not used to U.S. political customs and is trying to learn as much as he can.

I could really care less about what Rex is talking about. I look across at the empty chair that my dad should be sitting in, and wonder where he is.

My dad. What a complicated relationship we have. He always treated me older than what I was. Even when I was younger, he expected me to be more mature. Wanted me to act like I was in Sixth Grade when I was only in Fourth. I never had a chance to be a kid around him that much, was never allowed to make those silly mistakes kids make. I had to be better in his eyes.

It had its benefits, though. When I was eight I wanted a puppy. That's all I talked about for months. It was on my birthday list and then later that year, the only thing on my Christmas list. Mom would have none of it.

"It's too big of a responsibility for a child your age," she would say. "Wait a few years until you grow up."

"She's more mature than you think, Carol Ann," my dad would argue.

"James, you're always at the office or lab or school," Mom argued back, "You won't be the one to raise the dog. I will."

"Alex will help," he said back. But that was the end of the argument. Mom always got her way.

One night after a dinner out, my dad announced he had to stop at an Assistant's house to pick up some research results really quick. We pulled into the driveway and my dad suggested Mom and I come in to meet her.

When his Assistant opened the door, we walked in and three puppies came running up to us, barking and licking our feet. I stooped down to pet them all and after a while I looked up and saw a forth puppy cowering and shaking between the Lab Assistant's feet. I slowly crawled past the other puppies to the one that seemed super scared. I gently petted her back.

"I'm Alex," I whispered in her ear, "There's nothing to be scared about."

The puppy turned and licked my face. I picked him up and put him on my lap. I overheard my dad saying to my mom, "Try and say 'No' now."

That was my cue. "Can we keep him, Mom?" I begged. "Pleeeaseee?"

That night I had a new Yorkshire puppy sleeping in my bed with me. Dad checked on us and tucked me in.

"Thanks, Dad," I smiled.

"I expect you to take good care of him," he instructed. "I'm in big trouble with Mom now, so you have to help feed, walk, and train the puppy, understand?"

"Yes, Dad," I promised, "I'll take good care of him."

"What did you name him?" he said.

"Vito," I replied.

"A big name for such a little dog," he responded.

"I wanted him to have a strong name since he was so scared," I said.

"A name can mean everything, Alex," he said. "Now, get

some sleep. You're going to have a big day with Vito tomorrow since you'll start his training."

Dad may have not had the warmest heart, but it seems like he was always watching out for me. I feel like I'm failing him now and not holding up my end of things. He's out there somewhere in trouble, and I should be out looking for him instead of listening to Rex and getting a medal.

"So, with that, we're done," concluded Rex.

"Excellent," responded Frank. "I know exactly what we need to do now."

I look up to find Frank closing his protocol book and Rex shutting off the projector. Thank God Frank was paying attention, because I know nothing about what we need to do.

———————————

They seated Frank and me in the front row. There's an empty space for my dad in case he suddenly appears, and Senator Steiner is seated on the other side. The Senator finally stopped asking about our trip and where my dad is, and has turned to checking his messages on his wrist watch.

I'm trying to soak it all in and not worry about my dad as much. We're up on a platform with the steps of the Lincoln Memorial directly behind us. A large crowd has gathered around the Reflection Pool to watch the event. Howard believes they are all here to see me and commemorate the end of the war. I think they were all paid to be here and that this is some political move by the President to win some more votes. There's no way that all of them are here to see me get a medal. But I look out in the audience and see a lot of old people. Not as old as the black man that Frank met on the roof of President Mack's neighborhood, but close. A dozen or so people were in wheel chairs, a few have a lost limb or sorts. I realize that they are veterans. They must have fought in the war that extended years after I left. I came to understand that assassinating the American Nazi government and blowing up the B-52 over the ocean didn't end the war. It was only the beginning of the end. The rebels kept on fighting and were able to drive the Nazis army out of the U.S., but it took a long time.

"Colonel Eviston, Colonel Bouchard, I am so honored to be in your presence," speaks a booming voice. I look up to see a man about six feet tall with a perfectly cut blue suit and the kind of smile you see in toothpaste advertisements. "You make me proud to be a Buckeye."

"I'm sorry," I say, "I don't recognize you."

The man frowns a bit, "I'm Senator O'Brien. You've already met my fellow statesman, Senator Stiener but I haven't had a chance to meet you." Senator Stiener turns and waves, but goes back to his messages.

"Sorry, Senator," Frank offers his hand to shake, "Alex and I haven't been back long enough to familiarize ourselves with the politicians of the day and who's running the government."

"We should always be aware of our leaders," added another fellow. He was a white man in his late 50s, disheveled and a bit unkempt. His suit didn't quite fit and his shirt was wrinkled, but somehow he still commanded attention. Like that used car salesman that managed to make you feel bad for him so you paid a little too much than you should have.

"This is Senator Pappas, from Michigan," Senator O'Brien explains.

"Colonel Eviston, Colonel Bouchard, it is a huge honor to meet you. We are proud of your accomplishments and grateful for all you've done. You're both true American heroes. If there is anything I can do for you, please give my office a call."

"Senator Pappas," Frank wonders, "You know, the name does ring a bell. Alex's father was talking about you the other day."

"Really? Dr. Eviston was talking about me?" Senator Pappas beamed.

"Yes," Frank explained, "He said you voted down a critical Education Bill that would fund scholarships for the underprivileged. There are tens of thousands of teenagers who can't afford to go to college now. Great minds going to waste because of your No vote."

The four of us stared at each other for a moment. Then

Senator O'Brien smiled and said, "I'm sorry, the ceremony is about to start. We need to take our seats."

Both Senators quickly walk away.

"I told you that was a bad idea," mumbles Senator Pappas to Senator O'Brien.

I turn back around to the crowd and see a few veterans talking and pointing at me. They smile with a look of excitement and pride on their face. Maybe they are here for the medal ceremony and commemorate the end of the war. We all fought an amazing battle against the Nazis. Seeing them today gives me the energy to continue my fight. I want to make sure their efforts were not in vain. We can't slip back under Nazi control. I'm grateful by their presence and desire to be here so I stand and salute them. They all return my salute. Each one stands a little more erect, as tall as their elderly frame will let them. Even one in a wheel chair straightens up a bit. I give them a nod and sit back down. Throughout the crowd, pockets of applause begin then fade away.

"You shouldn't have done that," smiles Frank. "It's against the protocol. Weren't you paying attention?"

"When have you ever known me to follow protocol?" I smile back. Rex gives me a stern look and raises his finger in a warning manner to not do it again.

The murmuring on the platform quickly dissipates.

"We're beginning," voices say behind us and the band to our right begins *Hail To The Chief*.

The whole platform and Frank stand up and after a moment I do as well.

"You should have listened during the Protocol meeting," Frank whispers. "That Catholic intuition of when to stand and when to sit isn't going to help you much today."

The President reaches the podium, the band stops, and he says, "Thank you."

I sit down with everyone else on the platform perfectly timed. I glance at Frank and raise an eye brow with pride. He smiles back. I look to the empty seat and wish my dad was here, hoping that he's just somewhere caught up in his research.

"Good morning, fellow citizens of the United States of North America," booms President Austin. "Today is a great day to be an American. To be on free soil and breathe this sweet air. It is a great day to be with you all and it is a privilege to honor two Patriots today. Patriots who have faced the enemy, crushed it, and ignited the flame of freedom in all of us. They are an inspiration and deserve our honor today."

Applause erupts in the crowd and maintains for several moments.

"Thank you. I see you agree as well," smiles the President. "Please, Colonel Alexandria Eviston and Colonel Frank Bouchard, step forward to receive your Medals of Honor."

I have to admit, I forgot to think about this moment. I was so focused on developing a foolproof plan on warning the President about the Nazis, that I completely forgot about our prestigious thanks.

A Medal of Honor is the highest form of recognition a member of the military can receive. It takes an Act of Congress to approve it and it must be presented by the President. One of the first things the Congress did when we returned was pass a special act that designated Frank and I as recipients. This was done under secrecy so the announcement could be made public at the right political time.

The first Medal of Honor was given back in 1862 but there was a long period of time when the medals were not awarded due to the Nazi occupation. Congress resumed the recognition once the war ended. Frank will be the 2,999 recipient and I will be the 3000th.

So here we are today, in front of thousands of American Citizens and hundreds of veterans of the U.S. Second Revolutionary War, about to receive the highest honor one can receive. Many of these veterans in front of me have given much more for the war than I have. I see missing limbs, ragged clothes, canes, and wheelchairs. Frank and I were just the catalyst that made it happen and I don't feel quiet worthy compared to them. But from the veterans that are closest to the stage, I can see a look of pride and respect, as if I'm receiving this award for all of us.

I stand proud and walk over to the President as I'm directed to by Frank. My emotions finally begin to overwhelm me and I can't quite absorb everything the President is saying. I hear words like "Patriot.... True American... Fearless... Freedom... Sacrifice... Democracy... Liberty... Justice... Hero." Looking down the National Mall, I can't be any more in awe. Thousands of citizens watching this historic moment, a beautiful crystal clear reflection of the Washington Monument in the pool which ends with the World War II Memorial, and finally the Washington Monument standing proud and high as a beacon for this great nation. At this moment, I couldn't feel any more American. It fuels my anger even more that Nazis still live among us and have infiltrated some of the highest ranks of our government. I can't wait to hunt down each and every one of them and bring them to justice. Just another 30 minutes or so and we'll be able to ask the President for our assignment.

Frank steps forward to receive his medal first. I turn around to see if my dad has arrived but still see an empty seat. Where is he? I know he hates politicians but how could he miss this special moment for his daughter. I shudder to think something awful has happened.

"Alex," Frank whispers, "Step forward."

My mind returns back to the moment at hand. I see the President in front of me with the medal in his hands, waiting to place it around my neck. In fact, the whole crowd is waiting for me. I think I blush a little bit from being lost in my thoughts and finally step forward to receive my medal.

"For conspicuous gallantry and intrepidity," bellows the President, "At the risk of life above and beyond the call of duty, in the name of U.S. Congress, I, President Austin, hereby present the Medal of Honor to Colonel Alexandria Eviston."

The President places the medal around my neck and the crowd erupts in applause. After the applause dies down, Frank grabs me and has me stand next to him. I have the President to my left and Frank to my right. I want to take it all in and remember every emotion, but I'm guessing that something else is going to happen next and I don't want to miss my cue. Instead of looking forward to the crowd and accidentally get lost in thought, I focus in on the President and his closing words.

"This is an amazing day," starts the President. "We have honored two war heroes to which we owe so much. They are some of the strongest Patriots that have ever lived. They have sacrificed much to return this great nation of ours to freedom and liberty. So it is only fitting that after giving so much of themselves, that I accept their request for retirement. Effective immediately, with a special order from the Chairman of the Joint Chiefs of Staff, Colonel Alexandria Eviston and Colonel Frank Bouchard are relived from active duty and will retire from military and government service. No longer are they needed to hunt down the enemy and bring them to justice. They are now free to lead a civilian life. We wish them well in their new careers as researchers and professors at The Ohio State University. Thank you everyone. And God Bless America!"

The President winks at me and waves to the crowd as the band strikes up *Hail To The Chief*. He struts away with the secret service to his motorcade and drives off.

TEN

"What just happened?" I ask aloud, sitting on the steps of the Lincoln Memorial.

I know what happened but I'm in disbelief. It's about an hour after our medal ceremony which just turned into our surprise retirement ceremony. In essence, we've been kicked out of the military and government service. They no longer want us there with the power to meddle in their affairs.

Furthermore, we've been kicked out by the President of the United States. He's got to be in on it. We have a Nazi in the Oval Office.

On top of it all my dad is still missing and I'm guessing he's been kidnapped. Dad is absent minded at times because his research comes first. But I find it hard to believe he's in some lab right now trying to discover something. He's forgetful, but he is a proud father. He wouldn't miss my medal ceremony… or retirement ceremony if he knew that's what it was going to be.

I'm scared because my dad's missing, I'm worried because there are Nazis infiltrating the highest office of the United States, and I feel helpless because the only ace we had up our sleeves was us being assigned to Homeland Security in the D.C. office.

I haven't felt this bad since my mother died. Part of me wants to crawl in bed and sleep the day away under the covers like I used to every anniversary of my mother's death.

So now I'm sitting here, feeling miserable and defeated, with Frank by my side on the steps of the Lincoln Memorial. We're watching the last of the laborers tear down the scaffolding and PA system, as if they were dissembling my plan. A few spectators are still milling about the Reflection Pool, the World War II Memorial, and taking pictures of the Washington Monument.

"I can't believe this," I finally say. "Everything we did back in 1989 was all for nothing. Roach… Ella… they died in vain."

"No they didn't," Frank argues. "We changed the world."

"Are you crazy?" I snap back. "The Nazis are still running

the government here. The President is a wolf in sheep's clothing. Did you see that twinkle in his eye when he announced our retirement? They are onto us! The President is a Nazi! And worse, yet, there's nothing we can do about it. We're retired now. Researchers. Lecturers. Sure they'll give us labs at Wright-Patterson so they can watch us twenty-four by seven. We can't stop this from the inside, and we don't have a rebel army to join like we did in 1989. We can't fix any of this. It's over."

"Over?" Frank questions.

"Yes," I say feeling completely powerless. "There's nothing we can do. I'm out of Homeland Security! You're out of Homeland Security! God only knows where my dad is. You're all I got left, Frank, and if we get caught, and they take you away I'll have nothing. Mom's gone. Dad's gone. You'd be gone. Nothing."

Frank stares at me in disappointment.

"You know, when I found out I was assigned to work with you, well, I was pretty excited to say the least. You had a legendary-like reputation," Frank says. "Strong willed, independent, thrill-seeking. Looking for answers and didn't want to play by anyone's rules. You were an idol to many women who were trying to make it in academics, math, science, history. Not only was I going to meet The Alex Eviston, but I was going to work by her side. It made being assigned to 1989 all worth it. But when I met you some five years ago you were nothing like your reputation said you were. You were scared, confused, and worried about being alone. You were miserable to be with. In fact, you were kind of like you are right now."

"Frank," I say to him, "If this is supposed to be a pep talk, you're doing a terrible job."

"Here's the thing," Frank continues. "You were that strong, independent, thrill-seeking woman that everyone said you were, you just kept her hidden. See, over the past year or so, the true Alex Eviston came to life. Finally broke out of the shell that you built around yourself. Today, you have a choice.

You can retreat back into that shell, or continue to be who you were meant to be."

Great. Now Frank is lecturing me. He doesn't understand it. I can't control everything. I can't change fate.

"What can I do?" I shrug my shoulders. "It's over."

Frank stands up, grabs my arm and pulls me up toward the Lincoln Memorial.

"Come with me," he says. He leads me up the steps of the Lincoln Memorial. He ignores Daniel Chester French's statue of President Lincoln and we head straight to the south side chamber. We stop.

"Read this," Frank says pointing to the inscription on the wall.

It's the Gettysburg Address. Back when I was monitoring 1989, I read it every morning as I ran through Washington D.C. Frank knows I love this speech and knows it's been part of my life nearly every day for the past five years. He knows I did a report on it during my sophomore year of high school. The speech reiterated the founding principles of our country at a time when it was falling apart. In times of crisis, we must trust in our values more than ever. That was what was at the heart of what President Lincoln was trying to say.

"Aloud. Read it, aloud," Frank insisted.

I began to read it aloud, word for word. Frank joins in as well. We didn't just speak the words, we began to emote them as if we were President Lincoln himself, as if we believed in what we were saying. The last few words of the address stirs a passion in me that I have not felt in months.

> "...that this nation, under God, shall have a new birth of freedom -- and that government of the people, by the people, for the people, shall not perish from the earth."

Heavy silence fills the air as Frank and I take in the words that we just spoke. Frank finally turns to me.

"Are you going to let it perish?" Frank asks me.

"No," I say. "Hell, no."

"Me neither," he adds.

I have no idea how we're going to do this. We need to find my father and save the country from the Nazis who are hiding at the highest levels of the government. This will be a tough road ahead, much tougher than any I've had before me.

I grab Frank's hand and we start down the stairs of the Lincoln Memorial. The last of the scaffolding is gone from the stage and you can barely tell that there's been a ceremony here this morning. It's as if they've erased us already.

But at the very base of the Memorial is a group of veterans who have stayed behind to tour the National Mall. They are wearing their uniforms from the Second U.S. Revolutionary War, the end of World War II. Most are leaning on canes and one is in a wheelchair, missing his left leg.

"Colonel Eviston, Colonel Bouchard," one of them yells. "Ma'am, sir, a moment of your time, please."

"All the time in the world for my fellow veterans," Frank yells back to them. Frank revels in the military camaraderie, while I am always more of a loner. But I share a special connection with these men and I'm more than willing to talk.

"Thanks for taking the time to speak with us," one of the men say as we begin to shake hands. They are old, at least in their nineties.

"It's an honor to meet a fellow veteran," I explain. "Where you guys from?"

"Most of us are from Fort Bragg, North Carolina," the one in the wheelchair responds. "We served in special forces, hunting down Nazi vermin within our borders and bringing them to justice." He finishes with a grin as if he really meant killing them.

"Except for me. I'm from St. Louis," says the man who first spoke. He's much younger than the others and seems to be their tour guide. "My name is Zak Aholt. General Aholt is my great-grandmother. She always spoke highly of you. Said you were a leader and savior. She'd be thrilled for you today. It's a pleasure to meet you. You're one of kind."

Temporal Gravity has a crazy way of pushing us all in the right direction. General Aholt was the one who supported me back in the council at the St. Louis Zoo in 1990. She's here in spirit to support me today.

"Men," speaks Frank. "It's always great to meet a fellow veteran, especially ones like yourselves who have sacrificed so much."

"Congratulations on your medal, today," one of them says. "We didn't want to miss the opportunity to see the great Colonel Alex Eviston and Colonel Frank Bouchard. We had no idea that we were going to see your retirement ceremony, too. You guys are so young, it was a shock to us that you're leaving the military. Guess you've been through a lot."

"Yeah," I stumble out. "We have no idea what we're going to do with the rest of lives now."

"Here's the strange thing," one of the men slowly speaks. He's the oldest of the bunch with deep wrinkles, age spots, and a few hairs left on his head, all white gray. "We have a saying at Fort Bragg: once military, always military. They can retire you, but you're not going to stop being who you really are."

"What's that?" I ask.

"You're a rebel. Always have been. Always will," the man winks at me.

I pull the medal off of my shoulders, step forward, and place it around his neck.

"Meeting all of you today is the only honor I need," I say. "And your kind words are much more meaningful than anything this President can say or do. You men deserve this medal as much as I do. Take care of yourselves, and God Bless America."

All the men salute us.

"De oppresso liber," the man in the wheelchair declares with pride.

"De oppresso liber," repeats the other men.

Frank and I salute back with clean, crisp salutes.

"De oppresso liber," I respond.

Frank and I turn around and begin our next journey.

"What does 'De oppresso liber' mean?" Franks whispers.

"It means 'to liberate the oppressed'. It's the motto of the Special Forces," I explain.

"Sounds like our motto, too," Frank smiles.

I grab his hand.

"Let's go find my dad," I say, "And save the United States of America."

ELEVEN

Frank and I decide that our first step is to try and figure out what has happened to my dad. Now that we believe the President is in league with the Nazis, chances are the government has kidnapped my dad. If we can prove this, than we can start to expose the President and others for what they really are. If there is a chink in their armor, we will find it and exploit it.

So now, we're in the lobby of our hotel. Frank's at the front desk arguing with the Manager to give us access to my dad's room. Meanwhile, I'm trying to get a hold of him one more time. We scrapped our modern age ear bud communicator for an older model of a traditional Watch Phone. It's all about what's more easily traceable. The Watch Phone uses old technology, GPS, to track people's movement. The government can use it to find out where we are but only if it's activated. It also uses old G4 cell phone technology which can determine where we are but only through triangulation of signals from different towers. The technology is so old that it's going to take a while to discover our where abouts, which gives me just a few seconds to try and call my dad.

"Dad. Mobile," I speak into my watch. The screen flips to a picture of my dad with a graphic below that reads 'calling.' I wait several seconds to see if he answers.

"Five, six, seven, eight," I count to myself to make sure that they don't have enough time to track where I am. Before I get to ten I hang up. I didn't expect him to answer. We all agreed to go dark and not use technology to contact each other. I have to figure out a way to find him. I turn around in the lobby and see Frank still arguing with the manager.

"He's my future father-in-law," Frank yells at him. "He's missing. Let me into his room."

"I've explained to you several times now," says the Manager. "That's just not allowed."

I'm in no mood to deal with anymore roadblocks today so I march over to the front desk.

"Do you know who I am?" I tell the Manager.

"Yes," he states with authority.

"Do you know who I am?" I say it again but this time with even more force.

"Yes. You're -"

I cut him off. "Give me access to my father's room this instance," I instruct him.

"Ma'am, it's hotel policy not to give access to another guest's room without their permission," he nervously responses.

"Listen," I explain. "I'm going to give you a choice. You let me into my father's room or I explain to the world how insensitive your hotel was in my time of need. I was honored as a war hero today and my dad missed it. I hope he's not in his room, hurt or in need of medical attention."

The manager pauses for a moment, reading the look on my face. He must be considering what's a worse career move: breaking hotel policy, or pissing me off.

"Give me one moment," he whispers.

After a few seconds he steps out from behind the desk and leads us to the elevators. We get on, ride the elevator up in silence, and then head to Dad's room.

"Management," the Manager speaks outside the door. The lock clicks and disengages. He turns the door handle and we walk in.

Dad is nowhere to be found. In fact, the room looks immaculate, as if he's never been here. The beds are completely made. A luggage bag rests on one of the beds, opened, but still completely packed. His toiletry bag is on the bathroom counter, but it hasn't been opened. I unzip it and inspect his toothbrush. Dry. Probably hasn't been used in days.

"Did the maid come through, yet?" Frank asks.

"No," the Manager explains. "They're not scheduled to be on this floor for another hour."

I emerge from the bathroom. "He didn't sleep here last night," I conclude. "In fact, I'm not sure he slept here at all."

"Would you like me to call the police?" the manager asks.

"That won't be necessary," Frank explains. "Alex's father is kind of an absent minded professor. He's probably with a scientific colleague of his at one of the Smithsonian museums, looking at some important breakthrough research."

"Are you sure?" the Manager clarifies, as if he's again reviewing what the proper protocol is.

"We thank you so much for your time," I say to the Manager, offering my hand.

He pauses for a moment, surveying the situation, wondering what he should do. Finally, he turns back to me and take my hand. He shakes it.

"Glad I could help, Colonel Eviston," he says and starts to walk out the door. He stops and turns around. "I would appreciate if we kept this moment to ourselves. We have strict policies here, and in light of the fact that your father is safe somewhere doing research, well…"

"Your help was appreciated here," explains Frank, "But it will be forgotten." He smiles.

"Thank you," replies the Manager. He turns around, walks out, and closes the door behind him.

"Perfect," I say. "The Manager doesn't want anyone to know he gave us access either."

"Looks like your dad was never here," says Frank. "He checked in, dropped off his suitcase, and left. Did he say who he was meeting with these past few days?"

"A colleague, someone at the Smithsonian Air and Space Museum," I rattle off.

"I think that's our next stop," Frank says. "But first, let's head back to our room and change out of these dress clothes. Maybe it's best we look more like tourists."

Frank used to visit the Smithsonian Air and Space Museum all the time during our assignment in 1989 and we busted in here during our raid on Washington D.C. back in 1990. But in reality it's been almost a century since we've been here. There are decades of change since 1989 and it's definitely different than when I visited it as a teenager with Mom and Dad.

The obvious exhibit Dad would have been studying was a

Time Travel one. We walk through the doors and find the closest floor plan map.

"Time Travel," I speak.

Images shuffle in front of me. "There are two exhibitions on Time Travel at the National Air and Space Museum here in Washington, D.C.," a booming male voice from the map display explains. "The first is a permanent display here on the first floor commemorating the discovery of time travel by James Eviston, including such artifacts as the Rolling Stone magazine…"

"Next exhibit," I command, cutting the voice off. "Dad never liked public recognition," I explain to Frank.

"The second exhibit is called 'What if Time Travel Never Existed?' and explores history without the man-made changes," the voice continues.

"Location," I ask.

"Room 213, second floor, northeast section of the building," the voice directs.

We find the closest set of stairs and hurry up to the second floor. We walk down the hallway and find the exhibit. A large banner signals the display. Inside against the longest wall is a timeline of true history with the end of World War II listed as September 2, 1945. A special display in the corner shows key aberrations in time. Along the back wall is a replica of the day I traveled back in time to give fire to women. I'm drawn to it as I've never seen a bigger than life size image of me. I'm eight years younger in the picture. My hair is a little crazier and the lines on my face look much softer. I don't know if it's the airbrushing they did on the graphic or if I'm really starting to show my age.

"Alexandria Eviston changed the world forever," Frank reads aloud the headline over my picture.

"It wasn't that big of a deal," I reply. "It didn't change that much. The Commission that punished me made it out to be the most catastrophic event in temporal history."

"Well that's what the display says," Frank jeers.

I look at the rest of the display. There's a description that over dramatizes what actually happened along with more pictures and an illustration of me showing cave women how to start a fire. A side bar explains the Commission and how it works, along with a picture of them. I've never seen the full Commission before, only three of the lead members delivered my sentence to me. I was told the full Commission was compromised of elected officials and top scientists from around the country. There's about twenty people in the photograph. One face suddenly pops out at me.

"My dad was on the Commission?" I question, shocked.

"You didn't know that?" Frank questions. "Rumor has it that your dad was the final vote and pushed to have you assigned to 1989. The Commission originally wanted to just suspend you from research for a year, but your dad insisted that you go out to the field and specifically indicated the year. I thought you knew that."

"Why did Dad want me assigned to 1989?" I wondered aloud.

"Do you think he knew something?" Frank asked. "Like he knew you'd have to one day fight the Nazis and save the world?"

"Dad's an expert in time travel," I say, "But he knows nothing about the future. He's not a psychic. He's a scientist."

"Excuse me, Colonel Eviston?" a pleasant sounding woman says from behind me.

I turn around to see a woman in a black business suit. She has long straight brown hair fashioned into a French braid. She's managed to keep that strong business leader look with a hint of proper femininity. I'm totally jealous. I can never do that with my hair, or my looks. I'm either a field agent, a researcher, or a professor. It's impossible for me to blend my looks, and frankly, it's difficult for me to ever feel charming.

"Yes, I'm Alex Eviston," I admit. It's hard for me to deny it with a more than life size picture of me directly over my shoulder.

"I'm Dr. Leigh Pringle," she introduces herself and extends her hand. Underneath her other arm she's gently carrying a leather portfolio. "I'm the Deputy Under Secretary for Collections & Interdisciplinary Support here at the Smithsonian. First, I'd like to congratulate both you and Colonel Bouchard on your medals today. You are both patriots and great examples for the youth of today. Especially you, Alex. My daughter is a big admirer of yours."

I blush, "Thank you, Dr. Pringle."

"Second, one of my responsibilities is the Smithsonian Archives," she continues. "I have the package your Father requested. He said you may be by to pick it up."

My dad didn't say anything about a package yesterday. Or that I should stop by the Smithsonian to pick one up.

"Yes," I lie. "My dad wanted to be here himself but he's running late."

"He explained that he might be," explains Dr. Pringle. "He requested it yesterday but unfortunately I couldn't get it immediately. It was in our offsite fireproof storage in Virginia. As you could imagine, we wanted to take great care of it while it was on loan from your family. We had it on display in the Natural History Museum for a while but we do try to rotate exhibits. At the time we changed the exhibit, your dad asked us to store it safely as we indicated it might go back on display at some point. I must admit it was odd to have your dad show up out of the blue to request it in person, but it made sense once we realized he was in town for today's ceremony."

Dr. Pringle carefully passes the leather portfolio over to me. I gingerly take it from her.

"As you could imagine, I wanted to personally deliver it to you or your dad, as it is so important," she says.

I look down at the leather portfolio and instantly realize what it is. It's one of the most important research papers ever written in the past century but unfortunately was shadowed by my dad's discovery of Time Travel.

"I must tell you," adds Dr. Pringle, "Your mom was a hero of mine. She's why I went into science. This paper was an inspiration to me. It's been a huge honor to have it in our collection."

I read the title engraved on the leather cover, *The Evolution of Influence by Carol Ann Eviston.* My mom's groundbreaking research discovered the biological and environmental traits necessary to increase your influence over others. Consider pack dogs. How is their leader determined? There's a series of genetic elements that are necessary but in addition the leader must be raised a certain way with several outside factors. It's not nature vs. nurture. It's both. Mom discovered what these core determinates were and how they evolved from beginning of time. It rocked the field of Psychology and jettisoned it as one of the more important sciences to study. Unfortunately, months later my father proved his Theory of Temporal Gravity which outshined any other scientific discovery since the atom bomb. In fact, many felt the study of influence was unnecessary since we are all moving towards temporal gravity and our destiny is inevitable.

"Thank you," I say to Dr. Pringle. "And thank you for taking such great care of it." I want to look at it in detail but the leather portfolio is bound shut with a leather strap. I'll look at it later.

"Dr. Pringle, how did you know we'd be here today?" inquires Frank.

"I didn't," she explains. "Our security cameras and computers are programmed for face recognition. Your face and your dad's face were already in the computer, I just selected that it alert me whenever either of you entered any of our buildings."

"I understand," responds Frank. "Thank you for meeting us, but we must be going now. We have a dinner reception tonight that we have to get ready for."

"Sure," she says. "Please, whenever you come back to the Smithsonian, call ahead. I'll make sure you get special privileges and arrange for a behind the scenes tour."

We step away from Dr. Pringle and when we're out of earshot I whisper to Frank, "Why are we leaving? I want to know more about why my dad wanted this document."

"They know we're here," explains Frank. "If Dr. Pringle

was able to discover us on the security cameras so would anyone else. If they kidnapped your dad while he was visiting the exhibits or a colleague, then they can certainly kidnap us. I'm all for finding your dad but I don't want us to get kidnapped in the process."

"They are not going to capture us in public," I say.

Not a moment after the words come out of my mouth I spot a half a dozen of guards coming our way. We're in danger.

"Head down those stairs," I nod to our left. We change our direction suddenly and make a move towards the stairwell.

"Stop where you are," one of the guards yell at us.

Frank grabs my arm, quickens his pace, and pulls me along. "Come on," he instructs. "We've still got to get through the main doors."

I take off running, knowing Frank's right behind me. I bust through an emergency exit and down a stairwell. An alarm goes off throughout the building. We emerge onto the first floor and into a crowd of people, all pushing to the main entrance. Blending into the crowd, we pass by the gift shop I manage to snag a NASA themed baseball cap. I put it on and tuck as much of my red hair into it. I grab Frank's hand tightly, hold onto the leather portfolio in the other, and ride the wave of people out the front door.

Over the sirens and nosy crowd I can barely still hear the guards yelling, "Stop her. She has one of the artifacts from the exhibits. Stop her!" Nobody's paying attention to them. Instead, they are moving to the exits just like we are. We get out onto the front steps and onto the National Mall.

"What do we do now?" I ask. "We're fugitives. They can accuse us of stealing federal property, even though this portfolio is really mine. We need a place to sit and think for a while."

"A friend of mine owns the best safe house in town, one that would survive a full on nuclear attack," Frank smiles, "And fortunately I still have a key to the place."

We follow the crowd crossing over the National Mall and start making our way on foot towards Georgetown.

TWELVE

We're standing outside the door to the basement level of a brownstone. Ironically, the last time I was here we were running from the Nazis back in 1989. It's Mojmir's apartment and Frank and I are hoping it's been untouched for the past 100 years or so.

"He gave me a key during our fourth tour of duty so I could water his plants while he took a vacation," Frank explained. "He never asked for it back. Let's see if there's still a key hole that works."

The door shows it's age, as paint is peeling off in chunks and rust is building up where the paint has completely worn off. The good news is the door handle still seems attached well. Frank jiggles the key into to the lock and gently tries to twist it. After a moment it turns and we hear several locks disengage from inside. Frank slowly presses down on the latch and pulls the handle. The door creaks open and we step inside.

I flip a switch on the wall and the lights come on. The place looks exactly like we left it back in 1989. The iron walls and concrete floors haven't changed at all. Frank closes the door behind us, locking each of the deadbolts and pulls down the aluminum gate.

"Thankfully we left in a hurry and Mojmir didn't bolt and lock everything on the front entrance," Frank admits.

"Funny thing is nothing smells," I say. "You'd think there would be a musty odor since no one has been here for almost 100 years."

"This place is powered and fed by the geo-thermal electric plant downstairs," reminds Frank. "I'm sure Mojmir included some special air duct filtering. Remember how paranoid he was about a nuclear blast?"

"Mojmiristan," I acknowledge. "His bomb shelter."

"And his oasis," Frank adds. "Everything one would need to self-sustain themselves for decades. Even if the Nazis track us here and manage to get into his apartment, they'll never figure out there's a whole cavern below. Let's hide out in Mojmiristan for a while."

We head into the back bedroom. I find the closet door with the Bon Jovi poster and open it up. I reach down and uncover the false bottom, then open the trap door. Frank and I descend 500 feet into Mojmiristan. While the apartment upstairs looks the same, this place has changed. All the computers have stayed intact and everything was on timers, but nothing's been tended to. The field of vegetables and fruits have grown wild since no one's gardened it for over a hundred years. Fortunately, I can see corn and blueberries still growing. There are apples ripening on the apple trees and bananas on the banana plants. The goats, chicken, and cattle broke out of their pens and are roaming free. Somehow Mojmir had planned for just enough animals so each could sustain their herd. He set up self-sustaining food sources for all the animals and there is a stream fed by the same spring that helps power the geo-thermal electricity.

The main building with the living quarters looks a little decrepit, but it isn't that bad. There is still a patio table out front that looks pretty stable. It's the same one that Mojmir, Frank, and I ate Rice Krispies on and planned to escape to Canada.

"This place is perfect for us to hang out at for a while," Frank observes. "Only problem is that the lights are much dimmer than I remember them being."

I look up at the lights above which simulate the sun and find out that Frank is right. They seem to be fading before my eyes. Suddenly, street lights pop on around us.

"It must be dusk outside," I say. "My guess is Mojmiristan is closing down for the night." A wave of exhaustion comes over me and I suddenly feel really, really tired.

Frank yawns, "Maybe we should get some sleep. You know I can't think when I'm tired. If I remember correctly, Mojmir had a queen bed in the one of the rooms in the main house. What do you say we turn in for the night?"

I'm dying to open up my mom's portfolio and find out why my dad wanted it back. He's missing and I've got to figure out where he is. Nazis within the U.S. government are slowly hunting Frank and me down to do God knows what with us.

While the worries are circling around in my mind, my body is telling me that rest is the answer. Crawling into bed, snuggling up to Frank, and falling asleep in his arms seems like the best idea in the world right now.

My mom never liked me eating chocolate for lots of different reasons. She thought it wasn't healthy for me. All that sugar wasn't good for my system and it was just empty calories. But Mom couldn't just leave it at that. She'd say that cocoa comes from some of the poorest nations on earth and those that harvest the cocoa bean are treated like slaves, getting only a fraction of a penny from the $2.00 candy bar I liked to eat. So Mom would never, ever, buy me chocolate, even if I begged for it.

Dad on the other hand had a major sweet tooth. When I came home from school in fifth grade with my report card of all A's, he scooped me up and explained to mom that were we were going out shopping to reward me with something special. He was proud of my good work and this was his way of showing it. Dad headed straight to the local ice cream store and ordered two double scoops of dark chocolate ice cream cones with chocolate sprinkles.

"Dad," I exclaimed, "What are you doing? If Mom finds out you got me chocolate she's gonna blow a gasket!"

"Are you going to tell her?" Dad calmly asked me.

"No," I responded.

"Well," he smiled, "Neither am I. You had an amazing report card this quarter. I think you deserve a reward."

"Here you go, Dr. Eviston," the person behind the counter said as he handed us two ice cream cones. That's when I realized my dad was a frequent visitor and this was actually my first trip with him. We sat there happy as can be eating our ice cream in a secluded table towards the back of the shop. But I had to admit, after I was done I felt a little guilty. It didn't feel right to do something behind Mom's back.

"Dad, I don't feel good," I confessed.

"You ate way too quickly. You have an ice cream headache," he explained.

"No," I chuckled. "That's not it. I don't feel good about hiding this from mom."

Dad sighed, "This is our little secret."

"Secrets are wrong," I argued. "I don't want to keep a secret from mom."

"Sometimes keeping a secret is the best thing you can do," Dad instructed me as if he were teaching a class. It's how he acted when giving me life lessons. "I keep secrets all the time."

"That's because you do work for the government," I shot back. I was still not happy keeping this from Mom. She'd get the truth from me when I got home.

"Alexandria," Dad started, getting super serious and lowering his voice. "There are lots of secrets I keep. I keep secrets from you, from my colleagues, from the military, from the government, and some even from Mom. Everyone doesn't need to know everything that's going on in my mind and everything that I do. There are some things that are better off if I keep them to myself."

So the ice cream shop became the only secret that my dad and I kept from my mom. She would think we were going out to get groceries, gas, something for my school work, or anything else we could come up with. But in reality we were keeping a secret – two double scoops of dark chocolate with sprinkles.

THIRTEEN

I wake up and stretch. I look out the window and see the sun rising. Well, it's really not the sun. It's Mojmir's fake lighting that makes me think the sun is rising. I look to my left and Frank is still asleep. We have a long day ahead of us. We have to figure out why my dad wanted Mom's paper and then discover where the heck my dad is. I want to start my morning like I prefer – a hot shower and a cup of coffee. I know there's hot water here, the place is run by geo-thermal energy. I can only hope and pray there's coffee beans somewhere, but I'm guessing that's a fool's hope.

The water does a great job washing away yesterday's grime and clearing my head to think. Dad's disappeared. I'm guessing that the Nazis have something to with it but there's an outside chance that Dad has vanished by his own accord. He may not even know he's missing. He could even be in his lab back at Wright-Patterson researching something.

After considering this, I rule it out because he would have gone back for mom's paper. Something or someone prevented him from doing that. I'm convinced that Dad has been kidnapped by the Nazis and we have to find out why. My guess is he was keeping secrets from the government and the military and it finally caught up with him. We'll probably find some clues at his lab at Wright-Patterson and should head there later this morning. On the way we can try and figure out why Dad wanted Mom's paper.

The question that's been eating away at me is why does he want the original. There's lots of copies of her paper in just about every scientific library in the nation. There's dozen of links to electronic versions that he can read or have read to him. Why does he want the original? What's so important about it? We'll have to examine it against a copy.

I get out of the shower and towel off. I'm energized and ready to start the day. I'm not even sure if I need that cup of coffee. I step out of bathroom. Frank has woken up and left the bed. I'm hoping that he's out gathering breakfast for us. I put on my clothes from yesterday because it's all I've got and step out into the patio. Frank steps through the gate with a bowl of food.

"Morning, Sunshine. I've got blueberries, strawberries, almonds, cashews, and pistachios," he reveals. "I would have got some apples and bananas, but they weren't all the way ripe, yet. I think they're out of season. I can track down a goat if you'd like me to get some milk for you, but I'm not going to get a hog and make bacon."

"Thank you, honey," I say and kiss him on the cheek. "Where'd you put my mom's portfolio?"

"I left it inside on the dining room table," he points through the window. I go and retrieve the leather portfolio and return to the patio table to join Frank for breakfast.

"How'd you sleep last night?" he asks.

"Ugh," I say. "Dreams. About my dad."

"Bad dreams?" he cringes knowing how rocky my relationship with Dad is.

"No," I counter. "This one was kind of good. Happy memories."

"You have happy memories about your dad?" he asks.

"A few," I explain. "Dad and I had a thing for chocolate ice cream that we shared. And secrets, we shared secrets."

"I bet your dad kept a lot of secrets," adds Frank, "Working for the government and all. Do you think maybe they got to him?"

"Never," I say, knowing that Frank had to ask. "Dad's a scientist first and an American second. If there's secrets he's keeping, he's hiding them from the military."

"How do you know what he's thinking then?" replies Frank.

"Clues," I respond. "When I got older and was in high school, Dad would drop hints about meeting him for our ice cream chocolate fix, just like he left clues about the steak dinner last week. Mom's portfolio is a clue, and I'm convinced there are more clues at his lab."

Frank grabs the portfolio from the table. "Well if there are clues in here, let's take a look." Frank unwinds the string and opens the front flap. The paper has yellowed a tad from age, but the print is still crystal clear. He begins to quickly flip through the paper, looking for anything odd.

"You're not going to find something by just scanning through it. We have to read it. Somewhere in one of the sentences is a clue that Mom or Dad left for us."

"How could they have left a clue for us in a paper written by your mom over thirty years ago?" Frank scoffs. "They didn't even know this moment was going to happen. Like you said, your dad's not psychic."

Frank raises a good point. Maybe there's nothing in there and Dad just wanted what was rightfully his. I was hoping the paper led to something bigger.

"There has to be something in there," I say and grab a few more strawberries feeling more hopeless than before.

"Wait a minute," says Frank stopping on a page. He pulls the portfolio closer to him and examines it. "Holy crap, there's a notation in the margins on this copy."

"A notation?" my eyebrows raise. "There aren't any notations in my mother's work."

"There is on this copy," explains Frank. He turns it around and pushes it in my direction. He points to markings in the outer margins. "Right there is the markings 'A.E.', in your mom's handwriting."

"That's not my mom's handwriting," I clarify. "It's my dad's."

"What's your dad doing writing in your mom's paper?" questions Frank. "I thought your dad hated her paper. He publicly called it false beyond all measurement and analysis."

"I remember that," Alex adds. "Mom was not a happy camper after Dad did that. Maybe he was making a note of where he thought it was really off base."

Frank pulls the portfolio back towards him and takes a closer look. I see a smile come across his face, "I read the passage that your dad noted and figured out what A.E. stands for."

"Hey," I kick him under the table. "That's my clue. I'm

supposed to figure it out."

"Your mom wrote: pack leaders are unique amongst the other dogs. They have the biological need to be always on and in control, and therefore have a natural sense of fear that is balanced out by an overwhelming feeling of confidence. Along with this, pack leaders emit a particular pheromone that when inhaled by one of the others in the pack, it induces a calming feeling but comfortable excitement at the same time. The pheromone reaches the pleasure sensor of the brain and the rest of the pack crave it constantly since it produces a state of euphoria. Because of this, the pack leader has a deep sense of influence over the rest of the pack, as if it's feeding an addiction, and gets his or her way."

"Okay, smarty pants," I see him still smirking. "What's A.E. stand for?"

"A. E.," he says with a look of surprise that I haven't figured it out. "Alex Eviston. Your dad was noting that you're a pack leader. A.E. is you."

Me? A pack leader? Dad thinks I'm a pack leader? He never told me this. "Are there any other notations in mom's paper?" I ask Frank, afraid to look.

"Yeah," he says. "Here's another entry. It's probably the most famous section of your mom's paper. It's where she explains there's a higher power of influence."

"My dad hated that entry," I admit. "It basically says that some animals have a stronger influence within them, more than just simple influencing skills from mammals to mammals. This was influence over large groups and being able to change the world around them. Mom proved it wasn't just social psychology. She showed how politicians, religious leaders, and celebrities used a different part of their brain and emitted yet a different pheromone of attraction."

"It directly challenged your dad's theories," Frank added. "Wasn't it the basis of Dr. Savino's research?"

"Dr. Samuel Savino," I say aloud. "Now that's a name I haven't heard in decades. His name was taboo around our house, the university, and the air force base. He was Dad's rival and a stone in his shoe."

"Well you have something to do with this pheromone of attraction and Dr. Savino's work," Frank surmises, "Because your dad made the same A.E. notation next to that entry."

"Any other notations," I ask.

"One more," Frank flips to the last page, "At the very end, the last sentence. 'We do not know what the future holds, but we can count on those with higher influence evolving even more and deciding all our fates.' Your dad marked A.E. next to that specific sentence and traced over it several times, as if that was the most important thing he wanted to take note of."

Mom and Dad never told me about any of this. In fact, this paper was never talked about at home since it was such a sore argument between my mom and dad. But from these notes, it's obvious my dad read it and actually supported some of it. So much, that he thought I was the embodiment of some of its theories.

To my dad, believing in Mom's work is the equivalent of believing in Einstein's Static Universe, Spontaneous Generation, or that the earth is flat. It's just wrong. Mom claimed humans had influence over the world around them, Dad claimed we were all destined to move towards temporal gravity no matter what we did to temporarily change the world around us. Dad supporting her was like Pope Paul V agreeing with Copernicus. It just wasn't going to happen.

"We got to find my dad," I conclude. "I have to ask him what all this really means. It may be a key to defeating the Nazis."

"Your dad is not going to be easily found. We can't go marching through the streets of D.C. looking for him, asking people questions," counters Frank. "Look what happened at the Air and Space Museum. Just a simple investigation led to us being chased by security guards. Who knows? Maybe the police even want to bring us in for questioning."

"So what do we do?" I ask.

"If there are any more clues to your dad's whereabouts it's in his lab at Wright-Patterson," claims Frank. "I say that's where we head. We're like lions trapped in a cage here. We got to get out of D.C."

"Okay," I acquiesce. "How do we get there?"

"Mojmir had a backup plan for everything," Frank smiles. "He wouldn't shut up about how this place was fully equipped with all the modern day technologies. Remember the sound machines he had back in 1989? The ones that powered our train cart? There's got to be something here that we can use."

"Let's take a look around. I hope there's more than a few farm animals. I really don't want to be riding a goat to Dayton," I chuckle.

We start checking everywhere. Mojmir completely set himself up. He's got all the farm equipment you'd ever need to tend to a small plot of land, but besides a small riding tractor, there was nothing much of value we could use. Another shed stored all the parts to repair the modern day geo-thermal generator that's guaranteed for life and are known to never break. A final shed stored all of the house maintenance items you'd ever need: plumbing, electric, carpentry, you name it. While it was all modern technology, none of it was really useful as transportation.

"Our only option is the tractor," Frank sighs. "I could rebuild the engine to get it up to 30 miles per hour, but it would take us almost a full day to get there."

"And we'd look super funny driving a riding tractor on the freeway," I add. "They'd spot us in no time."

"This is so unlike Mojmir," Frank spouts off. "He's got parts for a geo-thermal generator that never goes bad, but he doesn't have a set of wheels to help him escape."

Escape. That triggers an idea.

"Remember the abandoned subway station outside?" I perk up.

"Where we got on the rail car?" Frank remembers.

"Maybe there's something out there?" I question.

We walk over to the closets against the back wall and open the farthest to our right. At the end of the long familiar hallway is the submarine blast door. We walk through that, through the second chamber and out onto the subway platform. It's pitch dark.

"Light," Frank speaks and his watch emits a soft bright light. He raises his hand high in the air. We see the subway platform with aging, crumbling concrete and rusted train tracks. The walls are covered in grime. Besides us and a mound of rubble, there's nothing here.

"No one has been down here in over a hundred years," I surmise. "This wasn't built out of the same life-lasting materials in Mojmiristan. The place is falling apart. I'm not sure it's even safe for us to be here."

Frank raises his hand to the ceiling to shine the light above us. "We're 500 feet below the surface," Frank states. "If this place was going to crumble it would have happened long time ago."

As Frank moves the light back down to the floor, I see a flash of something rusty in the ceiling.

"Move your hand back up there, to the right," I instruct.

We spot an old rusty bar ladder bolted to the wall, ending at some type of equally rusty trap door in the ceiling. Frank climbs down onto the track and crosses over to inspect the ladder.

"This is simulated rust," Frank says grabbing a hold of it. "It's made out of stainless platinum steel. Same thing the geo-thermo generator is made of. This metal doesn't rust and it's definitely advanced Russian technology. Someone painted it to make it look old and rusty. My guess is Mojmir."

Frank starts climbing up and after a few moments reaches the top. "I found a trap door in the ceiling," he yells.

He pulls the lever and pulls it down. He shines the light inside and takes a peek.

"What do you see?" I yell.

"It's a garage," Frank yells back. "Let's gather our stuff. I think we have a way to get back to Dayton."

Frank and I pack some food for the road, grab my mom's leather portfolio, say good-bye to the farm animals, and lock the doors behind us. I follow Frank up the ladder and he pulls me into the garage. He shuts the trap door and locks it from the inside.

Turns out Mojmir was quite the motor enthusiast. It's a room the size of half a football field filled with cars and motorcycles of various years. There's a 2002 Harley-Davidson V-Rod and a 1991 Harley-Davidson Fatboy. There's a 1971 Ranchero, 1955 BMW Roadster, 1963 Corvette and a 1981 DeLorean. But we're not looking for any historical vehicles. Although there's a gas pump in here and we can probably fill a tank, it won't get us far with any of these vehicles since there's no gas stations between here and Dayton. But there is one vehicle that is built for the road ahead.

"A Ford Golden Eagle," smiles Frank. "Mojmir certainly has taste in transportation."

The Ford Golden Eagle was truly step-change thinking in the motor industry. Launched in 2071, it was the first car that's propelled by sound waves, and rather than tiptoe quietly into this new technology, they jumped right into the deep end of the pool. It's a Ford muscle car built with the frame of an old Mustang, but a modern day look and feel. It's engine is quite remarkable. Fashioned from stainless steel, it never rusts and needs minimal lubrication. Here's the mind-blowing thing: it has no wheels. It sucks air in through the front of the car and jettisons the vehicle at a rate of up to 200 miles per hour while gently focusing sound waves down at the concrete to keep it elevated a foot off the ground. It makes for the smoothest, quickest ride you'll ever take. While in reality it's fifteen year old technology, with the temporal shift still settling, the car is brand new to 2086. Mojmir took a lot of risks time traveling it back to 1989, but I'm glad he did.

"This is what we need," Frank exclaims. "I saw one of these on the road back in Ohio. I know they exist in this version of the future."

My heart suddenly sinks. "Frank, we got one problem. They are solar powered. We're in an underground garage with no daylight and it's been sitting around for a little less than a hundred years."

"The early models had a gas tank," Frank reminds me while inspecting the side walls of the car. "Damn it! There's no gas tank on this one. We're screwed."

I don't know a lot about cars, but I do know something about the Ford Golden Eagle. I did a paper on it during Engineering 131, analyzing it's aerodynamics. To get maximum air fluidity across all parts of the car, they greatly reduced any cracks, crevasses, or seams in front and sides of the body. In some early designs, the passengers actually entered from the rear of the car through the trunk. My guess is they wouldn't interrupt the curve of the back side wall for a gas tank cap. I think they went old school. I walk around the back of the vehicle and try to pull down the license plate. It quickly gives.

"Voila!" I shout, "A fuel tank."

"Let's hope there's no ethanol in this gas," Frank says as he removes the handle from the gas pump. "As long as this is real gas from 1989 it should last for a long time. While I fill the tank up, see if you can figure out how to get out of here."

I start looking around the walls and find no doors. Porcelain tiles from floor to ceiling and wall to wall. The only way in or out is the trap door which seems impossible because how else would Mojmir gotten in all these vehicles. I start walking around the room to inspect the walls further, and that's when I trip over something. I look down on the ground and find a slightly raised metal platform about the size of a large vehicle. Right above us, in the ceiling is a large trap door.

"We're all gassed up!" Frank yells. "Did you find the doors out?"

"Yes!" I shout back, "They're in the ceiling."

"How do you expect me to drive this car through the ceiling?" Frank yells back.

"I think this is a pressure plate I'm standing on," I shout back. "Let's start up the car and drive it on."

Frank and I get into the Ford Golden Eagle. He starts it up. The engine wants to turn but it doesn't catch.

"Damn it," grumbles Frank. "Start already." Frank turns

the key again. This time the engine fires and the car revs up. Frank keeps on giving it gas. After a moment, Frank puts it into drive. The car slowly rises off the ground and floats onto the pressure plate. We sink a little bit and the doors above us open. When they are wide open, the pressure plate reengages and we start moving up in the air towards the ceiling, rising above all the other cars. We float through the trap door and finally come to a stop once the pressure plate is even with the floor of our new room. It's a small room, with just enough space for us to open the car doors and walk sideways around the vehicle. In front of us is a rollaway door that's closed. I step out of the car, find a latch, and disengage it.

"What do you think is on the other side of this door?" I ask Frank.

"Clueless," he replies, "But we're going to find out in a second. Go ahead and open her up."

I pull the door open and sun shines in. We're on a side road among small white buildings. Frank drives the car onto the street and I close the rollaway door. A latch engages and locks shut. I hop back into the car and Frank begins to slowly pull forward.

"Where are we?" I ask.

"I think this is the Russian Embassy," Frank whispers, pointing to a sign written in the Cyrillic alphabet. "Keep your head down."

I shrink down in my seat and try to look inconspicuous.

"I don't see anyone milling about," Frank says, "But they have to have cameras everywhere. If they caught us, I'd doubt they'd turn us over to the police. But they ain't gonna let us go, either."

Frank pulls around a corner and stops at what appears to be a back exit. The iron gate doors open and we drive on through.

I sit up straight in my seat and breathe a sigh of relief.

"That was too easy," Frank says.

"Maybe the car has a special chip in it that allowed the gate to open or something else that signified it was Mojmir's car," I say.

"That's what I'm really afraid of," Frank says. "There's only three people that could have had access to Mojmir's lair and one of them is currently in Moscow. The Russians know we're stateside and now they know exactly where."

"But they don't have any idea where we're going," I correct. "At 200 miles per hour on the open freeway, we'll be at Wright-Patterson Air Force Base in under 3 hours. There's the entrance to 66. Let's get started."

FOURTEEN

Halfway to Dayton, Frank wakes me up. I rub my eyes and look out the window. We're driving through the Appalachian Mountains.

"Have we left Pennsylvania, yet?" I ask groggily.

"We're five miles outside of Wheeling," Frank responds. "Shh... listen to the broadcast." He turns up the volume.

"It's very odd," the one reporter explains, "Of all the things that could have been stolen out of the Smithsonian, authorities say it was just a scientific paper from the archives."

"But what paper?" another reporter chimes in. "See, that's what I mean about the lack of transparency with this Administration. They know what's been stolen but they won't tell us what. They claim it's for international security reasons, but Ben, we're the largest, most powerful nation in the country. What do we have to worry about?"

"Exactly, Jonas," the other reporter responds, "We are the United States of America. We can defeat any country. The Russians. Any of the Europeans. The Chinese. What secrets do we need to keep?"

Frank lowers the volume. "It's one of the conspiracy theorists podcasts. They've been talking like this for the past twenty minutes. Only bit of news they've been saying is there was a theft at the Smithsonian yesterday. The PR person from the Smithsonian has been denying it, but these guys won't let it go."

"The government knows we have my mom's paper," I surmise. "I bet they're trying to figure out why. We can't make any stops before the Air Force base. They might catch our faces on a camera and know where we're headed."

Frank nods his head in agreement and hits the accelerator a little harder. He wants to get to Wright-Patterson before anyone even guesses that's where we're going.

"What are we going to do when we get there?" Frank asks.

"My dad kept a lot of secrets and I'm sure some are hidden in his lab," I say. "We just have to find the clues to discover them. Hopefully, they'll help point us to what he wants us to do next. Maybe even where he is. We just have to get inside."

"Getting into the lab is going to be the easy part," Frank argues. "It's getting out that's going to be the problem."

"What do you mean?" I ask.

"They are going to want us there," Frank explains, "And trap us once we get inside. They'll lock all the doors if they have to, keep us there as prisoners."

"Well," I smile, "We won't be using the doors to leave. We'll be using the particle accelerator. I figure we should time travel back to 1991, explain to President Mack that there are Nazis about and help him kick some ass."

"Sounds like a perfect plan," Frank agrees.

———————————

About an hour later, we arrive at the air force base and are ready to test the theory that they want to let us in. We drive up to the North Gate and the security guards stop us. Three guys step out from the guard house.

"This doesn't look good," I say. That's when I remember that we didn't pack any weapons. There was a stash of high-end sonic detonators and rifles in one of the closets back in Mojmiristan. We foolishly left them behind.

"Good afternoon, Colonel Bouchard," waves one of the guards. "I ain't never seen a Golden Eagle up close." He and the other guards circle the vehicle checking it out.

Frank rolls down the window. "You want to see the engine?" he yells.

"Hell, yeah!" responds another guard.

"Have you lost your mind?" I whisper. "Let's get in and get out of here."

"It's about building trust," Frank whispers back and pops the hood.

Frank steps out of the car, around to the front, and opens the hood. The guards gather around to take a peak. They all jibber jabber about horsepower, air injection speed, and some other things that I could care less about. Eventually, Frank closes the hood. I see the guys shaking his hand and patting him on the shoulder. Frank gets back into the car as the gate opens. The original guard waves him in.

"That was super close," Frank smiles and waves at the guards.

"What are you talking about?" I say. "Looks like you guys hit it off like old friends."

"We are on the "must have escort to enter" list," Frank he explains. "I told them there is probably some confusion after our retirement ceremony yesterday. We went from Military status to Scientific Researcher status. I claimed we still have our Top Secret Clearance."

"And they bought that?" I questioned.

"It's amazing how much a guy will believe when you show him his first 650 horse power engine," Frank smiles.

I tend to forget how smooth Frank is sometimes. He's a guy's guy and I'm glad he's my guy.

We pull around the side of the second building. It's called the Eviston Building, named after my dad, and it's where all the time traveling research is conducted. The main door is heavily guarded and my guess is we can't finesse our way in through there. Instead, we opt for the side entrance that's used by the elite scientists like my dad.

We open the first door and enter the vestibule. I wave to the only security guard working the desk. It's Isaac. He smiles at me and flags me through. A buzzer sounds and we open the second door.

"Well if it isn't Mr. and Mrs. Celebrity. You guys hit the big time, avoiding the main entrance and all the autograph seekers. Gotta come through the special royalty entrance," Isaac jeers.

"Thanks, Isaac," I smile. "You always know how to make a girl feel like a million dollars."

He blushes a little bit, "You're worth more than that." Isaac's been watching these doors almost ten years and has gotten close to my dad over that time. Either he's not paying attention to our new security clearance or he doesn't care.

Frank and I continue down the hallway unnoticed and stop at the elevator.

"The next moment of truth," I whisper. The only people

who use this elevator is someone going to my dad's lab. If security is watching it, they'll assume it's us. We'll see if they lets us take the journey down there.

We press the button and the doors open. Once we're inside, the doors close and we proceed downwards to dad's lab. It's a long ride down, and I'm holding my breath in anticipation the whole time. We make it all the way to the lab level and the doors open. That's when I remember that my dad's elevator feeds into Isaac's desk for monitoring and not the main security at the front desk. I exhale in relief and head down the hallway.

I can see from afar that something is wrong. The glass entrance doors to the lab are shattered. We pick up the pace and peer through the doors. My dad's lab is in ruin.

"I guess we don't have to worry about security access into the lab," jokes Frank and he carefully steps through the shattered glass doorway. I gingerly follow him, making sure I don't cut myself on broken glass. The inside of his lab is completely trashed. Computer screens have been busted into pieces, desk and tables over turned, and papers are everywhere.

Farther in is my dad's main office. Every drawer of every file cabinet has been removed and dumped. His computer and hard drive are gone. Family pictures that used to sit on his desk have been tossed across the room.

"Somebody beat us here," Frank states the obvious.

"How the heck are we going to find a clue in this mess?" I say. I open a desk drawer and discover it's empty because all its contents have been tossed on the ground. I slam it shut, and then start looking through the papers on the floor.

"We're gonna get through this," Frank says calmly. "We're going to find your dad."

"He's counting on me," I snap. "He's been giving me the clues, but I just can't figure it out. The portfolio, there's got to be more to the portfolio."

"I'm going to start looking through things here," Frank says. "He had to leave some clues in his office." He starts picking up the family pictures and placing them back on my dad's desk. He takes the last one and looks at it for a moment.

"Your parents look really happy in this picture," he says. "They're hiking in the mountains. Is this their honeymoon?"

"No," I say. "It was their trip to Italy. Like the picture in the living room in front of the church."

"This is when they studied at the University of Torino!" Frank smiles. "Your dad told me all about it during breakfast at the house last week. He said it was the most magical place. Told me I should take you there someday. Said that the mountains were romantic there. Recommended a villa resort. Explained you could stay there for a week and forget about the world forever. That the picturesque mountains would hold secrets that would last a lifetime."

"Secrets?" I perk up. "He used the word secrets?"

"Yeah," Frank replies.

"Hand me that frame," I stand up and inspect it, turning it over and opening it up. I remove the picture and look at the back. There's one word and a date scribbled on the back. As soon as I see it, I realize it's the clue we've been looking for.

Savino 2052

"We're going to Torino," I explain. "I need to see an old friend of my dad's."

"Now?" Frank asks, stunned.

"No, Torino in 2052," I explain and show Frank the back of the picture. "My dad's clue is to go see his scientific rival, Dr. Samuel Savino. He's been dropping hints this whole time. The picture of him and mom in front of the church in Italy. The story he told you about my mom and him visiting the University of Torino and retiring there. Dad wouldn't shut up at M.E. Swing's about how the Italian Roast coffee reminded him of Torino. The notes in Mom's portfolio. They all point to Dr. Savino. He'll have some answers."

"I'll fire up the particle accelerator," Frank says and heads towards the far end of the lab.

I have a renewed sense of energy now. Figuring out this

clue made me feel like we can find my dad. I'm beginning to believe in myself again. I take the picture and stuff it in my back pocket. It's going to take three minutes and eight seconds to warm up the accelerator, just enough time for security to make it down the elevator and stop us. I run back out to the lab's entrance and start pushing a long file cabinet in front of the doorway as a deterrent. I managed to push it about ten feet when Frank yells from the other side of the room.

"Alex," he calls. "Come over here. I've got bad news."

I race over to Frank who's gone back to the lower level of dad's lab where the main controls of the particle accelerator is. I enter the control room. It's been beat up and trashed as well.

"The accelerator isn't firing," Frank explains. He pushes a big red button on the control panel and nothing happens.

"It's gotta be the electromagnetic connection," I figure. We race out of the control room and down a service staircase to the main junction. We reach the bottom. The control panel has been busted open. I move the door aside to inspect the main connection, but there's nothing to inspect. Someone has taken a torch to it. The whole thing is charred.

"We aren't going anywhere," I explain. "The connection has been burnt to a crisp."

Suddenly a siren wails and red lights go flashing.

"Security has finally figured out we're here," I say.

"My guess is they knew we were here the whole time," counters Frank. "They trashed this place. Now they are going to find us here and blame it all on us. We're going to get framed."

"We gotta get out of here somehow," I say and start heading back up the service stairs two at a time. I run straight into black high heels and long legs. I look up to find Dr. Radkowski.

"What are you guys doing here?" she asks in shock.

"This is my dad's lab," I shoot back. "What are you doing here? I know you're a Nazi. I know this whole place is run by Nazis. Did you give the order to trash this place?"

"No," she says calmly, too calmly for someone that's been

caught red-handed. "A military team came in here last night."

"And that's who you told to trash it?" I accuse.

"I had nothing to do with it. I was able to sneak back down here today," she said. "To make sure no one found this." She pulls a small drive from underneath her belt and hands it to me.

"What is it?" I ask, taking it.

"It's the secret project your dad has been working on," she explains. "With Dr. Savino."

"What in God's name are you talking about?" Frank chimes in. "You're a German spy. Alex caught you talking to that guy in Hitchcock Hall."

I look at the small drive that Dr. Radkowski handed me. It's inscribed with the letters A.E. in my dad's handwriting.

"You're a double agent, aren't you?" I ask.

"Yes. I've been trying to lead the Nazis astray. But there's little time to explain," she says. "Security will be here in less than 90 seconds. Come with me." She grabs my hand and starts pulling me up the stairs. For a woman with long legs, high heels, and a pencil skirt she moves awfully fast.

"I met your dad five years ago as a Graduate Intern. You had just left for 1989 and I think he was looking for another daughter to raise so he gravitated towards me. I slowly started helping him on projects of increasing value until he finally brought me into his inner sanctum to work on the Inherent Energy Project."

"Inherent Energy Project?" I blurt out. "That's Dr. Savino's theory."

Instead of stopping at the Control Room floor, Dr. Radkowski keeps on scaling up the stairs high above the particle accelerator.

"I don't have time to give you all the details, why it's important to your dad, and why it's important to you as well," she says. "I must get you out of here safely."

"The particle accelerator is broken," Frank shouts over the siren. "There's no way we get to Torino 2052."

"You're going to Torino, all right," she explains. "But not

to 2052. You're flying there right now."

"Flying? How?" Frank asks.

We stop on a landing in front of a door marked fire exit.

"This base is the National Museum of the United States Air Force," she says.

"Okay, what's that have to do with Torino?" I ask.

"Remember the F18 you flew in your mission to destroy the Atomic Bomb over the Atlantic Ocean?" she asks.

"Sure," says Frank.

"It's a historic airplane," she says. "It's been restored, but gutted of its armament, radar system, and luckily its tracking and communication devices. It's also been renovated to be a two-seater. The airplane technology within is so old that today's towers and satellites don't know how to track it. The exact F18 Frank flew is now gassed up and on the museum runway ready for takeoff. All you have to do it start it up and fly it to Torino. Beyond this exit door is a set of stairs that leads to the museum's runway. Good luck."

"Thank you," I say. "I'm glad you're a Double Agent. It would have sucked trying to kick your ass."

She chuckles. "I'm a Triple Agent," she adds. "I have connections with the Russians as well. I'll make sure Mojmir is contacted so he can meet you at Dr. Savino's. You'll need his help. He knows what your next steps are. But first you must get to Torino. Now go."

Dr. Radkowski opens the door and we ascend several more flights. I don't know if we'll ever see her again, and I'm not sure if I fully trust her, but she did plan an escape route for us. That's got to count for something. At the top of the stairs is a storm door. Frank pushes it open and we're on a runway. Several feet away is the F18 with a ladder up into the cockpit.

"This plane is yours," I say. "Which means you're piloting it."

"I drove from D.C.," Frank argues.

"Doesn't matter," I jest. "You're tied to this plane. It doesn't feel right for me to fly it."

"All right, I'll fly it," laughs Frank. "Get in the plane."

I tuck my mom's portfolio into my pants and strap myself into the flight chair as Frank climbs in the one in front of me.

"Well, there's one nice thing about me flying the plane," he says.

"What's that?" I ask.

"I'm in front and I get to lead for a change," he says. "Buckle up, we're getting ready for takeoff."

Frank starts up the engines and drives the plane to the end of the runway. We're not going to ask for clearance and even if we wanted to, we couldn't because the radio has been ripped out. Frank turns the plane around with a long runway in front of us.

"Let's hope there's nothing else in the air," Frank says. "I'd hate for our journey to end here."

"Not gonna happen," I say. "Temporal gravity is pulling us somewhere else."

Frank pulls back the throttle and we shoot down the runway, lift off the ground and climb high into the sky. I look down and see the houses shrink to the size of my thumb. No other jets take off from the base. They may not even know we left. Today's radar looks for modern-day-technology airplanes that use sonic waves, to jam the radar. No one's looking for an object that absorbs sonic waves and that's what we're flying right now.

"Sit back and enjoy your flight," Frank jests. "We won't arrive for another four hours."

"Will there be beverage served on this flight?" I joke back.

"Please don't bother the captain while he's flying the plane," Frank chuckles.

"I'm going to catch some Z's then," I say and slouch to the right in my seat since it doesn't move backwards. I slowly drift off to sleep.

FIFTEEN

Eighth grade was one of my most challenging years as I was growing up, almost as bad as my senior year when Mom passed away. I was thirteen years old, my body was changing, my hair got even crazier and my legs were longer than the rest of me. My body was growing in odd ways and my sense of co-ordination was nonexistent. Adults referred to me as gangly and kids referred to me as clumsy.

I was constantly teased at school. I wasn't the cute one, the funny one, the popular one, or the athletic one. Things were so bad that even the science kids didn't want me hanging with them for fear the teasing directed my way would gravitate towards them as well.

To make things even worse, Mom started getting sick at this time. It wasn't like an instant "flip the switch" kind of sick, it was an intermittent "I'm not feeling well today, something strange is going on, I should see the doctor," kind of sick. I couldn't rely on her to be there for me because sometimes she'd be able to give me her full attention and other times she wasn't even there to listen. So rather than count on her, I pushed her away knowing that I couldn't rely on her when I needed to. Of course, my dad was my dad, buried in his research and distant as distant can be. I was left alone at the one age when a kid needs the most support.

Since my confidence was shot, my grades started to suffer. Normally, I could do all my school work blind-folded and in my sleep. Instead, I dreaded everything about eight grade and anything that had to do with school didn't make me feel good, including the classes, the extra studying, and the homework. I avoided it all.

Midway through winter quarter, I was failing Honors Algebra. It was new math for me and while normally I could quickly grasp the concept of number analysis, finding "x" became extremely difficult when I could barely find myself.

I kept my grades from my dad as long as I could. At first the school sent all the messages to my mom, but since she was sporadically going to doctor appointments, she was missing them. Unbeknownst to me, the math teacher, Mr. Harrisford, eventually called my dad to speak with him, man to man.

So one day in February, I was standing at my locker after school, waiting and hoping that some boy would ask me to that year's Valentine's Day dance. There was one geeky boy in my English Literature class who recently started talking to me and I was praying he would get up the nerve to ask me out. But instead, when I peered down the hallway past my locker, I found my dad walking straight towards me. The mass of students milling about parted as he stormed down the hallway. They all knew who he was, and saw this look of absolute anger on his face. I was crushed. Not because it wasn't the English Lit Boy, but because in that instant I knew I had failed my father.

"Where's this Mr. Harrisford's classroom?" he grunted out as I closed my locker.

"Follow me," I murmured, ready to accept my fate and punishment.

I plodded towards the math department and made it to room 230. "Here it is," I announced.

"Come in with me," Dad instructed and took a deep breath.

We entered the classroom to find Mr. Harrisford, at his desk grading some papers. My dad closed the door behind us and as it clicked shut my math teacher looked up.

"I'll be with you in one moment," said Mr. Harrisford and he turned back to grading papers.

Dad looked down at me with disgust. I knew he didn't want to be here. He'd rather be in his lab doing his research. I had taken him away from what mattered to him most.

Finally, Mr. Harrisford closed his grading folder and motioned to the desks in front of him. "Sit down," he told us, "Let's talk."

I thought I was uncomfortable in the eighth grade sized desks but my dad looked even worse and it made him angrier. When we got home, he was sure to let me have it and punish me for weeks. I tried to shrink down in my desk in the hope that I could hide myself somehow.

"I assume you're here about Alexandria's grades," Mr. Harrisford announced and began to go into a ten minute description of my poor performance, inattentiveness, unresponsiveness, and how I was the biggest failure out of all his students. It was embarrassing and I could see my dad's face getting redder and redder with each minute that went by. I was the daughter of the man who invented Time Travel, destined to do great things, but instead I was failing eighth grade math.

"I don't think math is her strong suit," concluded Mr. Harrisford. "She's not a high performer at algebra. In fact, she's not even an average performer. She should be demoted to basic math. I'm making that recommendation to the principal later this week."

My dad paused and took a deep breath. Instinctively I leaned back a bit knowing the anger was going to explode.

"Bill?" my dad started, "Can I call you Bill?"

"Sure," Mr. Harrisford acquiesced. I never heard any of the other teachers call him Bill. I'm not sure Mrs. Harrisford even calls him Bill.

"You have a degree in teaching, correct?" my dad asked.

"Yes," said Mr. Harrisford, "I have an advanced degree from Columbia and doctorate from Harvard in Education Leadership."

"Well, Bill," my dad said, "Then you would understand that in science, when an action doesn't give you the outcome you want, you try something different. Correct?"

"I don't see what you're getting at," said Mr. Harrisford, wrinkles growing on his face. He didn't understand where my dad was going with this and frankly, nor did I. There was a big "x" in this equation and neither Mr. Harrisford and I could find it.

"I'll explain," my dad started, "When I'm working in my lab deep in the heart of Wright-Patterson Air Force Base, and I'm teaching my league of graduate students about the intricacies of time travel, I tell them that if they don't get the outcome they desire, they as scientists are responsible for changing their actions to alter the outcome."

"I think that's brilliant advice," said Mr. Harrisford, still not quite understanding where my dad was going.

"Good," my dad smiled, "So you would understand, that as from one teacher to another, if you're not getting through to your students than maybe you should try a different method of teaching."

Silence.

"Are you saying that your daughter's failure is my fault?" Mr. Harrisford asked.

"My daughter has been calculating complex math equations since she was five," my dad explained, "She was doing long division while her classmates were still trying to count to one hundred, she was working with decimals before others even knew how to do fractions, she was defining and explaining proofs while others were trying to understand the difference between a square and a pyramid. She's aced every math test that's ever been given to her, until she came to your class. Is her failure your fault? No. But it's your responsibility. Don't tell my daughter what she can't do. Tell her what she can, and then figure out how to help her learn it."

Silence. Dead silence.

Mr. Harrisford turned red, then white. He was about to speak his mind when my dad interrupted him.

"I hope you're about to explain a plan of action for educating my daughter," my dad calmly stated, "Or do I need to talk to your Department Head about your performance?"

My dad sat back. He's done talking.

Mr. Harrisford nodded his head up and down in agreement.

"Good," my dad said, "Now, I have to get back to my lab. Alex, let's go."

We walked out of the classroom and into the hallway. Several feet away from the classroom door, my dad stopped and turned to me. He bent down, put his hands on my shoulder and looked me in the eye.

"Don't ever let anyone tell you what you can't do," he instructed. "You are poised to do astonishing things. Things that are more remarkable than even I have done. You just haven't realized them, yet."

My dad took me home, left to go off to his lab, and I started my homework in a happy mood. I had a feeling that eighth grade was about to get a little better.

The next day, I was called to the Principal's office. Per dad's request, I had been reassigned to a new advanced algebra teacher, Mr. Johnson. He was caring, fair, and helped me discover a new way of looking at algebra. Most importantly, he made me feel that I was better than I thought I was. By the end of the week, I was doing A work and ended up finishing strong in math for the year. I left eighth grade feeling like I could accomplish anything.

My dad may have not always given me what I wanted, but he certainly gave me what I needed.

SIXTEEN

I wake up a bit groggy from my nap, rub my eyes, and look out the window to see white capped mountains. We're most likely over the French-Italian Alps, close to Torino. It's about three in the morning here, although my body thinks it's more like 9 p.m. I'm hungry and thirsty since I haven't eaten since lunch.

"How far are we from the airport?" I ask.

"Good morning, Sunshine," Franks says, "We're about 30 minutes from Torino, but we're not going to the airport."

"No airport?" I'm shocked. "Torino is a valley at the base of the Italian Alps. There's no plot of land anywhere around here to land except for the airport."

"While you've been sleeping for the past four hours," says Frank, "I've been thinking about how to find Dr. Savino. My guess is he has an office somewhere at the University of Torino but he won't get there until another six hours or so. Italians go to work later than most Americans. That gives us a lot of time to get to the University."

"Okay," I agree. "Continue."

"Landing at the airport is a bad idea," Frank states. "I've thought about it for a long time. Even though it's 3 a.m. and the airport probably has minimum staffing right now, everybody there is going to know an F18 just touched down at their landing strip. There's only one F18 in the world that's missing right now and that's ours."

"So we're not going to land at the airport?" I'm confused.

"Only four people in the world know where we are right now: you, me, Dr. Radkowski, and Mojmir," Frank surmises. "I want to keep it that way. If we land at Torino airport then everyone on this earth is going to find out we're there the minute we arrive. The Americans and the Nazis will figure out we're going to see Dr. Savino. It's the only reason we'd be here. So, yes, we're not going to land at the airport."

"So we're going to land at a different airstrip somewhere else?" I ask.

"No," Frank continues. "You were right about Torino being a valley. There's no other place to safely land around here. Even if there was, they'd find the F18 and know we're in Italy."

"So where in God's name are we going to land the plane?" I shout.

"I'm not landing this plane," Frank says calmly.

"What?" I don't understand.

"I'm flying it into the side of the mountain," he states.

"Did you just say you're going to crash this plane!" I yell. "You're going to kill us both! I'm not wearing a parachute and I didn't see you put one on either."

"This F18 is fitted with ejection seats. All I have to do is flip a switch in the cockpit and we shoot out of here," he says.

I look around my seat and realize he's right. My legs are positioned in a type of gutter system that restrains them from flailing about. The headrest is really a parachute system and my seat restraint is connected to it. Frank has one, too. He's thought this all out during the past several hours and I should trust him. I'm just not that excited about being shot out of an F18 into mid-air with nothing but a parachute that could be over 100 years old.

"I'm not really thrilled about this," I shout up to Frank.

"You're the Falls Jumper," Frank chuckles. "Here's something else to add to your resume."

"Can I convince you out of this in the next thirty minutes?" I ask.

"No," he replies. "And we don't have thirty minutes, it's more like less than three."

"I thought you said we were thirty minutes from the airport!" I yell.

"Thirty minutes from the airport. Three minutes from the mountain," Frank instructs. "And we don't want to be in the plane when it hits the mountain, so you better adjust your seat belt now. Make sure it's nice and tight because I'm ejecting us in less than a minute."

I'm not ready for this. Not at all. But I remember my dad's words that I can do anything I want to. I take a deep breath and begin to check my straps. I pull them tight around my leg braces, waist, chest and shoulders. I'm snug as a bug in a rug. I adjust my mom's portfolio under my belt, and tuck it under my shirt.

"Cross your hands over your chest and hold onto the restraints," Frank instructs. "I'm opening up the windshield. It's gonna get loud and this is the last we'll be able to talk for a while. I'll see you on the ground, Sunshine."

"Okay," I respond. "I'm ready."

A few seconds later the windshield pops off of the cockpit and goes flying away. Wind rushes in and whirls around me, smacking my face. I can see the white capped mountains up ahead and they look way too close. Suddenly, I shoot out of the plane like a rocket, along with half of my seat. The seat back falls away and the chute automatically pops open. I start drifting in the wind. Frank's chute is about 100 feet to my left.

The F18 explodes into the side of the mountain and lights up the night sky. The city of Torino is nowhere to be seen. Frank probably crashed the plane on the other side of the mountain so no one would see the explosion. Great for our cover, but that means a lot of walking in the snow for us and I don't really have the clothes and shoes for it.

The descent in the parachute lasts some time. With the windy mountains, it takes a lot of effort and skill to keep my chute even and open. Frank has managed to get a little closer to me, but is keeping his distance. As the ground nears, I spy a flat ridge that's perfect to land on and try to time myself to hit that. Thankfully my timing is perfect as my feet touch the soft snow. I lose my footing a little and stumble through the drift but I manage to stay upright. I race to the side and gather up my chute because I know Frank's right behind me.

He's not as lucky as I was since he had to circle around once and make room for my landing. I watch him as he lands farther along the ridge than I did, stumbles forward, tucks and rolls, and immediately goes flying off the side of the mountain. I race over, full blast, to try and grabs his chute before it slips away as well. There's lots of length to it and I manage to firmly grab an armful of nylon fabric. I spin around once to twist it around my body then dig my legs into the snow and fall back on my butt. Part of the chute is now wrapped around my waist and I manage to pull a few strands of rope in my hands. I brace myself as the chute tightens, leaning back as the ropes hold stiff. The wind is swirling around on the ridge and blowing snow in my face. I haven't released my chute yet, and I can hear it flipping around behind me. I'm hoping the wind doesn't catch hold of it and start picking me off the ground, whisking both Frank and me off the side of the mountain. What's left of Frank's chute in front of me is also getting some wind pockets, but it's too tight for it to go airborne.

"Frank!" I yell, "Are you alive?"

"Yeah," he yells back. "You okay?"

"I'm fine for now," I yell back. "I've got your chute. Can you climb back up? Or do I need to pull you?"

"I can make it," Frank yells. "Hold tight, it may be awhile."

I brace myself and lean back farther. I can feel Frank slowly climbing back up the chute. After a few moments, the vibrations stop but there's still tension on the rope.

"Frank," I yell. "What's wrong?"

"Hold on tight," he yells back. "I'm about to swing myself over."

The rope is pulling out of my grasp as Frank swings back and forth, so I quickly wind it around my wrist a few times and it doesn't move anymore. The tension loosens and Frank comes barreling over the edge of the ridge. He lands several feet away and falls deep into the snow, leaving one of those Wile E. Coyote outlines.

I crawl over to him. "Frank," I yell. "Are you okay?"

Frank rolls over on his back, looks up at me and says, "That... was... AWESOME! That was the coolest thing ever. That's not a ridge or a cliff... it's a ledge! I was hanging from it, like twenty feet down with another fifty feet drop, and I completely pulled myself up, hand over hand, then swung myself up to freedom. Take THAT, Falls Jumper," he smiles.

"That was cool," I smile. "But you scared the crap out of me."

"You don't think I was scared when you went over the Falls?" he smiles.

Snow keeps on falling heavily around his face and he has to brush it off.

"We've got to get off this mountain," I say, "Before we're buried alive in snow."

"You gather up the parachutes," Frank instructs. "We'll need the nylon to stay warm. Neither of us are dressed to be hiking in a blizzard. We should grab the lines as well for rope. I'll look around and find a path downward."

We have two big parachutes and I fold each of them up into blankets we can wrap around us. I keep the lines attached, but arrange them into a gasket coil. This kind of looks strange because we have a nylon blanket with several coils of rope hanging off it.

"There's a small village at the bottom of this mountain," yells Frank. "It doesn't look that far away. If we follow this ridgeline we can make it down. The side I fell off of was a hard drop down, but we can maneuver down the other side. Nice blankets. You better wrap yourself in them," he smiles. I can see him shivering a bit and toss him one.

"You're cold as well," I say. "I need for you to stay warm, too."

Frank pulls the parachute around him. "I'll lead," he instructs. "You follow. It's not steep, but it's not flat ground either."

He pulls out a knife from his pocket, cuts off one of the ropes from his chute, and tosses me one end. "Wrap this around your waist and tie it off. I'll do the same," he says.

"So if one of us falls, both of us fall?" I start wrapping it around myself.

"No," Frank explains. "You move to me, lock yourself down and then I move forward. Like an inchworm. That way if one of us slips, someone is always anchored. We take it slow."

We start to move down the mountain and it takes forever. The village looks close, but it really isn't. About an hour later we're only a third of the way down the mountain. My face is frozen and icicles are forming around my eyebrows and inside my nose. I can't feel my toes, and my socks are wet with ice and snow. I slowly inch up to Frank who's anchored.

"This is worse than any Toronto snowstorm I've been in," Frank says while chatting his teeth. I snuggle up to him trying to share body heat but I'm as cold as he is.

"We'll get through this," I say.

"I'm thinking that maybe taking our chances on the Torino airport runway would have been a better idea," he says.

"No it wouldn't have. You made the right decision," I say, trying to stay positive.

"Let's move on," he smiles and it seems I've ignited a little bit of energy into him. It's amazing what a boost of confidence will do for a man.

Another hour gets us down a third of the way more. At this point my legs feel like solid ice, up past my shins, and my fingers are frozen together. I can barely keep a grip on the parachute wrapped around my body. It's the only protection against the elements, and if it flies off of me, I'm sure to die on the mountain. I pull it closer around my shoulders as I step forward. Doing two actions at once in this cold throws me off a bit. I lose my footing and stumble forward, slipping on an ice patch under the snow, and my whole body twists to the side. I fall shoulder first on to the hard snow and ice. A sharp pain shoots up my ankle.

Frank reaches down, grabs me by my shoulder and pulls me up.

"Are you okay?" he chatters.

"Yeah," I'm fine. I try to walk forward but as soon as I put pressure on my foot the pain gets intense. Too intense to go any further. So I start hopping on it.

"That's ridiculous," Frank says. "Put your arm around my shoulder."

I wrap my arm around Frank's shoulder, but he pulls me up on his back.

"You tricked me," I say in his ear.

"You wouldn't have listened," he replies.

After a few feet, Frank's able to maintain better footing. The snow isn't as deep at this point on the mountain but it is a little more icy. I can hear his teeth chattering away so I try to wrap the parachute around us both. Frank's bare skin is frozen blue and the tips of his ears are full white. The elements are getting to us and he's slowing down. It's as if a full minute goes by before he takes a step.

I'm starting to fade a little bit, too. Groggy is more like it. As if I've had too much wine for the evening. But I don't feel warm inside. I'm cold at the core.

Frank stumbles forward and takes me with him. We land face first in the ice and snow.

"Frank?" I mumble out.

He doesn't say anything. Neither of us move. We're both lying flat in the snow and can't go on. I look up and see a bright light approaching us.

"This is it," I say. "This is what dying looks like. I love you, Frank."

The light keeps shining bright, glowing, then a shadow falls across my face and body. I try to focus and realize I'm staring at a man who looks like Jesus. Long hair, long beard. I close my eyes and feel his hands scoop me up in his arms, and raise me up.

"I'll take you home to paradise city, where the grass is green, and the girls are pretty," he gravels out, "Princess."

I open my eyes. It's Mojmir.

SEVENTEEN

I wake up wrapped in soft, warm, thick blankets, lying on pillows in front a fireplace. Frank is lying on a couch a few feet away, wrapped in similar blankets, but still fast asleep. It looks as if we're in the main room of cabin that serves as a kitchen, dining room, and living room. There's an entry door that's bolted shut, and I can hear the wind whispering through it.

The left side of my body is much warmer than my right since it's closer to the fireplace. I try to roll over and adjust but I'm wrapped in blankets like a cocoon. I realize that I'm completely naked underneath the blanket and my pants, shirt, underwear, and socks are all draped over chairs to dry. With no one else in the room, and Frank fast asleep, I wiggle out of my cocoon. I check my clothes and they're still a little damp except for my underwear and bra which are toasty warm. I slip into them and it feels like putting on clothes when they are fresh out of the dryer.

Since the rest of my clothes are still wet, I pick up one of the big blankets that I was wrapped in and drape it around my body like a toga.

"When in Rome," I chuckle to myself.

My mom's portfolio is laying on the table and miraculously wasn't damaged.

I walk over to Frank who's still sleeping on the couch. He looks like one huge burrito in wool blankets. He's got a trapper's hat strapped around his head. Color is coming back to his face and his lips are pinkish.

I lean down and kiss him on the forehead. His body is still a little cool to the touch but I know it's better than it was when we were on the mountain. He's breathing normally so I know he's going to be all right.

There's a cast iron pot next to the fireplace. I pull off the lid with an oven mitt and discover stew inside. That's when I realize I'm starving. Gathering a bowl and spoon, I portion some stew into a bowl and sit down at the table to eat.

It's the best tasting stew I've ever had, and I'm not just saying that because I'm famished and recovering from a near death experience. The stew has oregano, basil, garlic gloves that melt in your mouth, and chunks of lamb, beef, mushrooms, and potatoes. I scoop it all up and then look around for bread. There's a loaf on the counter and I rip off a chunk then clean the bowl with it. The food warms my soul and brings me strength. I check my clothes again and they are still not dry. I turn them inside out, along with Frank's so they can dry quicker.

Taking my bowl over to what looks like a make-shift sink, I clean it along with the spoon, placing it to the side when I'm done. I sit on the couch next to Frank and wonder if laying in his arms will help transfer some of my body heat to him.

The door opens from the outside and wind and snow swirl in. A short little woman, bundled in a big huge jacket, shuffles into the cabin. She pulls off her trapper hat and short blonde hair falls out, barely touching her shoulders. She's an older woman, in her early sixties, and if it wasn't for her square jawline I'd say she was more French than Italian. She notices that I'm awake and gives me a scowl.

"Dormi! Dormi, Signora!" she points to the pillows I was laying on in front of the fire. "Resto di fronte al fuoco. Tuo marito si sveglia presto, troppo."

"I really appreciate all your hospitality but I don't understand a word you're saying," I stare confusingly.

"Sono il medico del paese, e quando dico alla gente di riposo, si deve riposare," she says arranging the pillows in front of the fireplace. She points to them again. "Si riposi ora."

I pat the pillows on the couch next to Frank, "Thank you but I'm fine right here."

She shrugs her shoulders and waves her hands at me in disgust. "Piccioncini," she says. "L'amore vi farà male!"

The woman yanks off her huge jacket and hangs it on a hook on the wall. She brushes the snow off her boots, unties them, and kicks them off by the door.

"Mi dispiace, signora," she exclaims. "Hai fame? Per favore, mi permetta di ottenere qualche cibo." She moves to get a bowl and spoon from the shelf and heads towards the pot on the fireplace.

"No, thank you," I say, making a waving motion with my hands.

She gives me the evil eye, a stronger look of disgust than when I refused her direction to sleep.

"Prima non mi ascolti, e ora rifiutate la mia cucina?" she scowls.

I pat my belly than point to bowl at the sink, then the partially eaten bread. "I already ate," I indicate. I remember the taste of the stew and instinctively my face fills with delight. "It was the best tasting stew I've ever had."

The woman's looks at the sink and then at the bread on the counter. Her face fills with pride and smiles at me warmly.

"Ti piace il mio stufato, capa rossa? E 'meglio di stufato irlandese di Dublino! Vieni, sedersi con me. Avere un po'," she motions for me to sit with her at the table. She gets my old bowl and spoon and pours me a fresh bowl of stew, then she takes the other bowl and pours another for herself. She rips off two huge chunks from the bread, giving one to me and keeping the other.

"Faremo mangiare tanto e lasciare nessuno per gli uomini," she chuckles and points to my bowl. "Il pane è fresco. Ho fatto questa mattina. Mangia! Mangia!" She begins eating.

I join her, wondering how on earth I could eat another bite since I'm full, but suddenly I'm devouring the stew because it tastes so good. Now I know why Italians are overweight. The food is so good they can't stop eating. I smile at my host.

"Grazie," I say. That's the only Italian I know.

"Prego! Prego! Prego!" she laughs, raises her hands in the air and kisses me on the forehead. It's a wet sloppy Italian stew kiss.

I chuckle back.

"Il tuo amico russo, Mojmir, tornerà presto," she says in between bites, pointing to the door.

"My name is Alex," I say, motioning to my chest to indicate I'm referring to me.

"Ah… mi chiamo es Liliana," she says pointing to herself.

"Sono il medico per questo villaggio, Novalesa," she points to the ground and then outside, "Mojmir si trova sulle piste e ha portato i due di voi per me qui. Altri trenta minuti e potrebbe essere stato morto. Ma il calore che ha salvato."

I'm clueless as to what she's saying, but she keeps on talking as if I understand her. I think it's an Italian, thing. They just like to talk, talk, talk, and eat.

"Mojmir sinistra per ottenere i vestiti migliori per entrambi. Tornerà presto," she continues then points to her bowl, lifting her eyes and smile. "Per ora, ci mangiamo più stufato."

She grabs my bowl and fills it again. She rips off more bread and then places it and the bowl in front of me. I don't want to be rude and ungrateful, so I eat more even though I know my stomach is full.

Frank stirs, "Alex? Where are we?"

"Frank?" I rush over to his side. Liliana is right beside me. She pulls off his hat and checks the temperature with her hand.

"Bene. Bene. Bene. E 'caldo al tatto e il colore è tornato al suo viso," says Liliana and starts to lift him into a sitting position. "Portiamolo e lo nutrono qualche stufato. Mangia. Mangia. Mangia!" She races off and gets a new bowl and spoon, and begins to dish out some stew for Frank.

Frank looks up at me and smiles.

"Hey, Sunshine, where are we?" Frank says groggily.

"An Italian village in the Alps," I reply.

"How'd we get here," he asks.

"Not exactly sure," I reply. "Mojmir found us."

"Mojmir's here?" Frank sits up, covered in blankets.

"Not right now," I correct. "I think he went out for a while."

"Who's the blonde with the stew?" he says.

"I think she's the village doctor," I say. "The food here is really, really yummy."

Frank wraps the blankets around himself and makes it over to the table. We all sit down and eat some more stew. Half-way into my third bowl, there's a knock on the door and Mojmir comes in.

"Princess!" he smiles, "It's great to see you well. I thought Frank and you were surely goners and I'd have to save your dad on my own."

"I can't tell you how glad we are that you found us," Frank says. "We're so lucky."

"Very lucky," I add. "But how in God's name did you find us?"

"Mackenzie, your dad's lab assistant, told me you're coming to Torino and flying the F18," Mojmir explained. "I beat you here since I was vacationing in Sochi. Once here, I used radar radio signals to determine where your plane was. I figured you weren't going to land anywhere conventional, so I made sure to track you closely. When your plane suddenly disappeared over the Italian mountains, I guessed you crashed it on purpose. I drove up here to Novalesa and borrowed the snow mobile from the abbey. I road it up the mountainside towards where you crashed. Found you just in time."

"Thanks, Mojmir," I smile. "I owe you one."

"We don't owe each other anything except friendship," Mojmir smiles back.

Frank licks the last of his stew out of the bowl with his tongue. "This is fabulous," he exclaims. "Best stew I've ever eaten."

"We should take some for the road," says Mojmir. "You have to get dressed and we need to go find Dr. Savino."

"Savino?" pipes up Liliana. "Samuele Savino? Il famoso professore e scienziato?"

"Sì," says Mojmir. "Sono abbastanza sano di lasciare?"

"Sì," says Liliana. A look of wonder comes across her face and then a smile. "Capa rossa! È lei. La figlia del viaggio nel tempo. È venuta per incontrare Savino! La mia casa è benedetta stasera. Non vedo l'ora di dire al resto del paese." She makes the sign of the cross and motions to the sky for thanks.

"No, no, no," Mojmir says to her. "Non si può dire un'anima che erano qui. Siamo in missione ultimo segreto per salvare il mondo."

"Non capisco," Liliana is confused. "La guerra è finita. Gli americani hanno vinto quasi un centinaio di anni fa."

"I nazisti hanno occhi e orecchie dappertutto," explains Mojmir. He waves his hands in the air and opens them. "Stanno tessendo loro ragnatele ovunque. Non possiamo fidarci di nessuno. Per Favore. La segretezza è un imperativo."

"Feccia nazista," says Liliana and spits on her floor. "Hanno ucciso mio nonno in guerra. Quasi lasciato mia Nonna a morire qui, in queste montagne. Sono onorato di avere il grande Alex Eviston e Frank Bouchard in casa mia. Manderò mille preghiere per tutti voi e vi auguro ogni bene per la sua missione. Entrambi sono sani per andare avanti. Temo se rimangono più a lungo, non avrò alcun cibo per il resto della settimana." Liliana laughs and begins to wrap the rest of the loaf of bread for us to take.

"What'd she say?" asks Frank.

"She's honored to have you here and will pray for your future. You have a clean bill of health and better leave before you eat all her food," responds Mojmir. "Get yourselves dressed. We need to go immediately. The sun is up and the roads out of the mountains are better by day. I brought warmer clothes for you in the bags by the door."

"Possono usare la mia camera per cambiare," Liliana says pointing to one of the doors.

"You can change in there," explains Mojmir.

I grab both bags and head to the back room. "Come on, fly boy," I say to Frank. "I want to make sure you don't look like a vagabond."

Frank, Mojmir, and I are heading to the University in a Fiat Sedici, a rental that Mojmir secured after he flew here from Sochi. He had a much safer landing since he flew commercial.

"How do you know Dr. Radkowski?" I ask, "How does the whole triple agent thing work? Can we trust her?"

"We can completely trust Mackenzie," affirms Mojmir. "She's my granddaughter."

"What?" shoots back Frank. "You never told us you were

married!"

"I wasn't," he says. "You don't need a marriage for children. I met a woman before I went into the Soviet Committee for Temporal Security. We had relations. She had the child after I left her. Didn't even knew about it until a decade or so ago. It was Mackenzie that sought me out, wanted to meet her famous grandfather."

"That's amazing," I say. "You must be proud."

"She takes after me," Mojmir explains. "All guts and glory. It's going to get her into trouble one day."

I've never imagined Mojmir as a father. He always seemed like the consummate bachelor.

"I can't believe you're a father, let alone a grandfather," I blurt out.

"I'm really not," admits Mojmir, "I never knew I was a dad. I don't really have a relationship with my daughter. I'm just another guy to her. I'm trying to make amends with my granddaughter, but she's older and in the States, where I'm considered a terrorist. Pretty hard to start a relationship with a time traveler."

We sit in silence for a while. Am I luckier than Mojmir's daughter? Although my dad is rather cold and distant, we know each other. We're able to have a dinner together, talk about things without getting into an argument. Sure, my dad drives me crazy and at times I wish he acted differently but chances are so does he. I don't think he ever told me he loves me. But deep down inside, I think he does.

We emerge out of the mountains and into the city of Torino, one of the most magnificent places in all of Europe. It's first major growth began during the Renaissance when so many beautiful buildings were built, but it's also had a modern day surge. Fiat's European headquarters are now here. It's considered the Hollywood of Italy. Olivetti manufactures all the microcomputer ear buds here and cyclic sound energy that powers every generator in the world was invented here at the University of Torino. It's over seven centuries old being established in the year 1404 and it's considered the top technological university between the Atlantic Ocean and Ural Mountains. It touts the most recipients of Nobel Prizes in Physics, more than Harvard, Columbia, and Cambridge, all of which were awarded in the past hundred years.

The Temporal Physics Department of the University of Torino is located a few blocks from Fiat's headquarters. Fiat's building is a marvel in itself because the test track for the cars is actually on the roof of the building. The company poured hundreds of millions of dollars into the Physics Department at the University to make it the research haven that it is today.

Doctor Samuel Savino is one of its most famous alumni, researchers, and educators. He has a building named after him on the Physics' campus and we head straight there. We squeeze into a parking spot on the street a few blocks away and take a brisk walk to his office. It feels good to get the blood flowing in our legs, but I can tell both Frank and I are walking a little slower than usual.

"Am I walking too fast for you two?" Mojmir asks.

"We're fine," Frank says trying to pick up his pace.

"Have you met Doctor Savino before?" I ask.

"Yes," Mojmir confesses. "I was sent here by my Commandant to take a semester class with him. That's how I learned Italian. It's amazing how quickly you can learn a language when you're immersed in it. Italians speak really quickly, too. If they didn't do all those hand gestures it would have taken much longer to figure out what they were saying."

We reach the doors to the building and Mojmir stops us.

"I have to warn you," Mojmir whispers, "Most people who talk to Savino think he's crazy and I've heard he's gotten worse with age. Rumor has it that the only reason the University lets him keep an office here is because he's received four Nobel Prizes in Physics, more than Albert Einstein, John Bardeen, and Marie Curie. But don't for a moment be fooled by any of the rumors. The guy is brilliant."

As we enter the building a bell sounds and students flood into the hallways, heading off to their next class. Mojmir stops a young girl.

"Scusi , dov'è l'ufficio di Savino?" he asks her something in Italian.

"Savino di in prigione, credo," she responds and points down the hallway. "Ma non sta spendendo il suo tempo nel suo ufficio in questi giorni. Lo troverai nel suo laboratorio sul retro dell'edificio. Assicurarsi di avere un'ora di ricambio se si va a parlare con lui. Lui è più loquace del tipico in questi giorni. Buona fortuna."

"Grazie, senorita," Mojmir responds then turns to us. "He's in his lab down the end of this hall," he points and we head in that general direction. "And this student just warned us that he's crazier than ever."

As we walk down the hall, I can see the students looking at me from the corner of their eyes. Some heads even do a double take. While we are dressed as typical Italian citizens, I've forgotten that my red hair is like a beacon that screams foreigner. Not to mention that I'm rather famous in the temporal scientific world. Some of these kids may actually be studying about me right now.

"So much for trying to stay undercover," Frank whispers to me. "You should have worn a hat."

"I can't help it," I reply.

We stop in front of double wooden doors at the end of a hallway. 'Savino's Casa Del Divertimento!' is scribbled on the doors in black magic marker.

"Here we go," says Mojmir. He takes a deep breath and opens the door. The first thing we see is a giant Newton's cradle hanging from the ceiling with the outer metal balls swinging back and forth. Click... click... click.... click, continually fills the air. Along one wall is a floor to ceiling bookshelf filled with papers, books, trinkets, awards, and boxes overflowing with more papers. There's a large static electricity orb stashed in the corner along with several other large crates. At the end of the room is what appears to be a live experiment. There are several ten feet high metal plates with pin holes in them. To the left of them is a large sonar meter, and on the right are four large Marshall Stack speakers and an Ampeg amplifier connected to an electric red Gibson guitar. Holding the guitar is an old Italian about the age of my father. His gray hair hangs a bit past his shoulders, along with thick gray locks on the side, but his gray goatee is trimmed short. He's got puffy big red cheeks like Santa Claus, but looks more like a waiter in a family owned Italian restaurant than old St. Nick.

He puts on huge green headphones, turns up his guitar, and pulls up his hand to strike a chord. The speakers hum with excitement. He moves his hand down and I instinctively cover my ears, but he stops in mid-stroke as he finally notices us. His jaw drop and he slowly lets down his hand. His face fills with shock that quickly turns to absolute joy.

"In the name of God almighty, is that you, Mojmir?" he shouts, "You? The Russian of all Russians? Time traveler extraordinaire? Last time I saw you, we were discussing the strength of temporal flow and how many teslas it would take to burst through, if I recall, you argued that it would take as much as fifty teslas, but I correctly surmised that it would be just a mere thirty-five teslas."

Dr. Savino races through his words like a cheetah sprinting across the plains after an antelope. He's one run-on sentence.

"Yes, yes, yes," he rattles off. "We were at the restaurant across the street, the Le Magie Del Forno, at least that's what it was called at the time, but now it's the Fiore in Fiore, food is not as good, it's a vegetarian place now, lots of salads, but they make a really good garlic antipasti, and when you pair it with the Brunello di Montalcino, you feel like you've died and gone to heaven. You're probably wondering what I'm doing with this guitar. I'm conducting an experiment this moment on how to isolate sound waves of electric guitar waves for better live recording of rock bands, one of the recording companies hired me to create the proper equipment, it's not glorious but it pays, I have to test it in between classes or the professor on the floor above gets angry when I interrupt her class, she's a real *rompicoglioni*, I keep on trying to explain that it's my building since they named it after me, but it does not seem to have any influence on her at all."

Dr. Savino pulls off his guitar and flips some switches off as he continues, "What brings you here to Torino? Who are your friends? I will pause my experiment for now so we can talk, the period break between classes is almost over anyways." He turns and starts walking down the stairs towards us. "I am almost done with the experiment, this was the final test, the plates are made out of Russian ore you know, best metal to direct resonance."

Dr. Savino stops half way down the stairs and his jaw drops. He slaps his forehead in shock, and shakes his head as if he's seeing a ghost. His face twists in confusion then his cheeks rise and he grins ear to ear. "Joy! Complete joy! Capa Rossa! Alexandria Eviston! In my lab! Mi dispiace! I did not know you would be here today as well, I would have cleaned up my lab a bit." He rushes down at me, full-body hugs me and lifts me in the air. He swings me around and puts me back on my feet. He stares at my face, still grinning ear to ear.

"You have your mother's eyes and nose," he observes, "You have her hair as well, but the eyes, oh, amazing blue, like the Grotta Azzurra in the isle of Capri, her eyes are burned into my memory like none I have ever seen, I have spent several evenings looking at her eyes, your father is a blessed man, brilliant man, the three of us would discuss the theories of time travel, of temporal fate, and of inherent energy, I have a lot to thank for your mom and dad on my research, it was such a shame they did not allow me to cite them on my papers, such a shame, odd, they didn't want any credit for it all, your dad made me swear on the grave of mia madre that we never talked, never discussed our theories, I was crushed when he discounted my works, told the world I was a fool, especially when he helped me come to many of my theoretical conclusions, but your mom called me and told me to be at peace, that he had done the same to her, she begged me not to reveal our conversations and work together, and for the sake of those blue eyes I pledged my secrecy, I should not even be telling you, but you are family. It's okay, right? You must know all about it since your mom called me."

Finally, Dr. Savino takes a breath, leans up against a lab table and crossed his arms. He stands about five foot six and is a thin man. He's got olive oil skin with some age spots, but besides that he looks great for how old he is.

"So, who is this strapping young man with you? French? Canadian? Oh," his face turns into wonderment, "Yes, yes, yes, it is the famous Frank Bouchard! I am triply blessed today by the trio that helped save America from the Nazis! Frank, Alex, and Mojmir! But what are you doing here? How did you get here? Do you know you are wanted by the government now? Fugitives! My computer told me you stole a plane or something? Along with your mother's paper on influence. Good paper, she wrote most of it while she was here. I took some of her theories and applied them to objects in temporal gravity, and came to some interesting conclusions. I really believe a few of your dad's theories have some holes in them, no joke intended, because given the right object, that object can push temporal gravity in a whole new direction. I haven't been able to test this, because I haven't found the right object, or human, it's really a human we're talking about because an inanimate object really can't do anything, but any way, I haven't found the right human that has such a strong influence over temporal space that they can bend gravity in a new direction, thus creating a brand new future for all of us. Imagine that, your father claims we all have a destiny, a place to go, a future planned out, predestination, now consider that you can control your own fate, that your mere presence in time can shift the future in a totally different direction! Amazing, truly, amazing."

"We're here looking for you," I finally get in.

"Me?" Dr. Savino is confused. "You're looking for... me?"

"Yes, you," I swing off my backpack and pull out the leather portfolio. "This is my mother's original copy of her paper. It's been in the Smithsonian for decades on loan. My dad recently asked for it back. Since then he's gone missing."

Dr. Savino gently takes the portfolio from me like it's a newborn baby and slowly pages through it.

"This is definitely the original portfolio," Dr. Savino explains. "Your mother wrote this while she was here in Torino. Those were some great several months, your father and I would drink wine and stay up late talking about temporal philosophy, then wake up early, go to the cafeteria, and drink espresso, talking about temporal physics. The way your dad thinks is like no other. His mind works even faster than mine. I took great pleasure in speaking with him because I never had to explain anything, he always immediately understood. Very brilliant. I am sorry about your mother's death. I know it was years ago, but I could not attend the funeral myself and I want to offer my condolences to you and your father. The world lost one of the best scientists it's known in the modern age."

Dr. Savino pauses for a moment and places his hand on my shoulder, offering me a smile of grace and comfort. His eye brows raise almost all the way up his long forehead, transitioning from confusion to absolute shock.

"James Eviston is missing? Your father? When? Where? How long? When was he last seen? This is not good news. No, no, no. Not good for him, not good for me. Certainly not good for you. Please tell me he wasn't in D.C. with you," Dr. Savino goes on. "Was he meeting with the U.S. National Board of Temporal Governance? They've been out to get him for some time now. Rumor has it that your dad was researching how the Nazis altered the past to change history and the Board was completely against his work. Said it was a violation of U.N. Temporal Treaties. It was simple research and the U.N. would never have brought charges against your dad. Never."

I know nothing about the U.S. National Board of Temporal Governance. The last I saw them was when I was sent back to 1989. If Dad was meeting with them, he didn't tell me that he was.

Dr. Savino looks at me as if he's reading my mind, "Your father was conducting those experiments, wasn't he? He had you and Frank going back in time to investigate where the manipulation was going on. He sent you back to the burning of the Reichstag Building, didn't he?"

"Yeah," blurts out Frank. "How'd you know?"

"Perfect Temporal Node," responds Dr. Savino. "I would have sent you there as well if I was investigating where they manipulated the past, first place I would have sent you to, it's the perfect place to accelerate the passion behind the war, if you remember your history correctly Hitler used that fire to rally the Nazis against the communists, in fact, if that didn't happen Germany might be under Russian rule instead, who knows what that means for the future, but I'm banking on the fact we wouldn't have had the genocide of so many Jews, and then the whole Israeli state wouldn't have happened, and then the hundreds of years of dispute, killings, and wars in the Jewish-Palestine conflict, which of course didn't happen in this reality because the war was extended."

"Savino," Mojmir interrupts. "We're on a time crunch here. We have reason to believe the Nazis may figure out where we are and send troops after us. We weren't safe in the States and I'm guessing we're not safe here. We need a solution and have to get out of here fast."

"Okay, okay, okay," Dr. Savino nods his head, "I'll get straight to the point: we need the map."

Dr. Savino stares at us. We stare back at him, waiting for him to continue.

"You know, the map, THE map, the map," he says again.

Again, staring contest ensues.

"Map?" I'm confused. "What do you mean by map?"

"I thought we were going to try to make this quick," Dr. Savino sighs.

Dr. Savino steps over to chalkboard on the wall with a bunch of writing on it then pulls down a fresh chalkboard that was hidden underneath it. "Time for a lecture," he begins and draws a typical temporal river on the chalkboard. "As you know, temporal gravity flows in one direction. When someone goes back in time and creates an aberration, temporal gravity expands slightly, compensating for the change, still pushing time forward. Now the compensation is less or greater depending on the force and importance of the node. For example, you send a trained inspector back in time, you are in essence putting a stick in the river, but since they are merely observers, they do not create a strong aberration and therefore the compensation is minimal, barely registering on the VanVliet Aberrational Force Scale, but if the node is of great importance and the change made is phantasmal, like teaching cave women to make fire centuries before their time, than the force of the node becomes greater than three VanVliets, and the expansion of Temporal Flow is huge, spanning years of correction."

Dr. Savino draws a new temporal river example, this one with a huge pear shaped aberration with a big dot in the middle. "Right here is the node with the huge aberration, now what the Nazis have done is looked for nodes beyond the initial node that would cause equal size aberrations and continue the split of Temporal Gravity, and in addition, the more aberrations you have in a row, the force exponentially increases making the aberrations stronger and last longer."

Dr. Savino adds more pear shaped aberrations with dots in the middle. "This is how the Nazis extended World War II and changed the past in their favor. See, all this can be calculated knowing where the original begins and where it stops. Because one VanVliet is equal to 12.431 years of aberration. But you need to know, where it starts, where it ends, and what the strength of each node is. You create this on a Temporal Map and you save that map so you know specifically what you did. Plus, you need to have a record of what actual history was. Somewhere in Berlin is a Temporal Map on which the Nazi scientists calculated this all out. If you find the map, you can go back to each event and stop it from happening, but you have to do it systematically, because if we start at the beginning, the next node will just take over and keep the chain reaction going."

"Sounds like we're heading into the lion's den," declares Frank, "How close is Berlin?"

"Are you crazy?" ask Dr. Savino. "Berlin is crawling with the enemy. You'll be crushed there, like when you drop a pretzel on the ground and accidentally step on it and it turns into a million pieces of pretzel dust? And then you step back and try to pick it up but you can never quite clean it. The residue that's left behind is unclear, is it salt? Is it pretzel? You can't tell because it's that small. It's been pulverized. That will be us if we go to Berlin. Crushed powered pretzel dust salt stuff. "

"We don't have a choice,' argues Mojmir. "We have to fix this and fix it for good. The only way is to systematically stop the Nazis from creating all those temporal nodes. We need the map and then we need access to a particle accelerator. Dr. Savino, we need your help for both."

Dr. Savino pauses for a moment. Several moments. It's the longest period of silence we've had since we arrived. It only lasts about 20 seconds, but it seems like a century in his world. I watch his facial expressions turn from apprehension, to confusion, to resolve.

"Your father is missing," remembers Dr. Savino. "They must need him."

"He was working on some type of secret project," I explain. "He didn't tell me, didn't tell anyone. I'm worried the Nazis have him and want to get all the details, use his research to permanently change time forever."

Dr. Savino pauses again. He brow drops and he stares off to his left. He's deep in thought.

"We have to get moving," explains Frank. "We think the Nazis know we're here."

"I cannot go with you," says Dr. Savino. "I cannot go into Germany. I must stay away from the Nazis and I am safest here at the University. Now if you'll excuse me, I have to get back to my research."

I'm taken aback. A few moments ago, Dr. Savino was happy to see us, happy to tell us his story and explain what he knew about the Temporal Shift. He's suddenly become distant and pushing us away.

"You have to come with us," argues Frank. "We need your expertise."

"My dad told me to come here," I plead. "He said to get your help."

"Did he?" responds Dr. Savino. "Did he tell you to come here to my lab and get me to help you invade Germany to get the temporal map? I know your father, I've been working with your father. He wouldn't have wanted you to come here."

Working with my father? That's right, Dr. Savino's been working with my dad. Dr. Radkowski gave me his drive. I rummage around in my pockets and find it tucked away with some cough drops.

"I have his drive," I say, pulling it out and handing it to him.

"What!" shouts Dr. Savino. "You cannot bring that information here. You cannot. If this gets into the wrong hands it can be catastrophic. Devastating. World-ending. Ka-boom type stuff."

"What's on it?" asks Mojmir.

"Yeah, what's this Inherent Energy research project?" Frank asks.

"Please Dr. Savino," I plead, "My dad is missing. With my mom gone, he's all I have. You're the only one that can help us now."

Dr. Savino stares off into space, thinking, remembering. "Your mother," he smiles. "She gave me the confidence that propelled me on my career as a researcher." He wipes his cheek and sniffles a little. "For your mother's memory, I will help, but just a bit. Too much could be catastrophic. Maybe it will help you find your father. Give me the drive," says Dr. Savino. "Let's take a look."

I hand over the drive, which pretty much looks like a postage stamp. Same size, but thinner. He steps over to a computer terminal and places it against the monitor. It sticks to it like a magnet and glows.

"*File aperti*," says Dr. Savino. "That's Italian for access the files," he explains.

We stand over his shoulder and watch the computer screen as it quickly opens document after document in a cascade effect. During the rapid fire building of documents on the screen, I catch glimpses of what look like scientific journals and papers. Finally the screen images slow down and stop. The last document opened is my mother's *The Evolution of Influence*.

"This is odd," says Dr. Savino. He starts clicking through the rest of the opened documents. They are all papers written by my mother. Research papers, scientific journals, and raw data, all from her. Absolutely nothing from my father.

"This can't be," exclaims Dr. Savino. "Your father was doing important research. Amazing research. Like the kind of research that scientists around the globe would read and immediately think, 'Wow, that's mind-boggling brilliant', the kind of research that gives you a Nobel prize. Your father and I were working on it together, but independently. Not to get the Nobel Prize, mind you. No, this was to help us right all the wrongs that's been put into place due to the invention of time travel. It would be a huge moment in history and a necessary correction. But there was much more needed. I thought maybe your father was using you to deliver this information to me, but this computer disc is not it. No, this is obviously your mother's work. Which mind you, is extremely important and scientifically significant, but it is not what I expected. Not what I need. I need your father's work if I am to complete mine."

"Then you must go with us," says Mojmir. "We are going to find the map and Dr. Eviston. Help us save her dad and the world."

"*Non dovrei*, I must not, it would be terrible for your father and I to be captured by the Nazis," argues Dr. Savino. "Your father kidnapped by them is one thing. It's tragic, but not world-ending. You can find him, you can save him. But if the Nazis have me as well, that…, that is truly a disaster. For both of us to be in their hands. Right now Inherent Energy is a concept that is a puzzle. A puzzle made of TWO puzzle pieces. One is in my brain, the other in your father's. If the Nazis just have the knowledge in his brain, they won't be able to figure it out. But if they have the knowledge from both your father and me, even a little bit of it, then they will be able to truly understand. Once they have that knowledge, they'll use it for their power. And a little bit of that knowledge in the wrong hands is dangerous. Evil. Terrible. Destructive. Your father and I needed more time to shape our thoughts together. But he knew they were onto him. Like I said, when you said you had the drive, I guessed your father shared all his research so I could finish his work. But your mother's work, as brilliant as it was and as beautiful as she was, no… I cannot use it. It's useless to me. Inutile."

"Listen, Dr. Savino," interrupts Frank. "Okay, I get that you don't want to go with us. But we're going to need your particle accelerator to go back in time to fix things and first we're going to need a quick summary on this Inherent Energy project."

"Okay, okay, okay" says Dr. Savino. "Yes, you can use my particle accelerator to fix the past. That won't be a problem. But explaining Inherent Energy will take some time. We can do it over food, I'm starving. I'm Italian, you know, if we're not eating or drinking every two hours, well, we die. It's simple as that. I'm joking of course, we really don't die. We just get grumpy. Grumpy Italians are not a good thing. We scowl and then we hit things. Not good."

"All right Savino," agrees Mojmir. "Let's go get some pasta."

"Most excellent idea," he responds. "There's this great place around the corner that-"

A bang, bang, bang, on the door shocks me into jumping several inches in the air.

"Dr. Savino," shouts a German voice, "Siamo qui per discutere il futuro finanziamento della vostra ricerca. Si prega di aprire la porta in modo che possiamo discutere qualche pagamento."

We look at Dr. Savino. His jaw drops and eyes open wide.

"Germans. They want to talk to me about funding my research. I wasn't planning on talking to any Germans today," he explains. "I don't like Germans. I don't want any Nazi money. I don't know what they are talking about."

"My guess is they aren't here to talk to you about funding anything," says Frank. "They are here to get the other piece of the puzzle. They have Alex's dad and now they want you. I say we open up the door and take them head on."

"Wait a second, fly boy," I say. "Let's figure out what we're up against. You got a peep hole on that door, Dr. Savino?"

The banging continues.

"Dr. Savino," yells the German. "Apre la porta per favore."

Dr. Savino returns to the computer terminal. "Telecamera di sicurezza," he says. "One of my graduate students installed security cameras outside the office door because she was getting harassed by a former boyfriend. Came in rather useful at the time. Didn't know I'd need it one day to save my life."

The screen fills up with a large image of a Nazi leader at the door with eight mercenary soldiers behind him.

"That's not a research funding party," I say. "And that's not a group we can take head on in a university hallway."

"You got a back door to this place?" asks Frank.

"Hmm," says Dr. Savino. "You mean rear exit door? No. We don't. But we do have a back door with a stairwell down to the particle accelerator and I believe there's a maintenance hallway that leads to other parts of the building. So if you're looking for a means to avoid the Nazis, that might be our best route."

BAM! BAM! BAM!

On the camera, the Nazis are already swinging a metal battering ram at the doors, trying to bust them open. I grab the portfolio and my father's drive from the computer screen, shoving it in my pocket.

"Let's get out of here, pronto," I say.

We follow Dr. Savino through a rear door in the lab and start descending down several flights of wrought iron stairs. After a few moments, we can't hear the banging on the office doors anymore. I don't know if it's because we're far enough away and the sound waves won't travel all the way down here, or because they've actually broken in. As we approach the last set of stairs, there's shouting above in German, so it looks like

I have my answer. Shots ring out.

"This way!" yells Dr. Savino, leading us to the only two double doors at the bottom of the stairwell. We enter the lab and find a huge particle accelerator in front of us.

"This is three times as large as the one at Wright-Patterson," says Frank in awe. "Why do you need one this big?"

Dr. Savino begins moving lab tables in front of double doors to help barricade our way. Mojmir, Frank, and I start giving him a hand.

"This particle accelerator was funded and constructed by Fiat," he explains. "They wanted it to be large enough to send cars through time so they designed the inner chamber to accommodate their vehicles. We've never used it for that, but the elevator they installed to transport the vehicles down here is a favorite make-out place for the grad students. They call it "La Corsa," which means the ride. Apparently, it's got lots of bumps since it's an old school elevator run on pulleys and cables."

"Wait a minute," says Frank. "There's an elevator? Where? That's our escape route!"

"Perfect," adds Mojmir.

"The elevator goes up to a back dock on the side of the building," explains Dr. Savino, " It will take several minutes for the Nazis to catch up to us. We can be gone by then."

"They'll still know we're here," I counter. "We can't be tracked or reported in. I have a better idea."

With that, the Nazis begin banging on the outer doors.

I'm squished in the bottom shelf of a table with a full vantage point of the whole lab. Mojmir is farthest from me, across the room by the particle accelerator controls. To my side is Frank, squatting down between two cabinets, trying to hide his wide frame but also keeping himself poised to leap into action. Moments ago, he shoved Dr. Savino into one of the cabinets and closed it shut. I could still hear him arguing the many ways why this wouldn't work through the closed door. After a few moments he stopped, knowing that his words could reveal to the Nazis where he was.

The banging on the door becomes louder and I can see the deadbolt mechanisms starting to splinter. A loud crack fills the lab and the doors open, shoving the barricade of lab tables to the side.

Mojmir programs the particle accelerator and then quickly dives underneath a nearby desk, completely out of everyone's view including mine. Whirling noise fills the air as the magnetic coils begin to spin. A low hum begins in the distance and as it accelerates closer the pitch rises.

The Nazis burst in as the humming noises collide in front of us and suddenly dissipate, sucking the heat from the room. Light bends slightly at the door of the time machine. The computer screen on the controls fades dark except a panel that reads the date: October 12, 65,431,852 B.C.

There are twelve Nazis and two of them begin yelling at each other in German. One of them opens the cargo door to the machine and begins to push the other ten soldiers in while the last one starts programming the time machine. The first leader closes the door behind him, locking the eleven of them inside with the twelfth man still at the control panel.

Frank springs into action, and with three large leaps, clears the distance between his hiding position and body checks the soldier into the control panel. He grabs the confused soldier by the shoulder and with his other hand he pulls back open the cargo door, tossing the twelfth man in to join his buddies. Frank slams the door shut, locks it from the outside, and holds it in place.

Mojmir leaps out of from under his desk back to the control panel and in a few simple clicks, starts the send sequence.

Just like before, the whirling noise begins and a low humming travels to the main chamber. Through the window of the cargo door I see the soldiers pulling on the door, but Frank holds it shut.

The humming noise increases and when the two sounds

collide, they dissipate, and the energy vacuum sucks all the heat from the room, bending the light again. I look up to find Frank breathing heavily, leaning against the door and Mojmir placing his hand on his shoulder.

"Well done, my friend," commends Mojmir. "Well done."

Frank reaches up and pats Mojmir's hand. "The Russian-Canadian connection strikes again."

I crawl out of my hiding place, impressed by Frank and Mojmir, and glad they helped save the day. Banging from one of the cabinets stirs my memory that Dr. Savino's locked up.

Frank opens one of the doors and Dr. Savino falls out, "Did it work? Are the Nazis gone? How many were there? It sounded like it worked. Ah, it looks like it worked. Nazis all gone. Did the light bend? I heard the low humming and the sonic boom twice like I should, but if the light didn't bend, it didn't trigger. Did it bend?"

"Yes," Mojmir replies. "It bent. Sucked in all the heat. It worked. They're gone. We better get out of here before they start the return sequence."

Frank stands up, "I'm ready. I know how to live on the run when you're being hunted by Nazis. Been there. Done that. Got a medal for it. Let's go."

"We're good, we don't have to worry," I instruct them, "There's no way they're coming back from where we sent them."

"What do you mean," questions Dr. Savino, "The Osmium Shell went back with them. All they have to do is trigger the return sequence."

"Nobody knows why I sent them back 65 million years on October 12, do you?" I ask.

All the men stare at me.

"The K-Pg event?" I add.

Again. Blank stares.

"October 12, 65,431,852 B.C. is when the Peterson Asteroid hit the bay off the coast of Genoa. The thing was huge, about a seventy-five miles wide. It was a catastrophic event that created instantaneous mass extinction around the globe. We just sent them within 200 miles of the point of impact. They're in the blast zone. They can't trigger the return sequence because they have metal iridium shards shooting through their body right now. I don't think we need to worry about them anymore."

"You are a genius," exclaims Frank. "It's moments like these that make you even more beautiful."

I blush and all the guys know it. I hate special attention like that. I was never comfortable with being singled out for my beauty, but I guess I'm gonna have to get used to Frank's flirtatious comments, hopefully for the rest of my life.

"All right," says Mojmir. "We lost the Nazis and it will be some time before the Germans send a scouting group to find out what happened to them. But little do they know, we're heading to them. Our path goes to Berlin. We need to find that map."

"Staying here doesn't make sense anymore for me," comments Dr. Savino. "After what I just saw, I'm going to take my chances with you guys instead of hiding here on my own, or in my villa in the Italian Alps, or trying to make a run of it myself. No, you make a great group of people to hide with. Plus, you may need my services along the way. I can decipher the map quicker than any of you, and figure out which nodes are the best to go after fixing the first. If you'll still have me, I'd like to come with you."

"We weren't going to let you get away, anyway," Mojmir chuckles. "You're staying with us, whether you like it or not."

Dr. Savino smiles back at him.

"We need a way into Germany," I say to Frank. "Get us there."

EIGHTEEN

We didn't think it was a good idea for us to stay with the particle accelerator nor hang out in Dr. Savino's busted up lab. So we tried to quickly clean up as much as we could, close the splintered main doors to the lab so it didn't look that conspicuous, and headed off to a coffee bar around the corner to plan our next steps.

Italian coffee is much, much different from Café Americano. Dr. Savino ordered us four espressos, which is darker, stronger, and more bitter than the American counterpart. It has a rich dark chocolate nutty flavor and you can feel the caffeine instantly coursing through your veins the moment the it hits your tongue. I can only imagine what hyper Dr. Savino is like jacked up on Italian coffee, guess I'm about to find out.

"Ah," Dr. Savino begins as he takes his first sip of coffee, "This bar is one of the few in the neighborhood that serves illy Caffee Scura. The others serve the more popular Lavazza blends, but the illy is so much darker and flavorful. Plus, it gives me much more of a caffeine boost and after the scuffle we just had, I need a serious pick me up. So, Berlin. We must get to Berlin. Now, who do we think is behind all this?"

"General Stefan Kaiser," I explain.

"Stefan," Dr. Savino repeats and nods his head, "I should have assumed that. Your father and I used to call him Tef back in the day. We teased that he had not made enough scientific achievements to have a multi-syllable name like Jimmy or Samuel so we called him Tef. We also added that real Germans speak in grunts so Tef would suit him better anyway. It used to really burn him up. He'd get so upset and usually storm out of any symposium we were having at the time. Those were the early days, though, back when there was more collaboration between scientists, and back when Stefan was actually a scientist and not the bureaucrat he is today."

"I didn't know Dad collaborated with the Germans," I say.

"Your father had nothing against the Germans," adds Dr. Savino, "Germans are good people. I'll friend one any day of the week, and two on Sunday. It's the Nazis that are truly evil. Don't mix up the two. Just because one is German doesn't mean they share the values of the Nazi's Regime. With that said, Stefan is a Nazi. He's the chief Nazi, head of the Gestapo now, second in command. Breaking into his office is going to be like breaking into the U.S. White House."

"Been there, done that," counters Frank.

"Oh, yeah," smiles Dr. Savino, "That's right. Anyway, we're going to need a lot of planning. The Bundeskanzleramt Building is much bigger than the White House. Stefan is the Vice Chancellor now, and I'm sure his offices are there."

"I don't think we need access to his offices," I say. "I think we need access to his lab. Where he does his work."

"He doesn't practice science anymore," counters Dr. Savino. "He doesn't have a lab. He hasn't had one since he left TU Berlin."

"He's got to have a lab," argues Mojmir. "And have access to a particle accelerator. Isn't one of the originals in Berlin?"

"Yes, yes, yes, yes, yes! You're exactly correct. In fact, Stefan built that one," Dr. Savino says, "Back when he was Head of the Institute of Temporal Engineering at TU Berlin, but recently it's been rebuilt. A few years ago he arranged for upgrades through a government grant while he was part of the University board."

"Yes! That's got to be it," Frank exclaims, the caffeine getting to him as well, "Stefan serves as a school trustee, he probably arranged for the upgrades to the particle accelerator to make all the adjustments he needed. My guess is the original one didn't have enough recovery speed so he built a new particle accelerator that was faster. That way, there would be less time between his time traveling trips. He could go back, make a change, come back, then immediately head to another place, instead of waiting for the machine to warm up. Stefan still has to have access to that machine."

"He's listed as a Professor Emeritus," says Mojmir, projecting the university's information page from his watch to the table. "Look, right there, General Stefan Kaiser. Vice-

Chancellor, Technical University of Berlin Board of Trustees, and Professor Emeritus of the Institute of Temporal Engineering. Office 520."

"Sounds like we figured out where he's doing his dirty work," I say, "And where we're headed to."

"Do you think he has Alex's dad there?" asks Frank.

"My hope and fear is that he is somewhere in the Institute," says Dr. Savino, "Stefan is probably been forcing your dad to work for him and to finish his research on Inherent Energy."

"Maybe we can save Alex's dad and get the map all at the same time?" offers Mojmir. "Kind of a two for one."

"Saving your father is just as much of a priority as finding the map and correcting time," claims Dr. Savino. "If the concept of Inherent Energy falls into the wrong hands, than it will make the Temporal Shift look like a minor earthquake."

"You're going to have to explain this whole Inherent Energy theory," I say, leaning back. "My dad never mentioned anything about it."

"I'll explain on the way to Berlin," says Dr. Savino. "You'll have to promise me my safety. Your father in the hands of the Nazis is bad enough, but the two of us there, with what each of us know, can be catastrophic. Remember the puzzle example about your father and me? Whoever has the knowledge in his brain, paired with the knowledge in mine, can figure out how to change time forever. If we get kidnapped, then the whole world is doomed."

"We haven't been stuck in a bad situation yet," smiles Frank. "We always find a way out. How do we get to Berlin? Fly?"

"I'm not flying with you again after that crash into the mountainside," I say. "We're taking a train."

"No trains," argues Mojmir. "That didn't go that well back in 1990. We're driving and staying in control."

"Driving won't get us there quick enough," counters Frank, "We have to get there soon."

Dr. Savino smiles, "We're gonna do a little of all three. I have this former graduate assistant who, let's just say has an affinity for older Italian men, she's the lead engineer at a top secret project over at Fiat. I may be able to convince her to let us take it for a road test."

NINETEEN

Dr. Savino definitely has a way with women. As soon as he raised an eyebrow and tilted his head a little bit, his former graduate assistant melted in an instant. She handed over the keys to him and gave Frank a quick lesson, never taking her eyes off of Dr. Savino. We left my mom's portfolio and my dad's drive with her for safe keeping, so that if we get caught they won't fall into the hands of the Nazis.

Dr. Savino explained they had an on again, off again relationship over the past twenty some years, as she was his graduate student back in the sixties. She looked more like Gina Lollobrigida than Sophia Loren, having a plain, calm inner beauty about herself and didn't flaunt it. That's something I respect and admire.

We had no idea what this Fiat car was really about until Frank started getting an overview. Turns out Fiat is designing every driver's dream, a car that can drive on a road, glide in the air, and function as a high speed train all in one.

Currently, we're flying over Lake Constance at the Northern foot hills of the Alps on the way to Berlin. And when I mean over it, I mean like six feet over it. The way the car works is similar to modern day sonic elevators. It emits sound waves directly below the vehicle, forcing it up off the ground. It sucks in the air in front of you, pulling you through the wind as if it was on an invisible pulley system. Kind of the same concept as the Ford Golden Eagle. It was a bit bumpy over the mountains. Since it was on uneven vertical dirt, the car had a hard time finding its footing. Now that we're on a flat surface it's functioning much better, especially over the glass-like water of Lake Constance.

"This ride is much smoother than it was over the Alps," comments Frank. "It was so rocky that for a while, I thought we were going to have to roll down a window so Mojmir could puke."

"There is much I can tolerate in this world," claims Mojmir. "I've lived through two concentration camps and decades of time travel. I've lived the revolution of 1990. Been in London during the plague. In China during the famine. I was able to stomach it all. I have the constitution of an elephant. But your driving sucks."

"It's not me," Frank jeers back. "It's the car. This thing drives itself. In fact, just on the other side of the lake is a train track that the car is flying itself to. We'll land on the tracks and take them several miles until we get to Berlin."

"My graduate assistant, Elisabetta, said this thing travels at 300 miles per hour in train mode. I can't wait to feel that," chimes in Dr. Savino. "It's the first of its kind and it's never been tested outside of Torino."

"Wait a minute," I shout, "You mean to tell me we just took an untested bleeding edge of technology vehicle through the Alps? We could have crashed. Are you guys crazy? How come no one told me this?"

Silence. Dead silence in the car. Even Dr. Savino's not saying a word. No one has the guts to admit they hid the truth from me.

"Look," Frank breaks the silence, points ahead, and tries to change the topic, "There's land and where the train tracks begin."

The Fiat begins to ease itself down, simultaneously diminishing the sound wave pressure on the ground while laying back on the air propulsion. We gently land right on the tracks and hear the electromagnetic wheels engage. The car moves forward slowly, as if to test its connection.

"*Allacciate le cinture di sicurezza*," a soothing Italian voice speaks.

"That voice is Elisabetta's," announces Dr. Savino, "She's telling us to fasten our seatbelts."

"I've been flying through the Alps for the past hour," I say, "My seatbelt was fastened during minute one."

"*D'accord. Andiamo. Parlare in inglese*," Dr. Savino says. "I told her we're ready and to start speaking in English."

The engine suddenly reeves up. Lights start blinking on the dashboard and a gauge in the middle starts slowly building lighted bars on top of each other.

"Brace yourself, people," commands Frank. "I got no idea what this is going to feel like, but I'm sure we're gonna get hit with a couple G-forces."

One by one the bars build on the gauge until the car is roaring and the gauge is filled. They go from bright red, to white.

"Calculating potential obstructions on the route," Elisabetta's voice speaks.

The engine rumbles and revs, waiting to unleash it's power.

"No obstructions," she says, "Clear for this sequence of your route."

The white bars on the dash turn from bright white to solid green, and the car takes off at rocket speed. I go flying back in my seat, the force of pressure holding me back. It's stronger than the feeling of taking off in an F-18. I look over to Frank. Although he doesn't have to steer, he's gripping the wheel as if he's in control. There's a look of thrill and excitement on his face. He's grinning ear to ear, loving every minute of it.

"What a rush," he says to me. "Awesome."

My brain is barely staying inside my skull right now, feeling like it's getting pushed out of my head, and Frank thinks this is a thrill ride. He's crazy.

I manage to turn a bit and see Dr. Savino sitting behind Frank. His upper body is flat against his seat with his arms crossed over his chest and his head pushed against the head rest. He's not enjoying himself, but he's managing.

"How you doing back there, comrade?" shouts Frank.

"Fine," Mojmir stifles out, "How long are we going to be like this?"

I glance over to Frank's side of the dashboard to see a map. There's a timer counting down. It's currently at 59 minutes and 23 seconds.

"Not that long," Frank lies. "We should be in Germany in no time."

An hour feeling like I'm racing down the longest roller coaster hill ever? This is crazy. I can't let all these g-forces bother me. Soon we'll be in Berlin and I'll have to make a decision about what to go after first, the map or my dad. Once I have the map, I can save the world again. But if I don't save my dad, I could lose yet another parent.

My relationship with him has always been strained at best, but he is my dad. I do love him and while he doesn't say it, I know he loves me. I try to relax, close my eyes, and think.

My dad loves games. He uses them to wind down. When I was a child, after dinner, he would always sit in his chair and do crossword puzzles, logic games, word finds, puzzles, mazes, and whatever else he could get his hands on. In fact, he did it whenever he had free time. Some dads would watch sports on the weekend, but my dad would even pass on Ohio State Football. Since he wasn't good at housework either, Mom would always make him keep an eye on me while she did chores.

Dad learned early on that I was much more amusing if I was doing something with him, so I'd become his sparring partner on whatever game was age appropriate. Early on it was Tiddlywinks, Chutes and Ladders and Checkers. We then graduated to Sorry, Battleship, and Mancala, then Life, Clue, and Risk. The ultimate, my pick whenever I got to choose, was Monopoly. It was a big kid game. It taught you how to make great financial decisions, negotiate, and put your competition out of business. Dad loved playing it as much as I did, it was one of the few things we actually enjoyed doing together. We went through three different boards over the years, and if you looked up at the closet shelf today, you'd find the box for the current set broken and wrapped together with a big rubber band.

When I first learned how to play, Dad used to call me a gorger and a hoarder. I'd buy up every property I could with every last dollar I had and then sit on them, never negotiating and never giving any up. That would cause me to run out of money super quickly and since I wasn't willing to trade properties, I'd never get a monopoly. Soon I'd end up on one of dad's properties, owe a bunch of rent, and he'd win the game.

Finally, Dad talked strategy to me. "You have to learn patience," he would say. "Figure out what properties you want to own and target your efforts on those. Think about it, you always go after Boardwalk and Park Place because they are the most expensive. But how often do you land on either? Rarely. But most people go to jail several times during the game, eventually they have to get out of jail and there's a high likelihood that they'll land on the purple or orange properties. Which is why I typically beat you. I go after orange every game."

"Which is why you always want to trade me for St. James or Tennessee," I conclude.

"Exactly. Monopoly is more complicated than chess. Chess you just set a plan of attack and move pieces around the board. In Monopoly, you have to convince someone to do something they may not want to do," my dad explained. "You have to develop your strategy early on but be flexible. See the *whole* board, understand what's going on, but most of all be patient. Your strategy at the beginning of the game may be different than at the end, but if you continually look at the big picture and adjust your play accordingly then you'll win more often than not."

That week I ran a bunch of simulations on my computer to determine which were the most visited properties on the board. Even though I was twelve, I was already on the path to being a scientist. I determined that Illinois, Indiana, and Kentucky were the more popular color set along with the Railroads. I'd trick my father from then on out, always trading him the orange properties for more money than I paid for them while at the same time gathering the red properties. I beat him the next five times we played.

He was proud of me. I learned the values of patience and planning. Most of all, I learned how to trick him by using what he wanted to do for my own benefit.

Later in life, I figured out these were my dad's teaching moments. They weren't games, they were lessons. I learned patterns with Connect Four, aggressiveness with Sorry, educated guessing with Battleship, discernment with Clue, strategic use of resources with Risk, and most importantly negotiation with Monopoly. Dad could easily teach me the lessons of Temporal Gravity with a chalkboard and some drawings, but the real things that would count in life he taught me through the help of Milton Bradley and Parker Brothers.

When I became a teenager, I started spending my weekends with friends or doing school work so Dad and I spent less and less game time together. Eventually, he went back to doing mazes and logic games over the weekend as he did during the week. Every now and then at Thanksgiving or Christmas we'd pull out the Monopoly board and recreate the few special father-daughter moments we had.

Maybe things weren't as bad as I thought it was with my dad. He was a busy man, trying to fix things in the world and provide for his family. When we did have time together, he tried to make it count.

After we save him from the Nazis and get him back home, one of the first things I'm going to do is beat him in Monopoly. I'm going after the Railroads this time. When I win, I'm going to make him take me out for chocolate ice cream to celebrate.

TWENTY

Berlin is the shining jewel of Europe, an architect's paint canvas. Buildings of black and red steel with gold mirrored glass, spiral, twist, and jut into the air as high as you can see. Berlin now lays claim to the top twelve tallest buildings in the world but the city is filled with at least forty-some skyscrapers that would tower over the highest in many major cities. It's expansive and seems to go on forever, each building shooting high into the sky, trying to disappear into the clouds and touch the sun.

It's not just the height that's a factor, it's the design as well. All are colored in German's state colors: a deep black, a burnt red-orange, and magnificent sparkling gold. Each building takes on a unique shape. One building, called Feuer Zunge, looks like a huge flame leaping up to the sky with its top floors forking out from each other and swirling around, giving the appearance of a dancing flame. Two other buildings called the Liebhabers, reach out and touch each other at the top, extending over a stunning five city block reach. The tallest building was a huge homage to the Nazi period, done in the Nazi-Neoclassical design. It towers over all the other buildings and at the top of it's spire is perched the Nazi eagle on a swastika, as a reminder of the political party that made Germany what it is today.

All of this reflects in the deep crystal blue rivers and lakes that wind through this lavish city, combining the softness of water with the opulence of each tower shimmering in the sunlight. There is no shortage of wealth in Berlin and its city is a testament to greatness and dominance.

The Fiat quickly decelerates, going from 300 mph to 45 mph in a few moments, just like a plane landing on a runway.

"Elisabetta said the transition from train to car still needed some work," Dr. Savino says as he braced himself behind my seat. "The car ride should be the best part of it, I mean, they are Fiat, that's what they do, right? Make cars. So I hope the car part is the best part."

As we move from train to car, wheels descend from the

bottom carriage and Frank turns off the railroad track and onto a road. The transition staggers a bit, but once the four wheels are on the ground the ride is super smooth.

"The fascinating thing," chimes in Frank, "Is that we've only expended 25% of the power. I'm not sure where it gets its fuel from. Maybe it's solar energy."

"Energy!" I shout, "Dr. Savino, you were going to explain to us about the Inherent Energy Theory you and my dad were working on."

"Yes, yes, yes," he says, "I will. I am. Here's the deal. Simple concept on my end. You know how everything flows towards temporal gravity. One direction, like the river going towards the falls. You're aware of that, right Alex? Anyway, imagine temporal gravity going in one direction, and it's hit from the side with a big huge force, so big that it's knocked off its path. A huge bundle of energy. BAM! It bends the path in a new direction."

"Kind of like the Big Bang?" Mojmir interrupts.

"Yes! Exactly like the Big Bang," confirms Dr. Savino, "The Big Bang is one of the things I am studying. My role in the research is to determine if the change in course is possible. Your father's role was a bit different, he was taking your mom's research and applying it to my theories to see if it was possible for a single object, more specifically a human being could be the catalyst, if they had such influence over temporal gravity that they could be the Big Bang within the flow, and in essence bend time forever. Your father wanted to know if people could change the course of time."

"That's like Copernicus's Earth revolves around the Sun discovery," Frank says, "How the heck were you going to convince the world of that?"

"We weren't," counters Dr. Savino, "We weren't going to tell a single soul. The information is too dangerous for anyone to know. I mean, look what happened when your father announced the ability to time travel, all the governments took it and made it a military weapon. That's why your father and I were working on it separately. Think about it for a moment. If the wrong person gets us together and is able to merge our ideas, then they can discover exactly what they need to do to bend time. And if they have the right person to bend it, they can change the course of history forever. No course correction. Things happen the way they want it to, not the way it's supposed to. The only reason your father and I were doing it was to satisfy our own curiosity."

"So what you're saying," asks Mojmir, "Is that there's someone out there with the ability to actually change the direction of temporal gravity?"

"That's what Alex's father and I were setting out to prove," says Dr. Savino. "I was almost finished with my part, and was hoping your father was done with his. That's why I was so eager to see that computer disc he gave you. I thought the answers were in there."

"Now I completely understand why you were so hesitant to come with us," I say, "Inherent Energy in the hands of the Nazis would be devastating."

"Yes," says Dr. Savino, "They haven't figured out what we're up to, but it looks like they discovered we're working on something together and it's big. If there's one thing that the Nazis want above all else, it's knowledge. They realized a long time ago that knowledge is power, and rather than come up with it yourself, it's easier to acquire it."

"Back in 1989, the Nazis had kidnapped all the younger versions of all the great scientists," Mojmir explains, "Probably just for that reason. Better for them to have Galileo discover gravity or Ben Franklin find electricity as a German."

So that's the Nazis' plan, I think to myself. All this time they didn't want land. They wanted knowledge and the ability to change the past so they could dominate all the greatest discoveries over the past several centuries. Currency in innovation.

"We have to stop them," I say aloud, "Technology only advances when the information is shared. If the Germans own all the discoveries, then science will come to a grinding halt."

"Well, in a few minutes you can tell that to Stefan yourself," states Frank, "TU Berlin is right ahead, with the Institute of Temporal Engineering at its center."

The University is on the eastern side of the city away from the opulent skyscrapers and governmental buildings. It's a beautiful spread of buildings, magnificently merging old world architecture with modern accents. The Institute of Temporal Engineering is most famous department of the University as it's made many of the advancements to time travel since my dad's initial discovery. The building shoots several stories above the other university buildings, and if you look closely, as the building grows so does it's architectural style. It's blurred the lines of early styles at its bottom, with more modern styles at the top. The Germans pride themselves in making statements with its landscape and the buildings here are evidence of that. It's artwork and engineering impossibilities weaved into one. They think if they can show the world they are smart enough to build an architectural marvel, they can do anything.

"I'm going to find a back alley way or loading dock to park at," says Frank, "While it's not strange to see a Fiat in Berlin, it's going to look out of place for an Irish-American, Canadian, Russian, and Italian stepping out of one. Especially someone that looks a lot like the woman who just saved the world and cast the Germans in a bad light."

Frank pulls down a roadway that leads behind the Institute. There are students milling about, but none of them recognize us through the windows. To them we're just another car driving down the street. Frank turns down a utility road and parks the car next to a garbage dumpster.

"What's the plan?" he turns to me.

I have no point of reference since I've never been to Berlin, let alone its Technical University. We have no resources, no weapons, no disguises, or anything of use. We have to find a temporal map, which is probably under lock and key, and save my dad, who may or may not be in this building. All we know is Stefan has an office on the Fifth floor, room 530. Once again, the team is counting on me to have a plan.

"We're going to kick some Nazi ass," I smile, "That's the plan."

Mojmir opens up his car door and begins to get out. "I love it when she doesn't have a plan," he admits, "It's more fun that way."

"I do have a plan," I argue, "Getting out of the car."

"You never have a plan at first," jeers Frank, "You make this stuff up as you go along and then act as if it was your idea the whole time."

I lead the team up a set of stairs and onto the loading dock. "Not true," I say, "I had a plan in Niagara."

"Really," says Frank, "You planned to jump over the Falls that day?"

"Well, sometimes you need to make things up as you go along," I argue, "It's called improvisation."

Frank grabs my shoulder. "Seriously," he says, "We don't have any guns. All we know is his office is 530. We have two of the most recognizable faces in the world right now. How we going to win this one?"

"Listen. We have a crazy Russian, a brilliant Italian, a strong Canadian, and a risk-taking American. If we can't figure this out, no one can," I respond. I open the dock door and immediately find a stairwell. "Come on, let's go."

I start walking down the flight of stairs.

"Alex," Frank shouts.

At the bottom of the first landing I stop and turn around to find Frank, Mojmir, and Dr. Savino still at the top of the stairs.

"Come on," I say, "What are you waiting for?"

"His office is on the fifth floor," says Frank pointing upward. "If we're going to catch him we have to hoof it up five stories."

I smile at Frank. "We're not after him, we're after his map. His office is on the fifth floor but we're looking for his lab. That lab needs to be near a particle accelerator. There's no space on the fifth floor to house a particle accelerator. That has to be in the subbasement. We're going down."

I turn around and head down the stairs as far as they will

take us.

At the bottom of the stairs is a utility door which leads into a hallway. I'm guessing that both my dad and the map are down here. Stefan wouldn't keep either of them up on the office and classroom floors, too much of a chance of being seen by students. He wouldn't keep my dad over at one of the government buildings because he'd want him close to his lab for research purposes. If he's trying to find out my dad's next big discovery, he's got to have him here. Likewise, the map would be down here, too. He's going to keep it under lock and key somewhere far away from anyone else. Stefan couldn't risk people knowing about the temporal shift. The less people who know the reality they are living in is wrong, the more people will accept it as the truth.

The hallway seems to be on the outside edge of the floor, with doors only on the inner walls. The outer walls are cold to the touch, which means there is earth behind them. We have to be about 100 feet or so down.

"None of the doors look like a prison cell door," I say. "They look mostly like office doors."

"It's not the doors you want to examine," instructs Mojmir. "Doors can be disguised to look like anything. It's the door knob and lock you want to examine."

I look at all the locks on the doors and they all seem normal as far as I can see. We walk down the hallway, slowly. We haven't run into anyone and if we do, all we have is our muscle to get out. Halfway down the hall are a set of double doors. I look through the windows and see an open lab with iron wrought stairs that lead down to the particle accelerator.

The next door down has a different lock than all the others.

"Here," I say, "There's something special in here. What do we do now?"

I look at the men and they all just shrug their shoulders at me.

"Turn it?" Dr. Savino suggests.

I grab the handle and try twisting it. It doesn't move.

"Identifizieren Sie sich," a female voice says from the door.

"It's a voice activated lock," explains Mojmir. "We're never going to get in there."

"Identifizieren Sie sich," the voice states again.

"Worse, yet," adds Frank, "It's going to figure out we're not the right person and send the police."

Out of the corner of my eye, I see Dr. Savino playing with his watch.

"Identifizieren Sie sich," a female voice says firmly.

Dr. Savino holds his watch in the air and touches its face. "General Stefan Kaiser," says the watch and Dr. Savino touches it again.

"Willkommen, general," says the voice and the locking mechanism disengages. We all look at Dr. Savino in shock.

"He called me a few years back," Dr. Savino explains. "I never clean out my voicemail."

We enter the room and it appears to be a general research lab. Tall desks are scattered around, completely clear and empty. There's a full bookshelf against the wall filled with history books in German. Frank starts opening drawers of the lab tables.

"Empty," he explains. "Nothing. Zero. Zilch."

Mojmir and Dr. Savino join the search, and from the looks of it, they find nothing as well.

The only thing in here are the lab tables and the books on the shelf. It's as if a moving company came in here and totally cleaned out the place. I rub my finger against the surface of a table and draw a line in the dust. My finger is now caked with dirt.

"No one has been in here for some time," I observe aloud.

"Because there's nothing in here," adds Frank. "Every drawer empty. We just got a bunch of German books."

"Why would they have kept this place locked, with special access to Stefan, if there wasn't something important in here?" I ponder.

"Maybe it's old access," thinks Mojmir, "Maybe he used this lab to do all his calculations and when it was over they cleaned it out. Maybe he hasn't been in here for some time."

"No," argues Dr. Savino, "After Alex defeated the Nazis back in 1990 he'd have to refer to the map. He'd have to know if there were any changes. The map shows real history and indicates where he manipulated things. He'd need to see the map after you all manipulated 1990 to see if it changed his plans."

"I think he looked at it more recently than that," says Frank, "Alex and I went back to the Reichstag fire just five days ago. He would have had to look at it then."

"Find a light switch and shut it off," I instruct, "Mojmir, hand me your flashlight."

Frank dowses the light and I shine the flashlight on the floor. It's thick with dust as well, but I can see the shuffling of all our feet throughout the room.

"Crap," murmurs Frank, "We totally destroyed any evidence."

"Look for different footprints," I explain, "Ones that aren't as recent and seem more like a man's dress shoe than a field boot."

I move the light along the floor, but all I can see is our shuffling. We've knocked up a lot of dirt so it's hard to tell what's fresh and what's not.

"There," shouts Mojmir. "Over by the bookshelf. Shine it over there again."

I move the light across the edge of the bookshelf and look at the dust on the floor. There's a layer of it that's been untouched by us since we've spent most our time walking around the lab tables. But three quarters down the length of the bookshelf, there's a spot where the dust isn't as thick. I move closer and find the exact prints I'm looking for - men's dress shoes. It appears as someone beside us was here recently. They've walked up to the book shelf and stopped.

"Maybe it's one of the books that's holding the map," guesses Frank.

"Can't be, the map needs to be extensive, very long and about this tall," Dr. Savino puts his hands in the air about three feet apart, "And rolled up so you can spread it out on a table and read it. There has to be a lot of points on it so you need to view it as one continuous timeline with lots of notations on the top and bottom. Historical facts, etc."

"He was in here," I say, "Standing right here. Are you sure it's not in any of these books?"

I look at the shelf and each title is in German. I have no idea what any of them mean. I'm hoping that one pops out at me. That one looks a bit odd or different, like one of those old cartoons where the piece of rock that the character is going to pick up is a bit off color so the animator knows where the action is.

"If I was a German scientist," I think aloud, "Which of these books would I put a map in."

"I'm telling you," explains Dr. Savino, "It's not in a book. You can't put this in a book. A smart German would put it on a scroll. And Stefan is a really, really, really smart German so there's no way he'd put it in a book."

I examine all the books on the shelf at eye level. They are faded colors of red, green, blue, and black. All have worn binders and gold lettering. They are all too similar, as if they were props on a movie set. Finally, I see book with a slight difference. The headband of one is significantly more worn than the others. I put my finger on the top of its spine and try to pull it from the shelf. Its base stays secure in the shelf but the top rotates down. I pull further and the whole shelf of books falls down as if the shelf is on some type of hinge.

"It's a false shelf," Frank exclaims, "There's something back there."

Laying lengthwise on two hooks is a circular leather case about three feet long with a shoulder strap. I grab it from its place, push the shelf back, and turn around to the table. I unlatch the top and find a rolled up parchment inside.

"That's it," confirms Dr. Savino, "That's his temporal map."

I start to slowly remove it when I hear a siren begin to wail and oscillate.

"They figured out we're here," yells Frank. "We can't do this now. We need to get out immediately."

I close the map back up and sling it over my back.

"To the stairs," yells Mojmir.

We bolt for the door and swing it open. I look down the hall towards the stairs, and it's empty.

"Good, no Nazis," Frank yells, "Let's make a run for it."

Before I take off, I look behind us. There's no Nazis there, either, but I find another door knob just like the one we found to the secret lab. It must be where they have my father.

"Frank!" I yell, "I have to save my dad."

"We don't have time to do a search for him," he yells and grabs my arm.

I pull his massive frame towards me.

"He's in this room," I shout and show him the lock.

"DR. SAVINO!" he yells down the hall. "GET US IN THIS ROOM!!!!"

Frank starts pounding on the door and checking it like a hockey player. It doesn't budge but I can hear the door's security voice, "Identifizieren Sie sich."

Suddenly Dr. Savino is by our side playing the voice mail over and over, holding it as high as he can so in can be heard over the siren. "General Stefan Kaiser," it repeats.

Just as we thought all hope was lost, the door lock disengages and opens.

Seated at a desk, reading, is my dad. He looks up at the door and when he recognizes me, his face turns from pride and then suddenly to anger. I race in, grab him by the arm, and pull him out into the hall.

"What are you doing here?" he yells. "You were supposed to go to Italy and hang out with Dr. Savino. He had important information for you. You should have not worried about me. You should have not come here."

Once again, my dad is disappointed in me. I know what torture they are capable of. I experienced what they did to my mom. I'll never win that emotional argument, so I try logic. "I did go to Italy, Dad, to see Dr. Savino," I yell back, "In fact, I brought him with me."

"Why on earth did you do that?" shouts my dad, getting angrier. "If we're captured together, along with you, then all is lost. I can't fix that. Time is running out."

"We're not planning on getting captured," I yell back, pushing him down the hallway.

Half way down the hallway we run right into Mojmir who has suddenly stops. He begins pushing us through the double doors and down towards the particle accelerator. "Get down there now," commands Mojmir. "They are coming."

Gun shots ring out as we start running down the utility stairs.

"Did Dr. Savino explain Inherent Energy to you?" shouts my dad.

"Yes," I reply.

"And Mom's paper," he adds, "Did you get your mom's paper from Dr. Pringle?"

"Yes," I yell back, "I saw the notations."

"And you have the disc from Radkowski?" he shouts.

"Yes," I confirm.

"Then you understand?" he asks.

"Dad," I say, "All that was on the disc was mom's research. There was nothing there from you."

Dad stops me and spins me around. The anger has left his face and he seems a bit more gentile now, but with a sense of urgency. "You need to see the bigger picture," he insists, "Look at the whole board. You're missing it."

Dad always told me to look at the whole board. Whether we were playing chess, Monopoly, Clue, or in the middle of a scientific breakthrough. He said my biggest flaw was I never looked at the whole board.

"Dad," I yell back, "For once can you just tell me the answer."

"Listen," he says kindly, "I appreciate you coming here to save me, but this isn't about me. You need to –"

Mojmir cuts him off.

"No time to talk," Mojmir yells, "We need to go now."

Mojmir pushes us deep into the lab.

"Get to the particle accelerator," shouts my dad.

We race across the lab floor and climb up to the particle accelerator. We all squeeze into its chamber. Before I can react, my dad closes the door on us and stays outside. I can see him through the window programming the panel. Lights blink on and off inside and a low whirling noise signals the start of the time traveling sequence.

I bang on the accelerator door.

"Dad!" I yell, "Open the door. Don't do this. You can come with us."

Shots fire out and my dad slumps against the window. Pools of blood form around his chest and he slides away leaving behind a streak of blood.

"NO!" I yell at the top of my lungs. I bang on the door, but it's too late. Frank grabs me and holds me. The low hum increases in pitch as the magnetic energy moves close to the Osmium core we're standing in. The pitch comes to its highest note and then the hum dissipates. Heat envelopes us and light bends. My dad and the Nazis that killed him are gone.

We've been sent somewhere back in time.

TWENTY-ONE

I bury my face in Frank's shoulder. I try not to wail because I don't know where we are and I shouldn't draw any attention to us, but I can't help the tears. Dad wasn't perfect, but he was all I had after Mom died. Now he's gone, too. I hold Frank tightly, knowing that I can't let go of him. I can't lose Frank, either. I feel the comforting hands of Mojmir and Dr. Savino on my shoulders.

"There, there, Princess," Mojmir whispers, "There. There."

Loss is painful. But with my mom I knew it was coming. I could prepare for it. There were no good-bye with my dad. No chance to tell him I love him.

But there's also no time for mourning when you're at war. I take a deep breath and try to pull myself together. I'll pay back Stefan at some point for killing my dad. I owe him that. But for now I'm on a mission. The best way I can show my love for my dad is by kicking some Nazi ass. I try to remember his last words, "See the whole board." I have to continue to think bigger picture and understand all my options. For now, we need to assess where we are.

I open my eyes and find the men huddled around me. At first I think it's because they're all trying to comfort me. Then I realize it's something more. We're crowded together in a small dark room that the four of us can barely fit in. My eyes adjust and I find medical supplies: scrubs, gloves, masks, cotton, bandages, depressors, syringes, masks, and bootees. If a hospital needs it, it's here.

"Where are we?" I ask.

"Don't know," says Frank, "But where ever we are, your dad sent us here."

I comb through my memory. What historical moment involves a hospital or surgery? Are we at some type of medical care for a Nazi general? Here to prevent President Woodrow Wilson's stroke?

I scan the shelves looking for a clue but find none. It's time to venture out. I dry my eyes with my sleeves and squeeze through everyone to get to the door.

"I'm going to take a peek outside," I say.

I slowly twist the door handle and crack it open. I peer outside with one eye.

It's definitely a hospital. There's hardwood polished floors with clinical white walls. Directly across from us is a nurse's station where they are going over patient charts. They are wearing white and blue scrubs, some with cartoon characters on them. There's a few glass panels projecting health information about the various patients on this floor. I can see curtains down the hall. A doctor pulls one open, steps out with his chart, and then pulls the curtain closed again. He walks towards me but then turns to the nurses' station and hands off his chart.

"Call Megan in Anesthesia," he instructs, "I need her to prep for surgery."

"Yes, doctor," the nurse responds.

I know this place. I've been here before. I step back from the door and slowly close it to not make a sound.

"Where are we?" asks Frank, "That sounds like English. Are we in Germany or England?"

"Neither," I explain. "We're in Columbus. This is the Emergency Department at Children's Hospital."

"This can't be one of the historical nodes," blurts out Dr. Savino, "There's nothing of historical significance that happened here. The Nazis never came here. Nor did the Germans. Why would your father send us here?"

"Dad chose a specific time and place to send us to," I say, "This one. He picked it for a reason. Now it's my job to figure it out."

I reach for the door handle to step out into the hall, but three hands grab for my shoulder and pull me back.

"First," starts Mojmir, "You're not going alone. Frank's going with you. Second, you're going in disguise."

Frank and I step out of the closet covered in light blue surgical scrubs with butterflies. My crazy red hair is stuffed in my cap and I have a mask covering my face. We both have surgical booties over our boots and have the uppers tucked into our scrub pants. We can't find any IDs to hang from our pockets, but since we're not planning on interacting with anyone, talking to them, or looking to go beyond the ER, we think we'll be safe.

We've decided to leave Mojmir and Dr. Savino back in the closet along with the temporal map. It would be harder for us to move a group of four than a group of two. This way Frank and I can stay close and quickly maneuver through the ER.

I've yet to figure out what year it is. Hospitals never seem to look any different. They always have that clinical clean feel with some type of central desk and rooms all around it. Health care interior design has maintained a bit of normalcy over the centuries. While strategies in efficiency ebb and flow, they still keep their overall look and feel.

We walk by the nurses' station, undetected and make our way out onto the main floor. We systematically look in each hospital bay trying to figure out what important person my dad sent us back to help, change, or kill.

I look in the first bay and there's no patient here. But what strikes me as odd is the technology. There's no plugs on the equipment. The television screens are pure black glass. The carts are made of a light-weight durable plastic called Caldwell, invented by Dupont, back in 2030. They didn't use it in computer monitors until 2050. The cordless electricity didn't have wide-spread use until 2060 when we learned how to power everything through sound waves emitted through the air.

I step back out into the hallway and run into Frank.

"We're not in the past," he says then corrects himself, "I mean past, past. Like history. Your dad sent us back to the sixties – this century. Only twenty years ago. This couldn't be on the Nazis temporal map. Or could it?"

"We don't know," I say, "If they had to keep the divisiveness between Germany and the U.S. until the future, there may be something here. Keep your eye out for Stefan. Remember, he may or may not know us. His journey to this year may have happened before the Temporal shift."

We continue to check each medical bay. There's a young girl complaining of intestinal pains. A grade school boy getting stiches on the bottom of his foot. A middle school girl being fitted for a wrist splint. A teenage boy hooked up to a heart monitor.

I meet back up with Frank in the hallway.

"What have you seen?" I whisper.

"Nothing suspicious," Frank says, "I did find a boy in hockey gear getting examined for a broken jaw, but I don't think your dad sent us back for me to see that."

"There's just a few more bays to check out," I say, "There's got to be something here."

A curtain swishes open from one of the back bays and a nurse comes down the hall right at us.

"Are you here to wheel the Eviston girl for her MRI?" asks the nurse.

A wave of shock goes over me. I know exactly where I am now. Exactly WHEN I am. My dad sent me back in time to see the nine year old version of myself in the Emergency Room, after I had been hit by a drunk driver while riding my bike.

The younger me is in the last ER bay with a broken right arm, a dislocated shoulder, and a cracked skull with swelling in the brain. There's also my mom and dad in there as well.

I break out in a cold sweat and can sense I've turned pale white. I feel a little woosy.

"Did you hear me?" asks the nurse. "Alexandria Eviston is in the last bay. She needs to go down to get an MRI. Be careful with her. Her father is THE James Eviston and her mom is head of the Psych Department at Ohio State."

"Will do," Frank responds.

The nurse steps away and I stumble a bit into Frank. He holds me up.

"Don't freak out," he whispers in my ear. "You can't freak out."

They warn you in Temporal school about seeing yourself in the past. They tell you not to make contact. That it can be mentally devastating. That seeing yourself can make you think you're that person again. That by reliving your own past, it becomes your present and you can't tell the difference between what's real and what's history. I'm about to see me at my worst ever, on the threshold of death's door. I know I make it out okay but I'm still nervous that I won't be able to control my emotions.

"Listen to me," Frank commands, "You helped me through the Temporal Shift in 1989, I'm going to help you through this. No matter what you see in there, remember that you pull through and heal. You survive. Let that thought guide you. Get strength from that. Have it feed you. You are a survivor."

Frank's right. I survive. I prepare to see the worst and take solace in the fact that I come out wonderfully.

"I'm ready," I say.

We take a few steps down the hallway and stand outside the curtain. I take a deep breath and pull it back. There in the middle of the room is nine year old me lying in bed. My head is taped in a foam brace at the end of the gurney. An ice pack lies on my right shoulder and the lower part of my right arm is in a plastic air cast. Caked blood runs through my matted red hair and a huge purplish red bruise grows above my right eye.

I want to reach out to her, tell her she's going to be okay. Tell her she's going to grow up to be a fine young woman, but I can't.

I turn and see my mom, in all her beauty with tears streaming down her face. My dad is squeezing her tightly, patting her back as he sometimes did. They are much younger looking than I remember. Dad's white hair is mostly black and the lines I'm used to seeing on mom's face are smooth and practically non-existent. But I can smell her perfume, with a touch of plum and jasmine, and it brings back sense memories. Deep down inside I want to hug them, feel their touch. I want to let them see me, show them that their daughter is going to turn into an amazing woman. I stare at them, trying to figure out how I can reveal myself without causing any damage. If anyone could handle the mental repercussions of seeing their daughter all grown up, my dad and mom can.

"Let's do this," Frank whispers. He brings me back to reality. Brings me back to our current mission.

"Are you here to wheel her down to the MRI?" my dad asks.

I look at Frank to respond. If I speak they'll recognize my voice.

"Yes," Frank says. "We're going now."

"How bad does she look to you?" my mom asks us, "I'm sure you've seen lots of kids in car accidents. How does she compare?"

"She's going to be fine," my dad said calmly.

"Look at her, James," my mom squeaks out as she chokes back tears, "Some drunk driver hit her going thirty miles an hour. She's not going to be the same."

"She's going to be fine," my dad repeats ever so sternly. "I know this. She's going to be okay."

"I'm not worried about her arm or her shoulder," mom says. "It's the swelling in her brain. I have medical training. I know what this means."

"And there are things I know," responds my dad, being more gentle than I've ever remembered. "She's special. She's going to be fine. She'll make it through this."

I look down and notice that my eyes are open. I remember this moment. I remember my mom and dad saying those words. The nine year old version of me closes her eyes again. This is the part I never heard. This is what my dad must have sent me here to see.

"Children don't usually survive things like this," my mom says, "Even the nurses here haven't said she looks okay."

"They don't need to," says my dad, "Carol Ann, your work, your paper, the research in Italy with Dr. Savino on influence and energy. She has it."

"You don't know that," my mom responds, "You don't know that."

"I've seen it in her," my dad insists, "I've seen her influence the world around her. If that drunk driver didn't hit her, he would have careened into the neighbor's yard and hit the dozen or so kids in the front yard playing kickball. She may have thrown herself into that car to stop it. She may have meant to hit that car."

I vaguely remember the two families at the end of the block that loved to play kick ball all the time. I don't remember the choice to drive into the car. But even at the young age of nine I had some heroic instincts.

"You, you think?" my mom asks.

"She's the daughter of the world's greatest psychologist and the man who discovered time travel," my dad smiles, "There are things inside her that she won't even understand. But I'm convinced that one day she'll change time forever. She will survive this, it's in her."

My dad pulls my mom closer. He never told me of his suspicions. Surely I can't change time forever? I can't have the inherent energy Dr. Savino talked about. I'm not that special.

"Nurse," says Frank, "Let's wheel her down to the MRI."

I nod my head in agreement. We begin to move the gurney into the hallway and through the ER. We really don't have any idea where we're going and hope that someone stops us to take over. I look down at my nine year old self and see my eyes open a bit.

"You're going to be all right," I tell myself, "Everything is going to be just fine."

My nine year old eyes close and I think I see a faint smile of relief on my face. I look up at Frank who gives me an evil eye. I shouldn't be talking to myself. It's against temporal law. But I can't help to take a little bit of liberty and a quick moment to console myself. I smile at Frank.

Approaching from behind Frank are two nurses dressed in the same clothes we are.

"Are you here for the Eviston girl?" I ask them.

"Yes," one says.

"The doctors are anxious to get her down for an MRI so we got you started," I say and pass my part of the gurney off to one of them.

"Thanks," the other one says as he takes his side from Frank.

"Be careful with her," Frank instructs, "She's special."

Frank and I watch the nine year old version of me be carted away down the hall. I remember that girl. She was really scared that something was going to go terribly wrong. That things weren't going to go her way. She never stopped worrying about that. Even as an older woman, I'm concerned that everything is going to go terribly wrong. The difference today is that I believe I can control it, and now I think I can change it.

We go back to the surgical closet and find Dr. Savino and Mojmir waiting for us. As we change back into our regular clothes we explain what happened.

"Your father didn't send you here to fix anything," explains Dr. Savino, "Instead he sent you here to discover something. To figure out that you were the center of his Inherent Energy study. It all makes sense now."

"The notations in your mom's paper," adds Frank. "A.E., pack leader, that's you. He's been studying you this whole time, even before you were nine years old."

"You may have been your dad's biggest discovery," chimes in Mojmir, "Bigger than time travel."

I blow it off. I don't want any more attention drawn to me than I already have. While I've gotten used to the accolades over the past several years, I still don't like being the center of attention. I just do the things I need to do because I need to, not to get attention.

"So what are the next steps?" asks Dr. Savino, "I know your father sent you back here. Do you think you've seen all that you need to see? That you were meant to see? Is there more? When we return back to the future, there will be lots of Nazis mercenaries waiting for us. They may kill some of us, they may capture us and send us to America, claiming it was us that killed your father. We can't just return like this. All we have is surgical scrubs, masks, and syringes. We need a plan."

"We don't have access to any guns," argues Mojmir, "We're not going to find any guns here in a children's hospital. Maybe on a few policeman, but not enough for us to defeat a bunch of Nazis."

I remember my dad's last words to me. See the whole board. There's a big picture here that I'm missing.

"What if we wait?" asks Frank. "Like really wait, hours, days, maybe weeks. Give them enough time to let their guard down, we send maybe one or two of us back as recon. Check things out."

"That could work out," says Mojmir. "We can find a place to hide out here and then when the time is right head back. We have all the time in the world."

"We don't know that," I counter, "They may have pulled my dad's theories out of him already, forced him to explain Inherent Energy. They are rather crafty with their torture techniques, they don't necessarily need to beat you to talk. I would have caved eventually back in Leavenworth watching my mom die every day."

Mojmir shivers a bit with the mention of Leavenworth as he has his own dark memories from that place. "Good point," he says, "The Nazis may have all the information they need. We got to go back as soon as we can and stop them."

"Well, we have to get out of this surgical closet before we get caught here," says Frank, "Alex, this is your home town. There's got to be place we can hang out."

I think about all the places I knew when I was nine. Back then my world consisted of my home, my mom's office, my dad's office, and his lab at Wright-Patterson. That's when it hits me like a ton of bricks. My nine year old world is all I need to defeat the Nazis. Dad sent me here for more reasons than I first thought. I have resources here.

"Dad and Mom are here at the hospital while I get the MRI done," I say, "We can head back to my house and get my dad's security ID."

"Why do we need that?" asks Mojmir.

"Because we're going to Wright-Patterson Air Force Base today," I say, "There's lots of fire power there. They have to have something we can use against the Nazis."

"Brilliant," notes Mojmir. "Completely brilliant."

"All right," says Frank, "Let's go acquire some transportation to your house."

We slowly step out of the closet and close the door behind us.

TWENTY-TWO

I feel bad for the family that owns the mini-van we hotwired in the parking garage. It was the first one we found that didn't have car seats so at least they don't have toddlers. I remember the streets exactly and heading back to my school-year home was like coming back for a high school reunion. My dad moved while I was in college, said he couldn't bare the pain of living there without mom. I never got to say good-bye to the house I grew up in. One day he called me and told me he moved. Gave me the new address and said that all my stuff was there now. He did move my mom's rosebush and other plants. In fact, he had a local gardener do it so he knew it was done correctly.

Since we're driving a stolen car, I decide to park it a few blocks away. We walk to my house and must look like a weird group of adults walking the neighborhood. We get to my block and thankfully there's no one out in their yards. I keep on glancing at windows hoping that no one sees us walking by. We sneak up the driveway, through the back wooden gate, and to the back door. I can hear my puppy, Vito, yapping inside at the kitchen door. I haven't seen him in over fifteen years when we had to put him to sleep. He's the cutest Yorkshire terrier and I can't wait to scratch his back and let him kiss my cheek.

But I remember we're here on a mission and have to get inside quickly before anyone sees us. I place my thumb against the biometric lock. The display confirms who I am and the lock disengages. I twist the door handle and enter into the back kitchen. An overwhelming flood of memories hit me.

I see my mom cooking Thanksgiving dinner for the family. Every year she'd make steaks instead of a turkey in the oven because that's what made Dad happy.

On the weekends Dad would make a huge salami sub sandwich complete with lettuce, tomatoes, pepper, cheese and olive oil. He'd cut it in thirds, take two for himself and give me the other.

In the morning, I'd wake up, feed Vito, and then sit on the floor in my pajamas playing fetch with him. He'd jump into my lap each time he returned.

I shake off the memories. I can't get lost here. I can't get absorbed back in time.

"We're here on a mission," Frank whispers in my ear. "Get the credentials and let's get out of here."

Vito is still yapping at our feet and it's turning into a growl. He's positioned himself in between us and the back bedroom where my dad keeps the keys for his lab at Wright-Patterson Air Force base. He must not recognize me, yet, since I look much older than he's used to. I reach up on the counter and grab some treats. I take one and put it in between my thumb and forefinger, and tap it down on the ground in front of me. Vito immediately stops barking and looks at me strangely. He knows this is our little secret signal. His ears drop and he slowly jumps towards me, then stops. I tap a little more. He jumps all the way and smells my hand. His tail starts wagging and he playfully jumps up towards my face. He recognizes me. I lean down to let him kiss me, and scratch his back then give him the treat.

"Good boy," I say. "Good, Vito."

"Sunshine," Frank says, "We don't have time for reunions. This is dangerous. We have to move on. We have to get you out of here."

I want so much to stay and play with my puppy. I miss him dearly. I miss this house. But Frank's right, I'm not here to play. My time here was done and over long ago. I must remove myself from this memory. I no longer live here. This is no longer mine. To detach myself from the emotions, I imagine this is someone else's history.

I stand up and start moving towards the back bedrooms.

"Someone keep the dog occupied or else he'll follow me," I instruct.

I walk down the hall and into the master bedroom, ignoring all the pictures on the wall and the many memories that call to me. I go straight to my dad's dresser, look in his valet, grab his ring of keys with several key fobs and walk out of the bedroom. Returning to the boys in the kitchen, I find them playing fetch with Vito. I press a button on the wall by the back door and the garage door starts to open.

"Leave some treats for the dog," I say. "And let's get going."

We pile into my dad's car and pull out of the driveway. I know we're taking a chance stealing my dad's car and driving it to Dayton, but it has special detectors mounted in the dashboard that allows us access through a special entrance gate at the rear of Wright-Patterson Air Force Base. We get onto Interstate 270 then head west on Interstate 70.

It's about an hour or so from Columbus to the Air Force Base and I decide our trip should be uneventful. I drive the speed limit in the middle lane, never getting over to the fast lane and driving any faster. There's no way we can look suspicious or get caught by the police.

It's pretty calm drive. I've taken it several times, but I try to put that out of my mind. Reliving memories in the past is a seriously bad thing for a time traveler. I force them out of my head. I forget about my mom, my dad, my dog, my youth, and all the times I drove from Columbus to Dayton. This is just another car ride to me. Just another trip on a freeway.

All the guys in the car take advantage of the drive and doze off. Dr. Savino is one of the loudest snorers I've met but his obnoxious arrhythmic snores keep me from fading into a memory. I see cornfields for miles, light traffic ahead, and a few cars behind me.

Way behind us is an SUV gaining ground in a big hurry. At first I think it's just some impatient driver that wants to get somewhere fast, but then my "expect the worst" instincts kick in. I smack Frank.

"Wake up everyone," I shout, "We may have a problem on our hands." Frank rubs his eyes and looks around but Mojmir's wide awake already and peering through the back window.

"Who is that?" he asks. "How long have they been following us?"

"My guess is Stefan was able to calculate where my dad traveled us to and sent some of his minions to track us," I surmise.

I look in the rearview mirror and see the SUV weaving in and out of traffic. It appears as if they are heading straight towards us. There's a stretch of road with no cars between us and they accelerate.

"We have to get off the freeway," shouts Mojmir from the backseat. "We can't have a major accident here. None of us have clearance to be here. We'll be returned to the future and jailed forever."

"Quick, get off at the next exit," agrees Frank.

I glance to my right and see open lanes of traffic. I swerve all the way to the far lane, over the ramp's shoulder and onto the exit ramp. I slow down to a stop, look for traffic and take a quick right turn down a state highway. The speed limit here is forty-five miles per hour but I'm doing about sixty. There are cornfields as far as I can see on either side of me with barns and farmhouses off in the distance.

The SUV got off the highway as well, but it is fair distance behind me. It's just us and them for a long stretch of land, but they are slowly catching up.

"Any ideas?" I shout out, "I don't think we can outrun them. They'll be catching up at some point."

"Any side roads ahead?" offers Mojmir from the back seat. "We could hide in a cornfield."

"I got nothing," I yell, "Just road for miles."

"Keep on driving fast," suggests Mojmir, "And look for something, anything to turn onto. There's no way we're going to beat them on a long stretch of road."

I look in my rearview mirror and discover Mojmir's right. They've closed more than half the distance between us and are gaining ground.

I put the pedal to the floor and accelerate as fast as I can, but my dad's car tops out at 90 miles per hour.

"This car isn't made to go that fast," Frank says, "They're practically on us."

They've gained about a hundred feet. The longer we go in this direction, the farther we get from Wright-Patterson. Deep down inside, I have hope that we can return to the future and save my dad, and that possibly he's survived the gun wounds and that we can get him to a doctor. I know this is a fool's hope, but I'm holding on to it.

The SUV weaves into the lane next to us and pulls along the driver's side. There's four men in the car, all dressed in black, two in the front, two in the back. The passenger reaches into his jacket, pulls out a 9mm, and aims it at Frank.

I slam on the brakes.

We all go flying forward and come to complete stop. I've given everyone a huge shock to their system but we're okay. Up ahead a hundred yards or so, the SUV has slowed down and is heading back in our direction.

"We have to take them out and get rid of the evidence," shouts Dr. Savino, "No one can know they were here. No one can know we were here either. None of us are supposed to be here. None. We have to fix this somehow."

"Hold on everyone," I shout. I slam on the accelerator and weave the car into the opposite lane. I drive straight towards the SUV.

"What in God's name are you doing?" yells Mojmir. "Are you trying to get us killed?"

"Just the opposite," I yelled back, "I'm trying to save us the only way I can. It's a game called chicken. You see who swerves first."

"What if they don't swerve?" yells back Mojmir.

"Then we don't have anything to worry about ever again," I say. We're quickly closing the gap between each other. I'm now in their lane pointed directly towards them. In another minute we'll hit.

"This is suicide," yells Frank. "There's got to be a different way."

"You have any guns or firepower?" I yell back. "Trust me on this, Frank. I trusted you over the Atlantic."

"Everyone brace for impact," Frank yells.

Frank puts his hands on the dashboard and behind me I feel Dr. Savino bury his head into the back of my seat. I keep my hands loose on the wheel. I can see the driver's face. I'm trying to decide if he's the type that's going to swerve left or swerve right.

We're fifty yards away.

Forty.

Twenty-five.

Ten.

Five.

At the last second the SUV swerves to his right, over the shoulder, rolls over into the ditch and lands top down in the cornfield. I chose not to swerve at all and kept on going straight. I slow down, turn around, and drive back up to the over turned SUV.

Throwing the car in park, I step out to investigate, finding four guys in the SUV. The two in the back seat have been crush by the roof of the car collapsing on in their heads. The driver is bloodied by the shattered windshield and is hanging upside down in his seat. He looks groggy and may be coming to. I can see the passenger moving around a bit. I reach into the driver's jacket and pull out a German-style Walther 9mm. I place it in my pants belt and walk around to the other side.

The passenger looks less banged up than the others and is messing with his seatbelt to try and get loose.

"Who sent you?" I ask.

The passenger sees me and reaches around for his 9mm. I punch him in his bloody shoulder and he gasps in pain. I reach onto the roof and grab his 9mm.

"Answer my question, who sent you?" I repeat.

"I will not tell you," he responds with a heavy German accent, "You Irish-American scum. You think you can stop us? You think that we are beatable? We are the superior race. We will win this. It is our people's destiny."

I look around the car for some clues to confirm that Stefan sent them. And from *when* they were sent. The car looks stolen. It's a family's SUV with a TV screen, dolls, Legos, and ear buds. The only thing these men have brought with them from the future is a lighter and a pack of HB cigarettes. It's a

German brand.

The passenger still tries to break free of his seatbelt. I reach into the car and pull out the cigarettes and zippo.

"This is such a nasty habit," I say. I flip open the zippo and strike it. It flames up. "You have a choice. You can die a slow painful death and burn alive, or you can tell me what year you're from and who sent you here."

The passenger turns white. "Don't burn me alive," he pleads. "Don't burn me."

"Tell me what I want to know," I say. "Or you'll be crispy German sausage within minutes."

Beads of sweat drip off his head. He's trained to keep secrets. He's trained to not reveal his mission. But he's not trained to tolerate being burnt alive.

"General Kaiser sent me," he cracks. "I'm on a special mission to kill the others and recover you."

"What year?" I yell. "What year?" I move the flame forward towards him.

"2086!" he screams. "2086!"

I step back and close the Zippo, "Thank you for your information." As I walk back to the car, I come face-to-face with Mojmir.

"We can't leave him here like this," he explains. "They'll find him and question him. We can't have him returning back to the future, either, and letting them know our plan."

Before I can figure out what he's doing, Mojmir grabs the gun and Zippo from my hand. In two quick actions, he shoots the passenger through the windshield and finishes off the groggy driver. He flicks open the Zippo, strikes a flame, and tosses it into the exposed undercarriage of the car.

"Let's get out of here," he grabs my arm and pulls me back to my dad's car. We both run up to the car. Frank's already in the driver seat. Mojmir hops into the backseat and I into the passenger seat. Frank takes off and in the rear view we see the car ignite in flames. As we get back to the highway ramp, it erupts in an explosion.

"How'd you know he was going to swerve right?" asks

Frank.

"I didn't," I say, "I just guessed."

Frank turns right, gets back on the highway, heads west, and drives towards Dayton like nothing ever happened.

We pull up to a service entrance used for scientific deliveries and parts for the particle accelerator. It's off the beaten path and not frequented by most people. My dad usually goes through a different entrance for scientists, but it's not odd for him to go through this entrance, either. The car has special Bluetooth beacons that raise the gate. During the day, cameras provide extra security but at night they place several guards here. Luckily, the guards haven't shown up for the evening shift, yet.

Frank pulls up to the gate and pauses. I breathe and say a little prayer. The gate rises and Frank pulls in.

"You'll have to take the service road around to the side," I say. "We can park the car there."

I have to admit. I had a plan on how to get through the gate, but this is where my plan ended. Now that we're here, I have no idea where to get some firepower. All I have is access to my dad's lab.

"We just need a couple rifles and a few hand grenades," claims Mojmir, as if he's reading my mind. "There has to be an outpost armory somewhere."

"This is an Air Force Base," says Frank. "They keep guns next to the barracks or in the hangers. We need to get into a hanger."

"The moment we leave this car, we'll be detected," adds Mojmir. "There are cameras everywhere. They'll do facial recognition and determine we're not allowed on the base. The MP's will converge on us and then we'll be captured."

"We need a plan," announces Dr. Savino, "One that is foolproof and well thought out. I can't think under stress like this. I need a cup of coffee and a moment to relax."

This is a huge base and there's only one place I have access to and that's my dad's lab. It wasn't guarded as much as the other buildings on the base because it was deemed rather harmless. There was a loading dock for getting parts in and out of the building and that was typically guarded by two or three infantry. The front door was monitored by Old Man Roberts through the evening. Sneaking by Old Man Roberts was going to be tough. He'd see us coming a mile away and alert the authorities.

"Pull around to the back dock of my dad's lab," I say, "There's a couple of sentry guards there. We can surprise them, take their gear, and then head back to the future. Once we're there, we can ambush whatever is waiting for us while Dr. Savino programs the particle accelerator to take us somewhere else."

"Okay, now we have a plan," says Frank with little enthusiasm.

It's a stretch and its success is dependent on a lot of things – us being able to take the guards on with only two 9mm guns, getting back to the future quickly, and most likely having to battle a dozen of Nazis waiting for us in the future. Plus it involves potentially killing American soldiers, which I'm not happy about at all. But it's the only idea I have.

"Frank, back the car into the loading dock as if you're making a delivery and then pop the trunk," I instruct.

We pull around to the back of my dad's building and spot the loading dock. There's no one on it, but I can see at least two soldiers in the guard house and hope there is no more than that. Frank turns the car around and slowly backs in. I hand the other 9mm to Mojmir.

"Don't use this," I instruct. "No blood. Got it?"

"Got it," he agrees.

"They will freak when they see a Russian with a German 9mm so be careful," I add.

"Trust me," he says, "I have no plans to die today."

Frank makes it to the rear of the dock and stops. He pops the trunk.

"What do we do now?" he asks.

"We wait," I command.

We sit there for what seems forever until we hear footsteps. Boots shuffle across the dock floor and jump down to the car level.

"Dr. Eviston," a soldier yells, "You need help with these boxes?"

I leap out of the car and race around to the trunk. I find one young soldier with a rifle slung over his soldier carrying boxes out of it. A look of sheer amazement and confusion floods his face and I take that opportunity to cold cock him in the jaw. He starts falling down and I hit him with the butt of my gun against the back of his skull. A loud crack confirms I've knocked him out for some time.

"Drop your weapon," a soldier commands from the loading dock. I look up to find his counterpart aiming his rifle at me. "I will shoot and kill."

"As will I," announces Mojmir, who emerged from the car seconds ago. He draws a bead on the soldier with his 9mm.

I aim my weapon at the guard who I knocked out. "You're outnumbered, soldier. You shoot me and both you and your friend get it. I think it's you that should drop your weapon. We mean no harm here."

The guard switches his aim from me, to Mojmir, and then back, gauging whether he can shoot the both of us within moments. Frank pops out of the car as well and races over to the knocked out soldier. Frank pulls the rifle from the guard's shoulder and takes aim on the dock guard as well.

"I'm an excellent shot," Frank calmly explains. "There's no way you can take all three of us."

"You don't need to be a hero," I say, "Stand down. All we need is your weapons and we'll be on our way."

The soldier thinks a little longer. I'm trying to figure out how far he wants to take this. Did he join the Air Force to save the world? Or did he join it for the pay and education? I'm guessing the later, or else he wouldn't be a dock guard for my dad's lab. He slowly lowers his gun.

"Don't shoot me, please," he asks with some dignity, "I have a wife at home, we just found out she's pregnant."

Frank steps up to the dock and takes his rifle from him, "It's going to be okay, soldier, we aren't going to hurt you."

"We've got our weapons," explains Mojmir. "We can head back."

"We need to blindfold them up first so they can't see where we're going," I argue, "Let's find a conference room inside that no one's using, stash them in there, and then get out of here."

"Savino," yells Mojmir, "Come out and help me move this kid." Dr. Savino sheepishly steps out of the backseat looking around.

"I'm done with all this shooting stuff. Why can't people just get along? Drink good coffee, eat tasty food," he blurts out, as if he's been holding it in for days. "I'm a scientist. I don't shoot things, I create things. I don't like all this war stuff. I shoot you, you shoot me. People die. For what? A piece of land? A flag? Honor?"

Dr. Savino bends down and helps Mojmir pick up the knocked out soldier.

"We do this for survival," explains Mojmir, "We do this so our children have a brighter tomorrow."

"So that your children will have a brighter tomorrow," says Dr. Savino, "The children of the people that lose don't have that bright of a tomorrow. They're going to be a little annoyed. May come back one day and get revenge. And then it starts all over again. Instead, give me a piece of paper. Make me think. Have me create something. That's awe inspiring."

I grab some rope and twine from the packaging area of the dock and start binding the other soldiers hands.

"I get what you're saying Dr. Savino," I understand, not surprised that he's finally coming out as a pacifist, "But here's the thing, if your country and my country have a problem with each other, than yeah, it's a stupid battle with one winner who's the oppressor and a loser that wants revenge."

"Like the Palestinians and the Jews," adds Frank.

"Exactly," I say, "But this isn't two countries against each other, Dr. Savino. This is one country, not even a country, this is one group of people within a great country who are saying they are better than everyone else. The Nazis are better than everyone. Doesn't matter if you're Italian, Russian, Canadian, African, Spanish, French, Chinese, Arab, Indian, or American. It doesn't matter. The Nazis want to rule you, to take your money and knowledge, or want you dead. That's why we're fighting. Not to save my kids, but to save the whole world."

"Wait a minute," interrupts the soldier, "You're Americans?"

"Yes," I explain, "Which is why I didn't shoot you or your partner. There are Nazis still here in this country and we're here to extinguish them."

Frank hits the back of his head with his gun and knocks him out, "He was asking too many questions. We couldn't have him discovering we're from the future. Let's get both of these guys into the guard booth."

We drag both bodies into the booth and lay them on the floor. We find an extra few 9mm in a gun case along with a few hand grenades. Frank smashes the glass and stuffs them in his jacket.

"Perfect," he announces, "This is enough firepower to take out at least a dozen or so Nazis. We'll have loads of time for Dr. Savino to program the particle accelerator and get us somewhere else."

"So once we return to 2086, I'll immediately start reprogramming the particle accelerator to take us back in time and avoid getting kidnapped by the Nazis," confirms Dr. Savino.

"Exactly," says Mojmir.

"To where?" asks Dr. Savino. "I mean, there are hundreds of places I could send you to. Lots and lots. I can send you back to deep history. Recent history. Literally, you name the time and place I can send you there."

"Send us back to 1990, Andrew Air Force Base," instructs Frank.

"Yes, that's perfect," agrees Mojmir, "To when after you and Alex left there to come back to the future. We can help

President Mack extinguish all the Nazis sympathizers. This time we'll do it right."

"That's a great idea," I add. I walk back onto the dock and look to see if we're missing anything. All I see are boxes and parts for the new particle accelerator my dad is currently building in his lab here. There's no more firepower or arms, just what was in the guard house.

"All right," announces Frank, "Is everyone ready?" He pulls out the retrieval stick and we all surround him tightly. I take one more look around knowing I'll never come back.

"One… two…" shouts Frank.

That's when it hits me. See the whole board.

"STOP!" I yell in his ear.

Frank stumbles back a bit.

"What the hell did you do that for?" he shouts, cupping his ear. "You shouted right in my eardrum. You were standing right next to me."

"I had to stop you," I say, "Returning to the future is the wrong decision, the wrong play. We don't need to go back."

"What do you mean?" questions Dr. Savino. "We go back to present day. Then reprogram the accelerator to 1990 to defeat more Nazis. What else do we need?"

"We have the map," I say, "Right?"

"Yes," confirms Mojmir.

"That's all we need," I announce proudly. "We shouldn't be going to 1990. We should travel to the different nodes and correct what the Nazis have changed instead."

"You're forgetting something, princess," adds Mojmir. "When we return the Nazis will be there. We won't have the time to travel to the different nodes with the Nazi's particle accelerator. We can't get to Dr. Savino's, either. If we're to travel through the nodes that the Nazi's changed, we need our own particle accelerator."

"We have one," I explain. "Several hundred feet below us. In fact, we have the FIRST particle accelerator used in time travel. The one my dad designed."

Mojmir's jaw drops.

Dr. Savino smiles and shakes his head.

Frank grabs me, raises me in the air, spins me around and kisses me. "YOU. ARE. AWESOME!" he yells, "That's exactly why I love you."

"Will you put me down," I blush. "We still have a war to win."

Frank sets me gently back on my feet. "I don't want to let you go, Sunshine. Ever," he whispers.

"Well you're going to have to for now," I say. I turn to the others, "There's an elevator right off the loading dock that leads down to the particle accelerator. Follow me."

I pull out my dad's key fob and hold it against a security box. Two double doors open and we all walk into the building. There's a long hallway that leads to offices but I set my destination to the right. We step around some wooden crates and find the service elevator. Frank raises up the door and we all walk in. I press the key fob against another security box and hit a button that reads accelerator.

The doors close automatically and the elevator starts its long decent.

Down on the lab floor, the doors open up and we step into a hallway. This looks familiar to Frank and me and he heads toward the accelerator.

"Let's go to the lab, first," I say, "We need to look at the map and figure out which node we're going to first."

"Don't we want to go to the first node, first?" Frank asks.

"No," explains Dr. Savino, "The first node might actually be the weakest one. It may not put anything else into motion, just only slightly splitting open the gap for the temporal shift. We want the most explosive nodes and only by looking at the map can we make a judgment call on that."

I lead everyone into my dad's lab and Dr. Savino begins spreading out the map on the closest empty table. It's several feet long and Frank has to wheel over a second table to lay the whole thing out.

Dr. Savino begins reading the map and a huge frown

appears on his face. His look of worry and concern grows deeper and deeper.

"Oh," he starts, "This is not good. Not good at all. I mean, if there was just a few points it would be manageable. I would say it is something we could possibly accomplish in a few hours with a little bit of luck. We don't need hours. We need more than days. We need weeks to fix this. Even if we correct the biggest node right now, we may not even shift anything. We'll have to correct several nodes. After two or three nodes, we may be discovered here."

"What if we time travel back to the future, but to your particle accelerator?" asks Frank.

"It doesn't work like that," Dr. Savino shakes his head, "A mass wants to always return to its normal state. You can send it back in time, and then further back in time, but when it returns to the future it wants to go exactly back to where it came from. Which in our case is Berlin."

"All right," I say, "We need a plan. If all we can hit is two to three nodes, then that's what we hit. Dr. Savino picks three of them and we split up. We each take one and Dr. Savino sends each of us back one by one to our nodes. While we're out fixing things, Dr. Savino picks the next three. First one back gets the next assignment. By the time we're caught we'll have nine or so nodes fixed. Who knows? We fix a few and maybe things start tilting our way."

"I think that's doable," says Dr. Savino, rolling up the map, "Let's head down to the particle accelerator."

Normally this area would be a hotbed of activity. Lab assistants and graduate students would be going crazy preparing things, running reports, and making calculations on whiteboards. But there's nothing going on today. The place is deserted. My guess is the crew knew that my dad wasn't coming into work today so there was no point in showing up. The good news is we have the place all to ourselves.

We travel several flights of stairs down to the lower levels of the lab to where the particle accelerator is. It's much smaller and longer than I remember. While the chamber itself is small, the accelerator is about fifteen miles long and only five feet in diameter. Dad is building a new one in the next lab over that would become his standard time traveling particle accelerator. This one was originally built for other scientific use then modified for dad's research.

We walk into the main room where the entry chamber is. Dr. Savino goes over, turns it on, and begins the startup sequence.

"I haven't used an older one in some time," Dr. Savino explains, "It's obviously the original model. We modified a similar one at CERN and that's what we used for the first European time travel. I headed up that team and we sent someone to listen to the first performance of Beethoven's Ninth Symphony back in 1824. It was our answer to your father going back to John Lennon. I wanted to go back to hear it as well, but we could only send one person at a time and in thirty minute intervals."

Dr. Savino stops.

"Oh Madonna," Dr. Savino stomps, "We won't be able to move as quickly. I can't send people back rapidly. We have to wait thirty minutes for the accelerator to recharge. Plus, I'm sure someone in Security will be monitoring energy usage and figure out it's being used because it sucks so much of it from the power grid. You all are going to have to move quickly through each assignment to get back here and move onto the next one. We may be able to get through five, maybe six nodes before they find us."

"All right, we can do this," I try to boost everyone's confidence, "Dr. Savino, let's pick the first few nodes so we can get mentally ready."

"Yes, yes, yes," he says, "I've been thinking about that. Pull out the map and spread it out on that table. There are three major points that are critical. One in the middle, one at the beginning and one that is recent. If you look at the map, dead in the center, is a node that made a major change. You may think it's saving Hitler from suicide. True, that's an important change, but it's not THE most important change from the war.

The thing that influenced World War II the most is D-Day and the Allied Invasion of Normandy. According to the map, Stefan was able to send someone back in time and influence French leadership to attack Pas de Calais instead of Normandy. This was a strategic flaw since the Nazis were ready for an attack there. They were able to destroy and kill close to a million Allied troops, leaving only Russia to fight on the Eastern front. I'm sending Frank back there since he may have influence on the French with his bloodline and background. But there are two other nodes that need to be addressed first. I'll be sending Mojmir to 1917, that's when Stefan went back to Russia and advised Alexander Kerensky on how to lead Russia's Provisional Government."

"Let me guess," says Mojmir, "That led to no Bolshevik Revolution, which led to no Lenin or Stalin."

"Exactly," says Dr. Savino, "Kerensky wasn't the best leader and without Stefan advising him, Russia and the Soviet Union would crumble. That paved the way for German dominance on the Eastern Front. Russia needed Lenin and Stalin's leadership to survive."

"So I'm going now?" asks Mojmir.

"No, Alex is going first, she needs the most time," explains Dr. Savino, "In Stefan's timeline, the Germans win. They conquer most of Europe, America, and Northern Africa. But they had to continue to quell the instinctive desire of Americans for a better tomorrow. Remember, in real history the U.S. experienced a post-war economic boom. When the Nazis manipulated time, that never happened. Agricultural technology never advanced and the U.S. lost some of their faith and spirit. Alex is going back to the Ohio Valley Corn Rebellion and help your ancestor General Tommy Eviston win that war. It's going to take the longest to accomplish, so I'm sending you there first. If they win that battle, the Americans start the rebellion much earlier and fuel their self-determination."

"How did I get the trip with the most bloodshed?" I ask.

"You need smarts and skill to win that battle," argues

Frank. "You'll do just fine. Now get into the chamber so we can all get started."

I have to admit, I'm kind of excited to get back to war. I try to remember all I learned from the New York Rebels about my great-great-great-great grandfather and the Ohio Valley Rebellion. The Rebels were outnumbered by the Nazis, so I'll have to help them muster more American soldiers. They won't know me, or maybe won't even trust me, but that hasn't stopped me before.

I check my weapons. I place my pistol in my belt and lay down in the chamber, placing my rifle on my chest. I'm ready to go back. Ready to help the rebels. This is the beginning of the rebellion, and I can't wait to get it started.

The beginning.

"I'm programming the particle accelerator right now. The sequence should start any moment," shouts Dr. Savino from the other side of the room. "Close the chamber."

Frank leans down and whispers in my ear, "I love you." He kisses me on the forehead.

I wasn't listening.

I was thinking.

See the whole board.

The beginning.

The start.

Go.

Frank starts to close the chamber door.

"WAIT!" I shout at the top of my lungs and pull back the chamber door. "STOP THE SQUENCE!"

Dr. Savino reaches over to a red button and the particle accelerator winds down. "What do you need?" ask Mojmir. "Do you need to remember something from the Rebellion?"

"No," I say, "We've had the answer all along. How completely stupid of me." I step out of the chamber and go back to the map.

"It's right here, plain as day," I announce looking at the map, "There's only one node we need to go back to. Only one. We fix that and we don't have to worry about anything else."

Dr. Savino steps down from the control panel and joins me at the lab table, "Alex, I've gone over all these nodes on the Temporal Map. Stefan has planned this thoroughly and considered every little detail. He's examined all the facts, historical documents, connected all the different scenarios, planned and predicted everything to a 'T'. He probably spent years going back in time doing research before he even changed anything. No one node makes a difference. They must be done together. The guy is a brilliant scientist and historian. He must have studied this for months and mapped it all out here. This plan is exquisite and he used it to change everything."

"And without it," I explain, "Any of it. He wouldn't have been able to create the Temporal Shift, correct?"

"Correct," informs Dr. Savino, "He needs all the events from the map to make such a huge shift."

"Then we go back to when he made the map," I say, "And stop him. I find Stefan and kill him before he ever completes it."

No one speaks.

I've stunned the room.

"That's brilliant," smiles Dr. Savino, "Absolutely brilliant. I've never seen intelligence like that. It's Nobel Prize winning thinking. Your father would be proud. Your mom even more. That's where you're going. You're going to have to do it."

"Wait a minute," argues Frank, "What about Temporal Gravity? Won't there just be someone else that comes along, makes the map, and creates a Temporal Shift?"

"No," explains Dr. Savino, "I don't think so. If Alex does this, she may be able to bend Temporal Gravity. If her dad is correct, she has Inherent Energy and can change the outcome. She kills Stefan before he goes back in time to change anything so then the world has a chance to come out of Nazi rule forever."

"So all we need is a when and where," announces Frank, "We just need to figure out when he finished the map."

I pick up a corner of the map.

"It's dated," I announce, "The map has a date on it. May 10, 2084."

"Perfect!" announces Frank, "We send Alex back to May 10, she kills Stefan, and 'Poof!' Everything's back to normal. The shift never happened. Everyone lives happily ever after. No Nazis. No world domination. No nothing. "

"No us," I add.

"What?" asks Frank.

"That's the first time machine built and the capsule is very small. There's only room for one person in that chamber," explains Dr. Savino, "Only one person can go back in time and it has to be Alex. If she goes back and is successful then this, all of this, never happened. You'll be giving up all your success, winning the war in 1990 never happened, teaming up with Mojmir. None of it."

"Our memories of Roach, Ella, Mack Truck," continues Mojmir, "Your attack on Niagara, our attack on D.C., gone. It never happened. Those moments will never have existed. You'll never remember it. None of us will remember it. Only Alex will."

"But we're removed from the Temporal Gravity," argues Frank, "All of us, we're independent masses. We're not subject to those rules."

"This Temporal Shift is so huge," explains Dr. Savino, "That Alex will actually have to bend time to keep it from happening again. It will start things over. It's like a reset. When it's all over, there will be a point in time that everyone will return to and not even know it. Everyone except Alex. She'll be the only one that remembers because she survived it. Are you all willing to make that sacrifice?"

"I don't want to keep running," I say, "I don't want the world to continue like this. I have to take this moment, I have to fix it."

"Fixing it means good-bye," says Mojmir. "I won't know you, princess."

"You'll get to know me," I smile, "I'll make sure of it." I give him a huge hug. "Thank you for everything."

"You will do good," he assures me, "There's no other person I'd want to save the world than you."

"Dr. Savino," I say, "Thank you for all your guidance. I thought you were my dad's rival, his arch-enemy. Turns out, you're a friend. I'll seek you out in the future and tell you the whole story. You of all people should understand."

"You can't," says Dr. Savino, "I won't be able to comprehend it and worse, yet, if I do, I'll want to study it and that might lead to some catastrophic tears in temporal gravity. No, it's best that you remain away. Don't tell a soul. Keep it a secret."

I turn to Frank. I try to keep it together but I can feel my eyes start welling up. We never were able to settle and have a real relationship. Now we're going to have to start over.

"Doing this means we won't have us," Frank says.

"I'll figure something out," I chuckle. "Now that I know you like me, I can convince you whenever we meet up again."

Frank shakes his head. "It's going to take a lot of convincing," Frank frowns, "I thought you were out of my league. Didn't even think I had a chance and gave up on you soon after I met you. You're going to have to work on me and make me believe."

"I'll try my hardest," I whisper and pull him tight to me, "If there's one thing I've proven is that if I want something done, I find a way. I'll find a way for us." I kiss him. I kiss him like it's my last kiss because that's exactly what it might be. Frank's been my ray of light in all of this and I don't want to let go. But if I'm going to save the world, I have to.

"All right, Dr. Savino," I say and turn away from Frank. "Start the sequence."

"I'm sending you to his lab in Berlin," explains Dr. Savino, "The morning of May 10. That should give you enough time to find him and destroy him. But close enough to the node that when you do kill him, it will bend time. Good luck to you."

I lay back down in the chamber with the rifle at my side. Frank kneels down next to me as the particle accelerator starts whirling. Mojmir stands over his shoulder, nodding in approval.

"Go get that son of bitch, princess," says Mojmir. "Kick his ass."

"Will do," I smile back.

"Promise me you won't stop trying to pull me in," says Frank.

"I promise," I say and smile at him.

Frank closes the chamber door and the whirling gets higher and louder. I can see him through the window staring at me longingly. I know he's not happy about this. I know he doesn't want to lose me. I mean, when you finally find someone you don't want to let go. We found that magical bond in each other that you don't walk away from and the sad thing is when I find him I'll have to try and create the magic all over again. But this time on my own.

I can't think about it anymore. I have a mission. Right now I have to save the world. After that, I'll figure out a way to save me. World first, me second. That's always how it is, right?

The whirling gets higher in pitch and I know the magnetic force is getting closer. Soon I'll be traveling through time. There's a countdown clock inside. Thirty seconds left. The other display is my destination - May 10, 2084 at 7:30 a.m.

I look out the window again and my breath has fogged up the panel. I can't see Frank's face anymore, everything is just blurry images. I've lost him.

Twenty seconds left. The pitch of the whirling increases.

I see movement through the window.

Suddenly the chamber door opens up. Sirens wail.

"Suck it in, Sunshine," Frank commands, "And make room for me. I'm not losing you."

I inhale and try to make myself as small I can while he squeezes in next to me. Mojmir closes the chamber door shut.

"Thank God in heaven that you're short and thin," says Frank, squishing down my head and smashing the rest of my body against the side of the chamber.

"I love you, too," is all that I can manage to get out.

From the corner of my eye I see the display. The whirling

stops, light bends, heat overwhelms us.
We're gone.

TWENTY-THREE

Even in the world's first particle accelerator, time travel is rather instantaneous. One second there's a bend of light, the next second you're there. Frank and I are lying next to each other on the floor of Stefan's lab. It's early morning and there's no one here.

"You can take your elbow out of my ribs now," Frank says to me.

"Hey," I tease, "You were the one that squeezed in at the last minute. I'd say you shoved your rib into my elbow."

Frank peels away from me and stands up. He extends his hand and offers to help pull me up. I grab his arm and he yanks me up off the ground.

"That was rather romantic of you," I say.

"Pulling you up off the ground?" he asks, "Any gentleman would do that."

"No, crawling into the particle accelerator with me," I smile.

"Yeah, well," Frank blushes, "I'm that kind of guy."

I punch his shoulder. "I'm glad you are," I respond.

I want to pull him close and kiss him, but there's really no time for that.

"Okay, Sunshine," smiles Frank, "What's our next move? You're running this rodeo."

"Let's look around and see what Stefan's up to," I instruct, "This is his lab. I wonder how far ahead he is."

Each lab table is covered in books, open and closed, along with piles of papers and folders. There are pens, markers, rulers and protractors on just about every table, too. The bookshelves are almost bare because all the books out on the lab tables. Everything's in German and we can't understand a thing. The center two tables are wheeled together with the map on them, spread out completely. We step over to the table and investigate it.

"It's almost finished," I observe, "There's twenty-one nodes on it. It's missing the first one." Although the notations are in German, I remember what Dr. Savino was describing on the map. "He must have calculated the first one today and went back in time to check his work. Once he comes back, he'll put in on the map then take his time putting all the pieces and parts in place."

"This must have taken him a lot of time and research," adds Frank. "He's much smarter than I thought he was."

"You have to give him credit," I say, "Instead of coming up with all the world's greatest innovations and inventions himself, he just manipulated time to make sure the Nazis absorbed all the knowledge they wanted. Acquire instead of create. That's his motivation. That's how he operates."

The door knob twists and Frank grabs me by my shoulders and pulls me down. I hear the door swing open and two sets of boots step into the room. Frank and I squeeze underneath a lab table. He motions for me to be silent.

"*Der general sagte, zu bereinigen, alle Bücher und Datei die Papiere,*" says one of the soldiers, "*Aber lassen Sie die großen Karte in der Mitte Tabellen unberührt.*"

I have no idea what he's saying and really wish I had taken German in college. Through the lab table legs I can see there are two soldiers. They begin clearing off the tables and piling the books back on the shelves.

"I think we've figured out all we can here," I whisper to Frank.

"Yeah," he agrees, "Hold tight here. I got this."

Frank rolls off of me and our lab table onto the floor. He army crawls down an aisle of tables a few feet and then starts slowly climbing through a few tables. He stops at the last row, rolls over on his back and aims up in the air.

As the German soldier walks by to the shelf, Frank leaps up and pressed his gun against a pile of books in the soldier's hands. He shoots and a soldier goes down with the books muffling the sound of the gun shot.

Frank whips around towards the other soldier. That soldier had dropped his books and is now reaching for his gun. Before the soldier can move any further, Frank fires a bullet into his head, splattering blood and brain matter all over the bookshelf.

"Ugh," I say, crawling out from under the lab table. "Kudos on the first one. Clean, quiet shot. But the second one? Well, there's no way I'm cleaning that up."

"Sorry," says Frank. "I couldn't help it. He was going to shoot. I had to do something."

"At least let's hide the bodies somehow," I say.

We pull the lifeless Nazis to the back of the lab and underneath a table. We hope that if someone comes in, they just notice the messy tables and that's it. Maybe they'll ignore the smell of dead bodies and avoid investigating. Maybe they won't need any books off the shelf and not see the brain matter. Hopefully, we'll change time before anyone comes in here.

"We're done, here, right?" asks Frank.

"Roll up the map," I instruct. "We have to take it with us. He can't complete it. In fact, we have to burn it."

"I remember a large ventilation hood in the lab down by the particle accelerator," Frank says, stuffing the map into his jacket.

I grab the pistols off the dead soldiers and stuff them in my belt. I check my gun as well. "All right," I say, "Let's head down to the particle accelerator."

Frank and I step to the edge of the door. He places his ear up against the metal door and listens.

"Nothing," he says. He turns the knob and slowly pulls back the door. Frank steps out first and looks up and down the hallway.

"It's empty. Looks just like it does in the future," he whispers. "Come on."

I follow him out and see the same hallway with an elevator at one end. We slowly step down to the middle doors that lead to the particle accelerator. Frank looks down through the window.

"Nothing," he says, "Maybe it's too early for the scientists to get here. Maybe they stay up late and sleep in during the morning."

"I don't know," I say, "But obviously there are still soldiers walking about. We just killed two of them. So let's not throw caution to the wind."

We slowly open the double doors, walk through, and start our way down the utility stairs. We try to stay quiet but our boots make some click clacking noise.

We reach the bottom without any surprises. The ventilation hood is about twenty feet away on the left. Most chemistry labs have them to mix chemicals with toxic fumes in it. Temporal Labs need them to clean some of the moving parts of the particle accelerator. We slowly walk over to the hood. Frank lifts up the door on the front and places the map inside.

"Unfold it," I instruct.

While Frank starts unfolding it and scrunching it up in the hood, I look for some flammable chemicals. There's got to be something here used for the cleaning of parts for the particle accelerator. I find a glass bottle full of clear liquid and uncap it. It smells like bad vodka.

"Isopropyl alcohol," I say. "Perfect."

I reach into the hood and douse the map with it.

Frank begins opening drawers and pulls out a burner lighter.

"Ready?" he asks.

I pull my hand out and back away. "Do it."

Frank reaches into the hood with his right hand holding the lighter. With his other hand he's holding the hood's door, ready to drop it closed. He flicks the lighter and pulls out his hand while a flame instantly engulfs the hood. He closes the door and we watch the map consumed by fire. After a minute or two, all that's left is black paper flakes floating around in the hood.

"It's going to take years for him to recreate that," says Frank.

"We need him dead if we're going to bend temporal gravity," I explain. "Now we need to hunt him down."

"What's the plan?" asks Frank.

"You should know me by now," I smile. "I never plan this far ahead. We've got a couple of choices. We sit and wait for him to show up in his lab or we go hunt him out."

"Well, I've never been one to sit and wait," says Frank, "I say we storm the castle. Take out every last Nazi in this building. Set the whole place on fire. Just in case someone else knows something or if there's another map printed somewhere."

At some point Stefan needs to come down to the lab. At some point he needs to finish the map. We know he doesn't alter any nodes until November because that's when we experienced the change back in 1989. That's when the whole temporal shift occurs and we know that today is the day he finishes the map. That was noted on the map itself. Where is he? Where are all his lab assistants?

Suddenly the a buzzer sounds from the particle accelerator. I can feel heat building up.

"Someone's coming back," says Frank.

"I'm guessing it's not just one person. It's Stefan and all his lab assistants," I say, "Let's hide."

Frank and I split up. He hides across the room behind a tall cabinet. I hide next to the hood. The heat increases from the particle accelerator and we see a bend in the light, as if we're suddenly looking through a prism. Someone has returned.

Stefan's particle accelerator is larger than normal. It had fit the four of us with room to spare. My guess is Stefan has five or six lab assistants with him. All scientists. Stefan is probably the only military man among them. Frank and I should be able to easily take them with the firepower we have.

Frank can see me across the room and he motions for me to be quiet. He gestures to have them pass us and attack from behind. I nod in approval.

We have to kill more than just Stefan. We'll have to kill his lab assistants as well. No one else can remember anything about this other than us. It will add an extra complication, but it's a task we'll have to complete. When I think of all the Americans, Canadians, and others that the Nazis have killed over the decades, a few of their lab assistants won't even compare. Sorry, but I'll have no remorse for these scientists.

The bright light fades away and the whirling slows down to nothing. The chamber door opens and out comes seven cheering Nazis, dressed in black, with rifles and side arms, followed by Stefan. They don't look like lab assistants, they must be soldiers. Our job just got seven times harder.

They all speak in German, seemingly congratulating each other, and must be happy about figuring out the last temporal node.

Stefan shakes hands and pats them all on the shoulder, "*Danke. Danke euch allen!*"

The soldiers begin making their way through the lab as Stefan congratulates them. Suddenly he stops and looks at the hood. He stares oddly at it.

He points at the hood and speaks German. The soldiers don't answer and keep on heading towards the stairs. Stefan repeats himself and shouts it at the top of his lungs.

I slip down to the floor, knowing that if the lead soldier turns around to look at the hood he'll have me in his view.

The soldiers do stop, all of them frozen, and turn towards the hood. Stefan begins yelling rapidly at them all, questioning them in accusatory tone. He figured out that it was recently used.

One of the soldiers shrugs and speaks back, "*Ich weiß nicht,*" he repeats, "*Ich weiß nicht.*"

Stefan yells at the closest soldier to the hood and motions for him to investigate. He starts stepping forward and I can't see him anymore. I know as he gets closer, he'll be able to see me. I sit there quietly. If these were lab assistants, I'd have all the faith in the world that we could quickly take out all seven and Stefan within seconds.

But I'm guessing they are all professionally trained soldiers. Probably the best Stefan could find. They are tougher than any group we've ever fought. Tougher than the soldiers at Niagara Falls. Tougher than the guards at the White House. They are most likely the guys we ran into at the Reichstag Fire.

I say a little prayer as I hear the boot steps getting closer. In a moment, he'll be right above me.

A gun shot rings out.

The soldier slumps down to his knees and completes his fall right in front of me. He's dead.

Stefan shouts in German and I hear quick shuffling of boots. Rifle shots ring out.

I peek over the table and find Nazis braced behind lab tables shooting in the direction of where Frank used to be standing. He's moved and I don't know to where. No one notices me standing there because all are looking in the opposite direction. I scan their heads looking for Stefan and can't find him anywhere. Stefan and Frank, both missing.

We're down to six soldiers. One of them raises his hand and shouts. All of them stop shooting. The soldier closest to the cabinet that Frank was standing at breaks his position and starts to creep forward.

I brace myself against the lab table in front of me, take aim at the back of the lead soldier's head, and fire. The bullet finds it's mark and shatters his skull. He falls forward then slumps to the right. Five.

I dive back down under the lab table as return gunfire showers the air above me. I army crawl towards the stairs, knowing that eventually Stefan has to make his way up to his lab. He has to find out if the map is still intact and write down his thoughts before he forgets them. My plan is to cut him off at the pass and shoot him.

I still have no idea where Frank is, but I have faith in the fact he can hold his own. Another soldier shouts in German and the gunfire stops.

Finally Stefan speaks up in English, "I don't know who you are but I do know you are outnumbered. These men are the best soldiers the German army has ever seen and I am one of the best generals, living or dead. I've trained them. They are the finest."

"You're German scum," yells Frank from across the room.

Gunfire ensues. They used an old trick to seek out their enemy. But Stefan and the soldiers may not be aware there are two of us.

I look up over a lab table and quickly survey the situation. Again, I can't see Stefan but there are five soldiers shooting towards the other side of the room. I take aim at the closest and shoot him in the back of the head. That makes four.

I quickly select another target and hit him as well. Down to three.

I dive back to the floor as the gunfire shifts my way. We can't continue this forever. The three remaining soldiers are going to get smarter and seek us out. I look around at my surroundings. There's a door a bit to my left marked "*Elektroschrank*" and then further on down the lab tables end. It's about ten yards to the stairs and several flights up to the double doors to the main hallway. If I make it to the stairs, I might be able to use the railings as some type of coverage. Chances are one of these guys is a sniper and can take me out. The better option may be the door to my left, I can get to it quickly and discover what's on the other side.

I hear a noise to my left and find Frank has crawled over to my side of the room. He maneuvers to the lab table next to me.

"We have to do something," I whisper, "Got any ideas?"

"We take out Stefan, now," he replies, "We kill him and it's over."

"No," I disagree, "These soldiers may know something, too. They probably went on every expedition with him. I recognize some of them from the Reichstag fire. We need to take them out first, and then Stefan. If Stefan dies before them, I may bend time but the soldiers may have enough information to still cause a war."

At that moment Stefan runs in between our two lab tables and through the door marked "Elektroschrank." The gun fire stops.

"Here's the plan," I say, "You kill these three soldiers and do it quickly. I'll take out Stefan."

"Divide and conquer?" asks Frank, "Are you sure?"

"Positive," I smile. "I'll give you ten minutes, then I'm taking out Stefan. Think that's enough time?"

"Perfect," says Frank, "I'll see you on the other side, Sunshine." He blows me a kiss.

I blow him one back and then race through the door after Stefan.

TWENTY-FOUR

I can barely see a few feet in front of me. The room is dimly lit by a few security lights and looks like some electrical utility closet. There's a bucket in the corner with a mop, broom, dustpan, and a five foot step ladder hanging from the wall. Several circuit breaker panels are screwed into the opposite wall. The room is small, about eight feet by eight feet square.

There's no Stefan.

There's got to be a false wall or something in here. He had to go somewhere. I start knocking and pushing on the walls. Everything is solid. Nothing is hollow.

He had to go somewhere. I search the floor for a trap door and find nothing there as well. I look up at the ceiling and that's when I realize there is no ceiling. Instead, it's a very tall shaft that goes up past as far as I can see. There's a ladder that starts seven feet above me with a cage around it. How far up it goes, I don't know.

The five foot step ladder is leaning against the wall and ends close to the first rung of the caged ladder. I climb the step ladder, reach up to the caged ladder and continue my climb.

The ladder is rather rusty and I can see some of the bolts into the wall are loose. It's a shaky journey to where ever I'm going. From the vibrations on the ladder, I can feel there is someone climbing up above me. This is the way Stefan must have gone. He's got a huge head start on me and with him still on the ladder, it must go on for several stories.

I pick up the pace, knowing that where ever I'm going, I'll probably be out of breath when I get there. But Stefan will most likely be worse since he was already on one mission this morning and has less energy to recover.

I see a light up above and a shadow move in front of it. It looks like the ladder exits to the roof and Stefan has made it to his destination. I'm about fifty yards below.

The shadow returns above me and gunfire reins down. I try to cover my head and hope and pray that a bullet doesn't find it's mark. I get lucky.

The shadow leaves and puts the cover back down on the

ladder. I double time my way up and get to the roof quickly. At the top of the ladder, I twist the handle to the trap door and try to swing it open. It doesn't budge. There's something holding the door down.

I step up a few more rungs and place one foot on the ladder and the other on the metal cage. I twist the handle and lean all my weight into the door. I get more leverage but instead of moving the door, I slowly start pulling the rusted bolts out of the wall. The top of the ladder starts leaning into the utility shaft, away from the door.

I shift my position a little and try again. This time something gives a little on the trap door, but the bolts holding the cage and ladder into the wall extend even farther out. I remove my feet from the ladder and push it against the wall. I push with all my might and whatever is holding the trap door shut starts sliding off. At the same time, I'm forcing the rusted ladder from the brick wall. The heavy weight on top of the trap door finally rolls off and the door swings open all the way as I push myself up over the ledge. The ladder falls away below me and my waist is dangling into the utility shaft with the bottom some ten stories down.

I pull myself up onto the roof and look down the shaft. The ladder has fallen and bent further down. There's no way Frank can make it up here even if he tried. I'm on my own.

I survey my surroundings. I'm on the roof of the Institute of Temporal Engineering. There's a large compressor laying on the roof next to the trap door. It must have been what was sitting on top and preventing me from getting out. Around the roof there are a few air conditioning units, vents, electrical and plumbing units, a shed, and what appears to be some maintenance closet that may lead to a stairwell down.

Stefan has either gone that way or is hiding behind one of the air conditioning units.

There's no time to catch my breath. I cautiously make my way over to the stairwell, glancing right to left, and checking if Stefan is near. I make it to the maintenance closet, and pull the handle. It's locked, from the inside. I sink down against the nearest air conditioner unit to think.

I may have lost Stefan down the stairwell. My choices are to return to Dr. Savino and Wright-Patterson Air Force Base now and be sent farther back in time to try and stop Stefan again, or continue to hunt him down here. Things back at Wright-Patterson might not be perfect. Security there may have already found Dr. Savino and Mojmir and they probably don't take kindly to an Italian and Russian wondering around in my dad's lab.

If they haven't been caught, maybe Dr. Savino sent Mojmir back to help since I left a half hour ago and the particle accelerator had enough time to recover. But if Mojmir's here, there's no way he'll be able to make it up to the roof to help. Nor can Frank for that matter. I'm on my own.

My best bet is figure out a way to hunt down Stefan.

"You've destroyed our only way off this roof," shouts Stefan from somewhere. "I can't escape down the locked stairwell or back down the broken electrical chute. We might as well finish this battle. Come out and show yourself."

Excellent. I didn't lose Stefan and I still have a chance to kill him and change time forever. I check the clip on my gun. I have no more bullets left. I left the rifle down in the lab by the particle accelerator. I'm weaponless. There's no way I'm stepping out and making myself known. I have no protection.

"My gun is empty," reveals Stefan. He waves it in the air from behind an air condition unit and then tosses it over the side of the roof. "My guess is that if you had any bullets you would have fired them by now."

Stefan stands up and shows himself. "Come on, American scum, let's battle as God intended us to, man-to-man."

I stand up from behind the air conditioning unit.

Stefan looks at me and stares oddly. His shock leads to a smile and then to a laugh. "You are a girl," he chuckles. "The great United States Military strength can send anyone back in time to defeat me. Anyone. I expected a huge strapping soldier, the best America had to offer. They send me a girl. A frizzy redheaded skinny short girl. It will be almost too easy to defeat you."

"You think you can defeat me?" I jeer. "What arrogance."

"Even if you do manage to wound me or kill me," he continues, "You cannot stop it. Temporal Gravity will see that another great Nazi leader comes about and changes time. It is our Temporal Destination to rule the world. It is what Germans will do. It's why the Nazis exist. You cannot change the flow of Temporal Gravity."

"You have no idea who I am?" I say to him, "It seems you keep meeting me over and over again for the first time."

"So we do meet in the future," he smiles, "Which means that my plans are successful. That the Temporal Shift comes to fruition. Good. I really don't care who you are. The outcome on this roof is meaningless. The Temporal Shift will happen."

"No, it won't," I say, "I've burned the map. You don't know what to manipulate. Even if you survive here, it will be years before you can recreate that map."

Stefan laughs, "You think I didn't create a back-up map? Sure, that was the original down in the lab, and I couldn't risk another copy getting into the wrong hands. That's why I did this." Stefan unbuttons his shirt and rips it off. He spreads his arms wide in a Christ on the cross like gesture. The map is tattooed across his arms and chest. The timeline goes from one palm to the other.

"Here is my back-up," he grins, "All I have to do now is ink on the last node and put my plan in place. You are just a speed bump. A flat tire. A stone in my shoe. It will be a pleasure killing you, but I doubt I'll remember it years from now. You are just some scruffy American girl they've sent to try and stop me. You're insignificant."

Stefan leaps across the roof and runs right at me. I brace myself for his arrival. This isn't the first time I've engaged in hand to hand combat with him. On impact, I step to the right a tad and let his weight take us down, having his body come to my side rather than into my gut. I raise his hips high which rotates him up to take a face first landing. I twist over him on top of his back and reach down at his head to drive it further into asphalt roofing and gravel.

Anticipating my move, Stefan jumps to his feet, throwing me off of him and pushing us backwards. I fall into a nearby air conditioning unit, tailbone first. Pain shoots up my spine and leaves me paralyzed for a second, shuddering with pain. I look up to find Stefan charging me again, hands outstretched ready for a choke hold. I have a split second to react, so I kick his arms away. He falls onto me, pushing me farther into the air conditioning unit.

I try to roll over and push him off, but he's driving his knee into my hip. "It is over," he grimaces. "You are finished."

He places his hands on my shoulders, pinning me down on the unit. He places his other knee on my chest, pushing his full weight onto my body. He moves his hands from my shoulders and wraps them around my throat. He closes his grip and starts to cut off my windpipe, choking me to death.

I feel like my eyes are popping out of my head. I scratch, pull and claw at his hands, but he doesn't loosen his grip. I can't move his hands from my neck and the pain is getting more and more intense. I hear my dad's voice in my head, "See the whole board."

It's not his hands that I should be focusing on. I can't gain any leverage there. I think through the various body pressure points I learned in training, to discover a meridian that will stop the electric current running through his nerve endings and release his grip.

I reach up past his forearm and with my thumb and fingernail I burrow into the flesh of arm just below the inside of his elbow. I push with all my might at his upper Ulnar nerve. It's commonly known as the Funny Bone and its exposed part is between the inside forearm and the elbow. The nerve itself connects all the way into the fingers. I finally break skin and hit the location I needed.

Stefan screams in pain and his arms loosen from around my neck, instinctively folding back. I take this opportunity to roll out from under him, and fall off the air conditioning unit onto my hip.

Stefan is still holding his arms up against his shoulders, in temporary pain while his nerve endings get their feeling back. This gives me a moment to catch my breath. I stand up on my feet, leaning over onto my knees.

I look around. There's got to be something I can use. Something that will give me an advantage. I find nothing. I'll have to use my brute force.

I dig into my deep reserves of energy and get a second wind. I charge Stefan, shoulder first, and send him flying across the roof, just as he started to recover the energy in his arms. He stumbles back and falls against the roof asphalt, smacking his skull on the roof. I leap on top of him and start pummeling him with my fist.

"You think you're better than me?" I shout at him. "You think you're better than an American? Better than a girl? You're nothing. Race, gender, nationality. None of it matters."

Stefan reaches up with his hand and shoves it against my face. He pushes me back. I try to hit him again but I can't extend my arms far enough. He pushes me farther away. He gets his legs up underneath my body and kicks hard, sending me several feet back. I stumble a few feet and almost trip over the electrical closet ladder that brought me up here.

I stand up, panting and look towards Stefan. He's standing up as well, trying to catch his breath. We're several feet from the edge of the roof. Behind him I can see downtown Berlin in all its brilliance, reconstructed over the years as the crown jewel of Europe.

Stefan turns and looks as well. "It's a beautiful city, isn't it," he says, "Built by the hands of strong Germans. We've come back from the war and regained our worldly dominance. We are the leaders of architecture, leaders of technology, and leaders of innovation. These are the things that matter the most. Land, riches, and military, they are nothing. Knowledge is power. That's what makes a nation strong. Knowledge. My plans will bring more knowledge to German. With it we can gather all the great minds over time and make sure their innovations happen under German rule, not some American culture that will waste it for their own capital gains, turning it into profits rather than the good of the nation. You can't stop us. Killing me here on this roof will not change anything. Temporal Gravity will have its way, girl."

"I'm not just a girl," I say, "I'm Alex Eviston and I'm changing time forever."

Stefan turns ghost white. He's realized who I am and understands I know more than the average girl. That I know what he's up to. That I'm one of the few people in history that can figure out a way to stop him.

"You say knowledge is power," I continue, "Well then, you must be familiar with how gravity works." I reach down and pick up the compressor that was on top of the trap door preventing me from opening it. With all my might, I heave it at Stefan. He catches it, but it's too big for him to handle. He stumbles back with it in his gut. He keeps on stumbling several feet until he hits the ledge of the roof. He trips backwards and falls over into the empty air.

I race to the ledge, kneel down, and peer over. I see him falling back several stories into a loading dock area. He lands into a huge trash bin. His skull cracking against the side as the weight of the compressor and his body pull him completely in. Immediately, rats emerge from the trash and begin eating his flesh. I see them rip and claw at the skin on his arms, destroying his tattoo.

Suddenly I'm hit with a wave of heat and energy. I'm thrown back and I trip over the open electric utility shaft. I fall down to the roof on my knees as another wave of energy hits me, this time from another direction, the light this time bends significantly, as if I'm looking through ripples of water. A third pulse hits me. Pressing me flat against the asphalt roof.

This must be the temporal shift. *I must have bent time* I think to myself.

Another wave of energy, stronger than the others hits me full force from above. The light around me completely bends, all the heat is absorbed from my body. I black out.

TWENTY-FIVE

I wake up with a headache. It takes my eyes a second or two to focus but I discover I'm in my apartment at the Watergate in Washington D.C. My room seems to look like it did when I left it back in the real 1989. The desk is covered in papers along with a shattered cassette tape. My old TV is back and the cable remote is on my nightstand. There are no posters on the wall, nothing on my dresser but some money and my make-up. The room is as plain as it's always been. The blankets and bedspread is the same electric blue and I have on pajamas with bunnies wearing Ray-ban sunglasses.

I touch my face and my body, and still feel the bruises from my battle with Stefan. I'm sore all over. The battle was real. Did I change time? Have I reverted everything back to the way it was? I sit up in bed and slowly move my legs to the side and stand up, wincing in pain.

My back is killing me and my tailbone is throbbing. I go into the bathroom and take a look at my face. My hair is a mess, more than it usually is, and my cheeks and forehead are all scratched up. My neck is bruised from the chokehold Stefan had on me, and I have a few cuts on my face, but that's the only visible signs of attack. I grab a wash cloth, rinse it with cold water, and try to clean the blood off my face.

It's time for the moment of truth, to see if all things are back to normal. I lean against my bathroom sink, take a deep breath and slowly exhale. Now that I'm okay, I have to make sure my surroundings are. I walk to the window and pull back the curtains.

There in full view is the Washington Monument, white and shiny against the morning sun. Fifty American flags circle it at its base. We're back and we're okay. God bless America.

The alarm clock radio clicks on.

It's Madonna.

"Come on girls. Do you believe in love?" she sings, "Cause I got something to say about it and it something goes like this." Her song, *Express Yourself*, continues in complete English.

The video that started it all. Thanks for the warning

Madonna. If Mojmir didn't like music as much as he does, I may have never known the Temporal Shift was coming. We may have never had a jump start and repaired things.

I sit down on my bed. It was really Frank. It was Frank that got the tape to me. Frank that helped me through everything. Frank was always there for me.

Frank!

I've got to go to the coffee shop and see if he's okay. Does he remember anything? Does he remember us? I run through the apartment, throw on some fresh clothes and a hat, and race over to M.E. Swings.

I hurry into the coffee shop, out of breath. Scanning the room, I see Frank at our typical table except this time he's joined by Mojmir. He smiles and waves at me to sit down with them.

"Alex," he shouts, "Come here, there's someone I'd like you to meet."

Has Frank forgotten everything that happened to us? He wasn't with me on the roof. It's possible that only I have bent time, that only I know about our history. Do I have to start over with Frank? I'm shaking a little. My heart is beating a freight train in my chest. I know that I can rebuild us, but I don't want to have to. I want to leap into his arms right now and have him kiss me. But I have to wait it out. If he doesn't remember anything, then a sudden kiss from me could drive him away. I have to wait. Unfortunately, patience is not my strong suit.

I approach the table and Mojmir stands. He bows, gestures dramatically and says, "Wow. I am in the presence of royalty. It is an honor to meet you Princess of Time." He stands upright and extends his hand for an official greeting.

Mojmir doesn't remember anything. To him, we've never met before. Our travels together don't exist in his mind.

"It's an absolute pleasure to meet you," I say, taking his hand.

"Woah," he responds shaking as well, "I did not expect an

American to be so warmly accepting of a Russian. You must be educated."

"Frank has told me a lot about you," I explain, trying to come up with a lie, "I think you can be trusted."

I've seen no sign from Frank, yet, that he remembers anything. No smile. No wink. No acknowledgment.

"I got you a dark roast this morning," says Frank, motioning to sit next to him, "They had your favorite. It's an Italian Roast. The blend is from Costa Rica." This is normal behavior for us. Back in 1989 he always ordered us coffee.

I sit down in the chair and join the two. Mojmir sips his coffee and looks at me for a moment.

"While this is the first time I've seen you, I have met your father before," he explains, "I try to catch a lecture from a great scientist whenever I travel somewhere. I heard your dad's lecture on the Law of Return."

I remember this story now. Mojmir told me this when we first met. He actually argued with my dad.

"I disagreed with some of his points," Mojmir goes on, "Told him there were some fallacies in his research."

I sip my coffee as Mojmir begins his story. Frank says nothing to me. The Temporal Bend may have been too much for him. He may not remember anything. What if I am the only one who knows about our history?

Well, now's the time to focus on me and what I need. I need Mojmir's friendship again. I made friends with him before, I can do it again. More importantly, I need Frank. I want Frank in my life, forever. I need someone who knows all that I've been through. Not just the time traveling, but knows my relationships with my mom and dad. Frank knows what makes me happy, and I know him. I want someone who I can share all my past and my future with.

If I have to start over with Frank, I can make that happen, too. There's Temporal Gravity. We were meant to be with each other so we will be, right? I mean even though I bent time and it can be changed, temporal gravity should keep on going. Unless the change in history put us on a new path, a path that separates us instead of pulls us together.

My thoughts come back to the conversation. Mojmir is continuing on about how my dad was wrong, injecting a few jabs at American arrogance of innovation. I look at Frank and roll my eyes. Then I smile at him and try to flirt a little, hoping I'm not pouring it on too thick but enough so he thinks something's different. If I have to build our relationship again, I might as well start now.

Underneath the table, out of Mojmir's view, Frank grabs my hand and squeezes. He looks at me and smiles back.

"It's wonderful to see you, Sunshine," he says.

He remembers.

THE END

EPILOGUE

The breeze through the open window blew the kitchen curtains over the sink. Yet again, Alex accidentally sprayed them with the faucet. She kept on forgetting to make ties for them to avoid having them blow everywhere, but there's only so much time in the day. When you have to cook, clean, and raise two young children, your time is prioritized a little differently. What might seem like a quick chore to make sashes for kitchen curtain turns into a three hour project. Instead, Alex spent her time focusing on educating her children about important things like history, math, and kindness.

Alex taught more than just her children, she taught all the kids in the village. Seven to be exact. It was an amalgamation of home schooling and the little school house on the prairie. Except it was in the Italian Alps.

After her retirement from the U.S. Homeland Security Office, she married her long time beau Frank Bouchard and they traveled to Italy. At first they thought it would be a great place to honeymoon, but then they never left. The place helped them forget about their past.

They bought a cottage in the Italian Alps, learned to speak the language, and assimilated themselves into the Italian way of life. Frank got a job at the locale Fiat plant working on a top secret project that would eventually become the world's first hover car. An associate of her parents, Professor Samuel Savino, got Alex a job lecturing at the University of Torino.

After a few years, Alex wanted to fill their family with love. They had their first son, naming him after her father and family friend, James Mojmir Bouchard, and then gave him a sister naming her after Frank's mom, Sara Ella.

Saturday mornings were lazy days for Alex. She typically sent the kids off to play in the backyard, then sat and sipped her coffee on the back porch. She enjoyed watching them frolic, run around, and most importantly laugh. Laughter was a common thing in the Bouchard household. Alex made sure there was plenty of laughter and love. She didn't want them to have the childhood she had. She didn't want them to feel alone. Alex's parents were focused on their work, especially her dad. While she understood her dad's accomplishments were for the betterment of the whole world, she was never quite happy with him sacrificing his time with her for scientific improvements.

Now that she had children, she compared her parenting to that of her mom and dad often. One memory with her dad that she did cherish was Saturday morning family time and she chose to emulate it. So after she was done with her coffee, she'd go out and play with her kids. Tag. Hide and Go Seek. Bacci. Horse Shoes. It didn't matter what they did, she just wanted to spend time with them. Typically, Frank was home, too, and would join in on the fun.

But this wasn't your typical Saturday morning. Frank was called into the Fiat plant to address a manufacturing issue, which left Alex alone to get ready for Sunday's party. The next day was the Festa della Liberazione, celebrating Italy's liberation after World War II. Not too many people celebrated anymore, but it was always a huge party and feast in the Bouchard household. At first the villagers didn't understand why some foreigners embraced the festival so strongly, but after a while they came to accept the settlers' love of the holiday. After a few years, many neighboring villagers started coming to their cottage for the celebration and it's become a huge party.

So this Saturday, Alex was cleaning the whole cottage in preparation for all the guests. She wiped her hands on a dish towel and hung it neatly on a rack to dry. She looked out the back window one more time to check on the children. At eight and ten years old, they were an absolute joy. Old enough to have some freedom to be on their own, yet young enough to still enjoy the blissfulness of being a kid.

"I'm really blessed," said Alex to herself. She could have chosen so many other paths. Head of Homeland Security. Top Research Scientist. Chair at the Department of Temporal Engineering at The Ohio State University. Instead she chose the career of mother. She had no idea what she'll do when

Sara turns eighteen and goes off to college but that's a decade away and she'll figure it out then. For now, she was happy as the village teacher and preparing her children for the world ahead of them.

Alex moved into the living room and began dusting the mantel. Dust accumulated quicker up in the mountains this time of year and Alex had to change her routine to dust twice a week instead of once.

She bent down to pick up a book off the floor and didn't see the bending of light on her front lawn, as if the picture window was suddenly replaced with a prism that she had to look through. If she saw the bend, she would have been stopped in her tracks since she was very familiar with its significance.

Instead, she turned to dust the pictures on the wall. The children. The wedding photos of her and Frank. Frank's parents. Her mom, and finally her dad.

She paused at her dad. They had a tumultuous relationship at best. It was one of distance. She would have never chosen him to be her dad. But in the end, he served her well. He helped her through some difficult challenges. Alex often wondered how life would have been different if both her parents were still alive.

A knock at the door pulled her out of her daydream.

"The festival doesn't start until tomorrow," she yelled.

Another knock on the door, this time louder.

"*Il festival inizia domani*," she yelled again but this time in Italian.

A third knock with a rap that sounded urgent, a life or death matter. Alex put down her duster. She went to the front door, unlocked the bolt, and opened it.

She was shocked by what she saw.

It was her dad. Or at least someone who looked like him.

"Alexandria," he smiled warmly. Tears welled up in his eyes. "You've grown into such a beautiful woman. Look at you. You're amazing. I wish your mom was here to see you." He lifted his hand to his face, as if to hold back the outpouring of emotion that he could barely control. He wiped his eyes and smiled at her again.

This man looked like her father, but she sensed something different. He was acting strange. He had a huge grin on his face and stared at her with loving, kind eyes. His hands were at his side and in his right hand he held a single red rose. He was not the cold and distant man that he was as she was growing up. He would always avoid any physical contact. This was not the father she knew, but he certainly looked like it. Even more odd, was that her father was no longer alive. It was biologically unfeasible for him to be there at that moment.

"Dad?" she wondered aloud, "How can this be you? You're dead."

"Honey," he explained, "I invented Time Travel. I know how to travel through time."

She was confused. This couldn't possibly be her father, for both emotional and physical reasons. It was impossible.

"But backwards," she corrected, "You discovered how to go back in time and return. Everyone knows that. But only backwards."

"Alex," he said, "Don't you think the next logical step would be to discover how to go forward in time? Once I discovered how to go back in time, I immediately started researching how to go forward. But I was smarter with the second discovery. I saw how the government used time travel as a military weapon. Going back in time and changing things had a major effect on the world as you know. Can you imagine if travel to the future was just as accessible? What type of weapon that would become in the hands of the wrong person? No, I kept this a secret, only using it on special occasions. Like right now. I had to see you."

"Dad," Alex was confused, "But, you're not yourself. This can't be you. You're acting different. You look happy. You were never happy. This isn't you."

"Please darling," her dad said, placing his hand on her shoulder, "I don't have much time. The Nazis are watching my lab. If my superiors see I'm gone too long, they'll come investigating. Maybe even try to figure out where I went. I can't risk them finding out I went to the future. If they ask questions of where I was, well, you know I don't do well under questioning and I can't tell them I went into the future to see you."

"What are you doing here?" she said, "You're breaking so many time travel laws right now. Not to mention, the emotional repercussions can be devastating. I mean, I'm looking and talking with my dead father right now. This can't be good for me. Mom would be livid with you."

"This was mom's idea," her dad explained, "Here. This rose is from her bush." He handed her a freshly cut rose from her mother's memorial rose bush that was planted in their family's backyard. Alex hesitantly took it from him and smelled it. She remembered the aroma.

"She told me to come here," her dad continued, "Made me promise. She explained it would bring resolution to everything."

"She did?" Alex questioned. Mom would have never violated any laws like this, and the rules she established of temporal parental contact like this was strictly forbidden. It was like going back in time to see yourself. Even though Alex had broken that rule before, she felt justified since her dad was the one that actually sent her there.

She paused for a moment and stared at her dad's face. She realized that Dad has a pretense for breaking the rules. He must have known and understood that it doesn't have the impact that everyone widely and willingly accepts.

"Dad?" she said, "It's really you, isn't it." She reached out and touched his face.

"Yes," he smiled and took her hand, "It really is. It's the real me."

He embraced her and squeezed her tight, like he had never done before. Her father had never hugged her. Never kissed her. Never even put his hand on her shoulder in a comforting way. Dad rarely gave her affection.

Her dad pulled away from the embrace and looked her in

the eye.

"I've come here to say I'm sorry," he said as tears start streaming down his eyes. "I'm sorry for how I treated you. I'm sorry that I wasn't the father you wanted me to be."

Alexandria's eyes started to water. These were not the words she expected to hear today. She never expected to hear them in her life time. Her dad was a distant figure to her. Not just in time, but emotionally as well.

"See, Alex, honey," her dad explained, "Once I was able to travel to the future I saw what the Nazis had planned. I saw they had achieved world dominance. I knew they had to be stopped. Your mom and I theorized that you had Inherent Energy and that you could stop them. We had tried several iterations to get you to save the world, but our first three tries didn't end successfully. We had to keep on reverting time back to before you were born to try again. Finally, your mom and I created a temporal and psychological map to win the war. She theorized that if we did things certain ways, that you would become the person you needed to be to lead the revolution and win the war. Unfortunately, that plan included me being the Dad I was to you. Distant, uncompassionate, authoritative, and demanding. It killed me inside to treat you like that. To be mean to you, unkind, unloving. I did it because that's what you needed to become the person you had to be. To be a leader. To save the world."

Alex stood there, frozen in shock. How was this possible? Multiple iterations of time? She didn't understand. She knew that different folds of time existed in time travel, that there were almost a dozen major temporal shifts in history, but having those shifts center around her? She was having a tough time absorbing all.

"Listen, honey," said her father, trying to comfort her. He obviously knew it was difficult for her to wrap her head around it. "I'm not asking you to comprehend it all. I'm just here to say I'm sorry. I'm sorry, and I love you."

He squeezed Alex quickly and kissed her on the forehead, just like she does with her children.

"I have to go," her father said and started walking back to the front yard. "You did well, Alex. You did a phenomenal job at seeing the whole board. You won. You've made me a very proud father."

Alex looked out at her dad on the front lawn. He pulled out his return wand to start the squeeze to go back to his present time. They looked at each other one final moment. She didn't see a time traveler or an inventor. She didn't see an absent-minded professor or a distant, cold father. She didn't see the man he was. She saw deeper now. She knew it was all an act. She saw a man who risked it all to make sure that his daughter saved the world, and gave up the one thing that he wanted the most – to be a loving father.

Alex raced across the front lawn and leapt into his arms. She held him tight, as if she could squeeze out all the pain, all the lonely nights, all the times when she wanted so much more than just his approval. It was all forgiven now.

"I love you, too, Dad," she whispered in his ear. "I love you, too."

She stepped back and kissed him on the cheek for the first time ever, and wiped away his tears.

"I have to go," her dad said, "But this is the moment I'll always remember." He pressed his button and the osmium orb encased him. With a bend of light he was gone.

Alex's children, James and Sara, ran around to the front of the house.

"Mommy, Mommy," shouted Sara, "We heard a noise. Why are you crying? Is everything okay?"

Alex knelt down and hugged both her children.

"Everything is perfect," she said.

ABOUT THE AUTHOR

Wal Ozello (1971 - TBD) is a child of the 80s. He was born in Cleveland, Ohio and attended film school at The Ohio State University, where he was a founding member of the Columbus hairband, Armada. After graduating, Wal moved to New York City's Upper West Side, worked in broadcast television, and sang for the prestigious Saint Patrick's Cathedral Choir. *Sacrifice 2086: Daughter of Time Travel* is Wal's third full length novel in a series of three. He currently resides in Upper Arlington, Ohio with his wife, two young boys, and the world's most amazing dog, Vito. His favorite writing place is Colin's Coffee where if he isn't working on a novel, he's blogging for the website, Pencilstorm. Wal wishes he could time travel to San Francisco in July of 1983 to see his favorite band, Journey.

ACKNOWLEDGEMENTS

It's not every day that you finish the third and last book of your Time Travel series. It's been an awesome ride and it will be sad to leave Alex, Frank, Mojmir, and the whole gang behind. But I think Alex has finally found herself and she'll be okay on her own.

This journey would have not been as fulfilling without the support of so many friends and family. I'm grateful for their help and love. My wife, Kate, and sons, Jay and Sam, have sacrificed a lot for me as I spent so much time working on these books. Jay served as a story editor for me this time around and Kate helped bring the book to its final version. Sam was supportive and understanding, as well as being the inspiration for Dr. Savino's personality. And then there's the world's most amazing dog, Vito, who did a fabulous job of keeping the house safe from squirrels while I worked at the kitchen table.

I received additional editing help from Aggie Ozello, James Ozello, and my friend, Kelly Poggaili. These are the people that keep me from making crazy grammar mistakes and question when things don't quite make sense. They make the story better and I'm eternally grateful for their help. A special shout out goes to Ray Barben who explained to me what happens during a military retirement.

I'm so overwhelmed by the deep support I've received from fans and friends. Your excitement for the completion of this book, my work, and the lives of Alex and Frank have pleasantly taken me by surprise. I never realized how many people would be eagerly anticipating the last installment of this series. Your kind words and declarations to "get it done, already!" every time I provided an update was the inspiration to work harder. Thanks to each and every one of you. I hope the story is everything you wished it would be.

Thanks to my fellow bloggers at Pencilstorm.com and book authors Tom Hobbs, Kelly Durham, and Don Ozello for your support over the past year. Tom runs the independent authors website, Kindle Mojo, and provides wonderful resources for everyone in the writing community. If you're looking for great books to read, check it out.

Finally, I need to thank my friend Colin Gawel and the whole staff at Colin's Coffee. I sat in his shop just about every morning working on this book. The staff there kept my coffee cup filled with the Dark Roast of the Day and served me up an egg and bacon sandwich on a bagel. The regulars were equally supportive, asking about progress in between conversations about Buckeye Football. If you're ever in Upper Arlington, Ohio make sure to stop by Colin's Coffee. I recommend the McRoy… with an extra dash of salt.

June 17, 2015